OCTOBER'S END

HALLOWEEN HORROR STORIES

KEVIN LUCIA, JEREMY BATES, AND JASON PARENT

BOOK 3 IN CRYSTAL LAKE'S DARK TIDE SERIES

Let the world know:
#IGotMyCLPBook!

Crystal Lake Publishing
www.CrystalLakePub.com

WELCOME
TO ANOTHER

CRYSTAL LAKE PUBLISHING
CREATION

Join today at www.crystallakepub.com & www.patreon.com/CLP

Subscribe to Crystal Lake Publishing's Dark Tide series for updates, specials, behind-the-scenes content, and a special selection of bonus stories - http://eepurl.com/hKVGkr

DAUGHTER OF THE MISTS

KEVIN LUCIA

November 1st

SHERIFF CHRIS BAKER stood outside the Clifton Heights police department's only interrogation room, trying to gather his thoughts. Clifton Heights was a strange town where odd things happened. Working here was never boring, though he sometimes wished it was. Life in Clifton Heights was often fascinating, as well as exasperating, eerie, and sometimes, terrifying.

It was his home, however. For whatever unknowable reason, by whatever unseen hand, he'd been brought here to watch over this paradoxically charming, enigmatic, and sometimes dangerous town. It was his job. His duty. His *calling*. Nothing would ever change that.

Over stretches like this, however, he often flirted with thoughts of early retirement. His only daughter Meg lived in Raleigh, North Carolina. Besides his "duty" and a handful of close friends, nothing was keeping him here. His friends would miss him, should he leave, but they'd also understand. As for his duty?

After a month like this, Chris sometimes thought his duty could get stuffed. In a town where strange things routinely occurred, October in Clifton Heights—a time when legends say the walls between worlds thinned—served up its own unique brand of strangeness in triple doses. Things always seemed off balance in this town, but between October 1st and 31st, the whole place felt askew.

Even so, this year had been a bad one. More strange occurrences than usual, with greater intensity. Cryptid and ghost sightings, vandalism, hikers disappearing in the woods, out-of-towners going missing, their belongings left in discarded heaps in their rooms at The Motor Lodge. This had proved to be a banner October for Clifton Heights, for sure.

Even so.

None of it compared to what he had to face, now.

Sheriff Chris Baker, custodian of the mostly good but often strange and sometimes lethal town of Clifton Heights took a deep breath, released it, reached out and pushed open the interrogation room door for what he believed could be his most nerve-jangling interview in many years.

Just another October in Clifton Heights, of course.

1.

Tuesday, October 4ᵗʰ

Regardless of the weather, Earl Flanagan left for work on foot every morning at 7:30 AM, after a breakfast of grapefruit and two fried eggs. From his home on Ford Street, he turned left onto Owen Avenue. Then right onto Boden Street, which eventually crossed Black Creek Bridge, leading to his place of employment, Bassler Memorial Library.

He always walked alone. Sometimes, passing cars honked, and he waved. He rarely saw anyone walking near him. If so, Earl passed them with a spare nod and a polite smile.

Fall in the Adirondacks bit with notoriously crisp teeth. So, on Tuesday morning, October 4ᵗʰ, Earl wore a jacket against the morning chill. Hands in his pockets, shoulders hunched, he walked in silence to Black Creek Bridge. Over the bridge, his footsteps beat out a pleasing staccato rhythm. It occurred to him—as it often did—that the rhythm served as a reassuring reflection of his ordered existence.

He'd almost reached the other side when he saw it. A piece of paper fluttering on the bridge's edge. A strong gust of wind would send it floating away.

For some reason, his stride quickened. As the paper fluttered, a strange urge compelled him into a trot. The breeze lifted the paper several inches higher. In a surprising burst of energy, he broke into a run. A stronger breeze finally puffed the paper into the air.

Earl leaped and reached out. A small part of him realized with dismay that his trajectory was carrying his torso precariously over the bridge's railing. For some reason that didn't matter. Heeding an odd compulsion, Earl knew he *needed* to see that paper.

The wind lifted it. His belly pressing against the cold iron railing, Earl's fingers snagged it. Gasping, feeling strangely elated, Earl stepped away from the railing. With two hands he beheld what he'd rescued from a watery death.

As he read, however, his elation faded, replaced by another emotion which felt just as strange. Anger. It began as a dull throb in his guts. As he read, it pulsed with a liquid fire he'd never felt before.

"No," he muttered. "This isn't right. They can't do this . . . they *can't*. It's not *right*."

His anger turned to rage. He crumpled the paper in a fist. Stuffed it into his jacket pocket, and proceeded to Bassler Memorial Library in a stiff-legged gait, his anger pulsing with his heartbeat.

2.

Until the age of thirty-five, Earl Flanagan had lived an uneventful life. He wouldn't call it happy, but he wouldn't call it sad, either. It simply *was*. For the most part he felt content. That was enough.

It had always been such. In high school, he'd endured a largely invisible existence. No one bullied him. No one trashed his locker, or knocked his books from his hands. No muscle-bound jocks smeared Icee-Hot in his gym shorts. No one hung 'kick me' signs on his back.

However, no one invited him to dances or parties. While he didn't drink or do drugs, he never won any citizenship awards, never did anything outstanding for the community or his fellow students. He never flunked a class, but never earned higher than a 'B'. He never got into trouble with his parents, but they never showed much more than a dutiful interest in him. He simply existed amicably in the same space as they.

His adult life ran a similar course. He enjoyed studying cinema at nearby Webb Community College, where he drifted unnoticed across campus for two years. However, to become a film critic, he would've had to move somewhere like New York City, Los Angeles, or at the very least, Syracuse. The thought of living in such big cities unnerved him, so he took the first job he found after college. Clerk at Bassler Memorial Library, in his hometown, Clifton Heights.

He moved back in with his parents Edna and Paul. They eventually retired to Florida, leaving him the house. Ever since, he'd lived there quietly. Working at Bassler Library, continuing his uneventful, ordered existence.

A rare visitor would find Earl's decorating tastes pedestrian. His parents had last re-decorated in the nineties. After they moved out, he'd left everything the same. The tan wallpaper, furniture and carpets in the dining room, living room, and his bedroom were unremarkable. His generic kitchen looked like a picture snipped from a catalog. Identical to thousands of kitchens elsewhere.

In the unlikely instance someone was to visit, *one* room would stand out, though it was just as unlikely he'd ever allow visitors inside. His theater. The only place Earl personalized after his parents left. He'd colored it with the one bright flame which burned in his gray life. Classic black and white horror movies.

The walls he'd painted a deep wine-red. He removed the carpet and polished the oak floor to a shine. The wainscoting and trim he'd painted black. The stucco ceiling, black also. The walls he'd adorned with framed posters of the most famous movie monsters to ever grace the silver screen.

He'd lined both sides of the room with black book shelves. On them, he'd meticulously arranged every single VHS, Laserdisk, DVD and Blu-ray monster movie he'd collected over the years. They ranged from classic movies from Universal Pictures, Paramount, to RKO Radio Pictures, and other lesser-known studios. One whole bookshelf consisted of books about classic monster movies, and biographies of the greats. Peter Cushing. Boris Karloff. Vincent Price. Bela Lugosi. Val Lewiston, and more.

In the back of the room sat a well-stocked mini-bar. Earl drank in moderation, and only while watching his beloved films. Usually two fingers of Chivas Regal or Crown Royal blended whiskey, on the rocks. Tasteful drinks meant to enhance his viewing experience.

In the center of the room, before a 50-inch flat-screen wall-mounted television, sat a black leather chair. One chair, for Earl alone. Only he could enter this room and watch his movies. Only he understood their value.

The thought of allowing someone into his most private place filled him with a bone-jarring trepidation. Letting someone into his den represented change, which frightened him in a way he couldn't verbalize.

That fear of change fueled his agitation as he stalked to Bassler Memorial Library on the morning of October 4th. The pamphlet he'd rescued angered him in a way he'd never felt. Earl Flanagan didn't get angry. Ever. He remained calm. In control. His emotions *didn't* change.

However, the pamphlet represented *change*, which had made him *angry*. This anger represented an internal change which, perhaps, Earl feared even more. It flickered and crackled, eager to burn. Earl was afraid that if he fed it, let it out . . .

It might burn everything down, with no hesitation, and with frightening glee.

3.

Working at Bassler Memorial Library proved ideal for Earl. People rarely frequented his shift. Those who did showed little interest in conversation past checking out books. He usually spent most of his shift re-shelving books and using the computer at the front desk to work on his movie review columns. He wrote three. One for a weekly Arts and Entertainment circular based in Utica, called *The Celluloid Times*. One for the monthly newsletter of his college Alma mater's Film Society, *Webb Filmography*. Finally, a weekly blog for ClassicFrights.com. He wasn't paid and he didn't know if anyone read them. In the six years he'd blogged for ClassicFights, no one had ever commented.

His columns met a personal need, however. A need to remind the world that horror films far nobler than the latest slasher film existed. He occasionally suffered moments of self-doubt as to whether or not he made any difference. The world had grown harsh. There seemed no interest in the misunderstood monsters he'd grown up with on late Saturday nights. All anyone cared about anymore were blood-drenched breasts and bodies hacked to pieces by shallow, one-dimensional villains.

Usually he comforted himself with the reassurance that his editors expected his submissions, which must mean *something*. Someone, somewhere found his articles worthy. He'd keep writing, reminding the world of what it had lost.

The morning he'd saved the pamphlet from Black Creek, however, all Earl could do was stare at a blank screen. Anger fought with despair. He couldn't make the words come. It seemed as if his quest had been dismissed in several keystrokes.

"Earl? You all right?"

Earl turned to see Ms. Bassler at his elbow, wearing a concerned smile. Head librarian and related in some vague way to those whom the library was dedicated, Lida Bassler was the epitome of everyone's favorite grandmother. Short, rotund, wearing mounded white hair with never a curl askew. Young eyes sparkled behind round spectacles. Ms. Bassler had run the library since she'd retired from teaching English at Clifton Heights High, though Earl couldn't say when that was, exactly.

He flickered a fake smile. "I'm fine, Lida. Just stayed up a little too late last night, is all."

Ms. Bassler narrowed her eyes. "Are you sure? You're usually deep into your articles by now. You haven't written a word."

Earl shrugged, feeling guilty, as if he'd gotten caught not doing his homework. "It's nothing," he lied. "I'm distracted, is all."

Though she didn't look satisfied with his answer, she relented. "Well, I'm not surprised. Your big night is coming up. Halloween. I think it's wonderful what you do. A nice break from all these sex-filled slasher movies. I just wish the town's youth appreciated it more, is all."

Earl swallowed down a bitter taste, repressing thoughts of the pamphlet. "As a matter of fact," he said, forcing a more upbeat tone, "I was wondering if I could take a little extra time on my lunch today. I need to talk with Mr. Phillips. Finalize some details."

Ms. Bassler nodded, still looking inquisitive, but not pressing the matter. "Of course. You haven't taken a sick or personal day in years. Take all the time you need. In fact, why not go a little early? That way you can talk with Mr. Philips and still eat lunch."

Earl clicked the mouse on the slightly antiquated desktop computer and closed the blank document. "Thank you, Lida. I won't be long, I promise."

November 1ˢᵗ

In his time as sheriff, Chris had seen things which he'd never forget. Things ranging from the odd to the bizarre, and some things—in their own ways—horrifying. He'd seen enough that, every time he entered the interrogation room, he thought there wasn't anything left which could possibly shock him. He'd thought this, of course, now.

Still, the sight of Earl Flanagan, sitting at the lone table in the middle of the room, wrists shackled in handcuffs which had been welded to a metal ring in the center of the table (Chris had always wondered which of his predecessors had welded those handcuffs there and why, but always decided he didn't really want to know). The normally orderly and meticulous library clerk was a mess. Hair disheveled, shirt untucked, and smeared with blood. Blood which streaked his pants, coated the soles of his shoes, and was splattered all over his face. Blood which wasn't his.

Chris paused. Cracked his neck, put on his most affable smile, and approached the table and the blood-splattered, glassy-eyed Earl Flanagan.

"Morning, Earl. Hope you slept okay last night. The bunks in the cells aren't terrible, but they aren't all that great, either. From what I hear, anyway. Never had cause to sleep on them myself."

He paused, pulled back the chair on the other side of the table across from Earl, and sat down. He leaned forward, folded his hands on the table and continued, while Earl stared at some distant point over Chris' shoulder.

"Listen, Earl. I'm going to jump right in. County police will be here soon, and given the severity of last night's . . . incident, they've instructed me to remand custody of you to them immediately. There isn't anything I can do about that."

He held up a finger. "However. There's conflicting reports about what happened last night. Lots of people saying they saw things they can't explain, and some of those stories don't match up. If there's anything you can say which might shed some light on what *really* happened, then maybe we can . . . "

Earl's eyes flickered.

His gaze snapped to and met Chris' almost instantly, his slack features sharpened, his jaw clenching, eyes hooded and flashing. It almost seemed as if his face narrowed, giving him a leering expression.

"Chosen," he said in a flat, emotionless voice.

Though the sudden transformation jolted him, Chris kept his expression passive. "Pardon?"

"I was chosen," Earl Flanagan said in clipped tones which don't at *all* sound like the quiet, reserved man Chris had admittedly only known in passing. "I was chosen. It was my fate. My destiny."

He leaned forward, eyes suddenly alive and bright with an intensity which made Chris' stomach turn over. "It was my destiny, but I rejected it. Threw it away. And because of that . . . I *paid the price.*"

4.

October 4th

It was a short walk to Town Hall. The entire way, Earl's anger seethed. In his thus far uneventful life, he'd never felt furious. Not even slightly angry. The most he'd suffered was irritation. Usually when *change* invaded his carefully structured existence. Normally, those feelings quickly passed as he regained his coveted equilibrium.

Walking stiffly down the sidewalk, however, hands stuck into his pockets, he felt both frightened and strangely delighted by his anger. Frightened, because he was *imagining* physical violence toward Bob Phillips, Town Board Chairman. How was he capable of such thoughts? He could barely comprehend it.

However, a strange elation filled him, too. He'd been done an injustice. Something drastic had changed his life without his permission. He refused to take it. He would remedy things . . . or else. Of course, he'd no clear idea what *or else* meant. Most likely it meant nothing, but he clung to it, regardless.

He reached the town hall building, between the police station and town court, sooner than expected. The sight of the unassuming edifice (no peaked gable, no columns, just unremarkable front steps and two glass doors) blunted his anger. What was he going to say? Would it make any more difference than the articles he diligently wrote but which no one ever read?

He stopped at the front steps and stared at the glass doors, across which was stenciled in plain black: CLIFTON HEIGHTS TOWN HALL.

He wavered on the edge of despair and fury. One second, he felt absolutely convinced of his righteous anger. The next, he felt cowed by his insecurity, compelled to walk away.

As he was about to slink back to the library, however, his hand clenched the crumpled pamphlet in his pocket. His anger flickered back to life. Fanning the flames, Earl hurried up the steps, desperate to complete his journey before his fire died.

5.

Bob Philips looked up from signing forms as his secretary ushered Earl inside. "Morning, Earl," he said, grin exposing immaculate white teeth. "What can I do for you? Things ready for Halloween?"

Earl opened his mouth, but Bob continued. "You know, I don't think we've ever told you how much we appreciate FrightFest. If it wasn't for you, the Raedeker Park amphitheater would be in ruins because of disuse. Your event alone keeps its upkeep in the town budget."

Earl opened his mouth again, but Bob kept going. "I remember those old black and whites Shep Lombardo showed back in the day. Those were real screamers." He flashed his million-watt smile. "It's been great, these past ten years. The way you've assumed his mantle."

Earl couldn't take any more of Bob's condescension. Before his nerve failed, he withdrew the crushed pamphlet from his pocket. With slightly shaking hands he uncrumpled it, then held it up. "Really? Then explain this."

Bob's eyes narrowed, confused at first. Very quickly, however, his eyes widened. To Earl's surprise, he looked genuinely regretful. "Ah, *hell*. Didn't Norman call you about this? He was supposed to weeks ago. It must've fallen through the cracks."

Norman Fuller, Clifton Height's one and only All-State insurance broker, was an unpleasant, pear-shaped man with thinning black hair and bad breath. A divorcee who drank too much, he had a wheedling manner which reminded Earl of a shady door-to-door Bible salesman. He felt little surprise Norman's supposed call had "fallen through the cracks."

Bob leaned forward, folding his hands on his desk. "Look, Earl. It's like this. At August's board meeting we tallied the attendance numbers for the last five years of FrightFest. It's dropped a little every year. In fact, attendance has been dropping for a while now. Mostly among the teens. Sheriff Baker's also noticed an increase of mischief around town that night. More kids out and about sneaking booze, pot, or sneaking off to . . . well, I'm sure you can imagine."

Bob sat back in his chair. He shrugged and said, almost looking embarrassed, "The board wondered if maybe the kids aren't coming anymore because they're not as engaged as they used to be . . . "

"Boring," Earl spat out with a surprising vehemence. "You think my movies are boring."

Shaking his head, Bob opened a drawer in his desk and looked for something inside. Again, it struck Earl how genuine his discomfort seemed.

As Bob searched his desk drawer, Earl looked around. The chairman's office was plain and modern. No polished oak paneling or other ornate touches. Adorning the walls, however, were the numerous awards Bob had won over the years. Citizenship and business awards from his days as lead salesman at Rich's Auto. Recent pictures as Chairman at dinner in upscale restaurants with sports and television "celebrities" from the Utica and Syracuse areas. His high school and college diplomas, and several plaques from awards he'd won for his high school and college athletic prowess.

It struck Earl, then. That deep-seated anger which scared him with its intensity. The sensation felt strange. In high school, he'd never paid attention to popular kids like Bob Phillips. He hadn't felt left out or under their thumb. Nor had he envied them. He'd shared space with them in the hallway. That was all. They'd ignored him; he'd returned the favor.

But now something like *hatred* pulsed through him. Hatred for all the Bob Phillips' of the world. Hatred for their accolades. Had he felt this way his whole life? Regardless, it suddenly didn't matter that Bob's regret seemed genuine.

"Here it is." Bob pulled out a folder. He set it on his desk, opened it, and withdrew a pamphlet. Even upside-down, Earl could tell it was the original he'd sent the board back in July.

Bob glanced down at the paper, then back up at Earl. "Look. The classic monster movies are one thing. *Frankenstein, Wolfman, the Mummy, the Creature from the Black Lagoon, Dracula.* The Board probably wouldn't have voted to change those."

He gestured at the flyer. "But I've never heard of these. 'Dark Priestess.' 'Daughter of the Mists.' 'She Walks in Beauty and in Darkness.'" He regarded the pamphlet again, frowning, looking confused. "All starring Contessa Victoria Williams. Whom I've never heard of, either."

Earl forced himself not to grind his teeth. Again, a sensation which felt strange. "Contessa Victoria Williams was a tent-pole actress for Into the Abyss Films. She starred in over fifteen of their gothic movies between 1930 and 1945."

Bob replaced the pamphlet in the manila folder and folded his hands in his lap. "Look, I get it. These old films are your passion. BUT." He gestured at the original pamphlet. "The board decided against showing films this obscure. Opted for something more current."

Earl snorted. "Current. 'Hacksaw Avenue.' 'Slaughter House.' 'Chainsaw Alley.'"

Bob shrugged again. "It's what the kids are watching these days. So far, registration and ticket sales have been through the roof. Double that of last year. There won't be an empty seat this Halloween."

Bob leaned forward, wearing sympathy like an ill-fitting mask. "Look. If you want to bow out of FrightFest, we'd understand. However, believe it or not, you're as much a part of it as these films. It was *your* proposition to bring FrightFest back ten years ago. We'd hate like hell for you to quit. And you know what—we'll make a concession. Pick one of the classics. *Dracula, Frankenstein, Wolfman*, whichever. We'll replace 'Hacksaw Avenue' with it. I think the kids will come and sit through a classic movie if they know something more . . . contemporary is next."

Earl almost snorted again, but somehow he kept himself in check, maintaining what he hoped was a neutral expression. His old survival instincts were finally kicking in. Don't buck the current, don't make waves. Get along. Don't rail against the wind. Things were changing, and he didn't like it, but fighting it? That only invited more chaos.

He nodded stiffly. "Perhaps *Frankenstein Meets Wolfman*? I've yet to show that."

Bob's smile blazed again. He looked as if he'd solved the world's energy crisis. "Perfect! A monster fight to start things off. I'll let the Board know of the change. We'll print some new pamphlets. Get the word out."

Bob didn't even stand to shake Earl's hand. He simply picked up his pen—a brazen, gaudy gold-plated thing, the kind no doubt engraved with is name—and asked, "Anything else?"

Earl forced a smile and shook his head. "No. I'm fine."

Without waiting for Bob's answer, Earl turned on one heel and left.

6.

Earl first discovered classic monster movies near the end of his sixth grade year. The library received four new picture books from MCA Publishing. Adapted screenplays of *The Mummy, Frankenstein, The Wolfman,* and *The Creature from the Black Lagoon.* At the time, he didn't possess the vocabulary to understand why he felt so drawn to them. He checked them out so often, Ms. Bassler, (in charge even back then) ordered a ten-book set which included *Dracula, Dracula's Daughter,* and *The Invisible Man,* among others. He spent the summer reading and re-reading about lonely, shunned creatures. Creatures shunned much like him, he would only understand years later.

That summer he saw his first monster movie at the Raedeker Park amphitheater. *Creature from the Black Lagoon.* He sat next to his father, enthralled. As credits rolled, he sided with the creature. Decided it was a tragic figure, long before Earl rightly understood what 'tragic' meant.

He didn't discover the work of Contessa Victoria Williams until four years after he finished college, in the summer of 1999, via the newly installed broadband internet computers of Bassler Memorial Library. His parents had enjoyed internet for several years by then, but only dial-up modem access. Slow and ponderous, it held little interest.

However, when 'broadband' internet arrived at the library, his first act was to search for his beloved classic movie monsters. Information which was once available only through obscure magazines was now keystrokes away. He quickly found not only websites about his favorite monsters, but websites about other movies from the same era. Val Lewiston's movies (*The Cat People, Isle of the Dead*), and the full RKO Radio Films catalog, for starters. Years before Amazon, Earl used a then-fledgling website called Ebay to build his personal collection of monster movies.

He downloaded his first clip of Contessa Victoria Williams that August, from a pre-YouTube website called "shareyourworld.com." He followed a link from a message board at a very home-spun website called goldenagemonstermovies.com. Before the days of high-definition streaming video, all he could download were grainy two-minute clips.

Even so, from the moment he first saw Contessa Victoria Williams stride boldly from the fog in a clip from *Daughter of the Mists,* he felt enraptured by her alabaster skin, raven black hair, and ethereal eyes. A voice inside promised he'd never be the same.

Over the years, he tracked down every available film she made for Into the Abyss Films, scouring the ever-more comprehensive internet for information about her career. Copies of her films in VHS, (and eventually remastered DVDs), were often ridiculously priced back then, but what else did Earl spend his money on?

Even so, as the internet was still in its infancy, it proved difficult to track down her movies. It took him nearly ten years to find them all.

He still loved his other monster movies, of course. He believed them far superior to the monsters of today. More than slobbering demons or flesh-eating, mindless zombies, the monsters of the golden age represented the outsiders of society. Those who forever longed to be a part of the human race, but through no choice of their own, were doomed to exist on the outside. They *hungered* for belonging. A belonging which dangled forever out of their reach.

Despite her relative obscurity, (even among his fellow monster movie aficionados), Contessa Victoria Williams' characters became the epitome of this tragedy. Forever longing to touch others. Doomed to know it meant certain death for anyone who dared. He'd planned on finally sharing her with a younger generation this Halloween, in hopes of showing them her awful beauty.

But he had been dismissed. Waved aside. Marginalized, just as all his beloved monsters, but helpless and weak, without any of their destructive power.

7.

Earl finished work in a daze. Luckily, few people visited the library during the remainder of his shift. A handful of mothers with toddlers checking out picture books and asking about next Saturday morning's read-along. An elderly man wondering when the most recent issue of AARP would arrive. Between them and shelving last night's returns, Earl managed to stay busy, keeping Bob Phillips' dismissal from his thoughts.

He tried several times during slow moments to write his

articles, with no success. He was supposed to review the remastered Blu-Ray of *The Wolfman*, (starring Lon Chaney Jr.) for the newspaper. For classicfrights.com, he owed a blog about the "otherness" of classic movie monsters and how they reflected feelings of exile for certain groups of people during specific times in American history. For the Film Society journal, a retrospective of Bela Lugosi's Dracula, and the superiority of Lugosi's version to contemporary versions, especially Christopher Lee's for Hammer Films.

The words refused to come. A crippling despair paralyzed his thoughts. Throughout the rest of the day, he couldn't manage more than a sentence or two, all of which he inevitably deleted.

Ms. Bassler might have sensed his distress, but she kept her distance. She'd come to know him over the years and she'd surely sensed he didn't want to talk. On one hand, he took comfort in her respectful boundaries. She understood him.

On the other hand, part of him *wanted* to talk about it. Rant about it. Vent his *rage* about the injustice done to him, Contessa Victoria Williams, and the classic monsters in general. But he couldn't make himself lower his defenses.

After clocking out and grabbing his jacket, Earl walked home in the same daze. The brilliant autumn colors he usually enjoyed couldn't penetrate the cloud of despair hanging over him. When he reached home he decided he wasn't hungry and headed for his study. He made himself a whiskey, neat, and selected the remastered DVD of one of the movies the town board had rejected. The source of the first clip of Contessa he'd ever seen: *Daughter of the Mists*. He inserted the DVD into his multi-deck player, turned on the flat screen, and sat in his chair. Uncharacteristically, he brought the bottle of Chivas Regal with him.

In this film, Contessa Victoria Williams played one of her reoccurring characters. Earl felt sure if she'd enjoyed the same fame as Boris Karloff and Lon Chaney, the role would've become just as iconic as the Wolfman and Frankenstein's monster.

Arglwyddes y Cors. An ancient Druid goddess of the moors which fed on the life-force of men. Befitting her tragic nature, Contessa never portrayed Arglwyddes as villainous or seductive, but as one eternally doomed to destroy everything she touched. Forever yearning for companionship, but destined to kill those whom she loved.

The other two movies he'd proposed for FrightFest offered similar scenarios. A totem of some kind came into the possession of marginalized men. In each film, these men invariably summoned Contessa unknowingly. She brought them love and passion, also fortune and power. At a terrible price, of course. Their essence. Their life-force. Until nothing of them remained.

Daughter of the Mists played out a bit differently, however. In this particular film, a lowly museum clerk at an invented Chicago museum of antiquities discovered Arglwyddes' totem, mysteriously displaced in the storeroom. When the clerk inevitably summoned her, he not only recognized her, but also managed to convince her to drain the life-force of all those who had diminished him.

During the course of the film, she fed on his persecutors, while he quickly rose up the museum's ranks. The movie—unlike her other two movies about Arglwyddes—ended with the implication that their joint reign of terror had only begun. It was by far his favorite of her films, and her most popular among her small but dedicated fan base.

The film's parallels to his situation weren't lost on him. He was the dismissed museum clerk, ignored by the Town Board. A collection of self-involved grown-up versions of the high school glamour crowd. If his life was that movie, he'd have no qualms offering them to the goddess Arglwyddes as sacrifices. He'd do it with a smile.

He wasn't sure how he felt about that. What it said about *him*. In some ways, he shrank back from the malevolence he felt growing inside. It alarmed him. That he could harbor such ill-will toward others, when his whole life he'd practiced a studied indifference to them.

As he watched Arglwyddes meticulously consume every obstacle standing in the museum clerk's way, he drank glass after glass of whiskey (far exceeding his usual limits), the malevolence spreading through him. He gloried in it. He lived in the real world, of course. A goddess who drained the life-forces of your enemies didn't exist. But if she did . . .

He'd gladly summon her into existence.

As he continued to drink, the movie grew fuzzier. Scenes, settings, and characters blurred together, until he no longer knew what he was seeing. In fact, he didn't know how long he had been watching. It occurred to him—in his hazy state—that perhaps the movie should've ended hours ago. Still, the blurry scenes kept flowing together.

One aspect of *Mists* remained clear. Indeed, seemed to become clearer the more he drank. Contessa Victoria Williams. As the rest of the movie faded into an incomprehensible haze, she blazed with a ghostly effulgence which outshined everything else. In fact, nothing mattered but Contessa Victoria Williams, as she gazed from the flat-screen with her wide, deep, ethereal eyes. Gazed at *him*. From out of her black and white world, across the expired years, and into his soul.

A sudden paroxysm of anger struck him. How dare those *bastards* take away the only thing he contributed to this town? The one thing which he'd been called to do? Even worse, how dare they disrespect Contessa in this way? Couldn't they see her eternal beauty? See the wonderful Otherness lingering in her eyes?

Compelled by a surge of anger, Earl lurched out of his recliner, still clutching his half-empty glass of whiskey. He wasn't sure how many he'd had. Too many, by the way he stumbled toward his flat-screen.

Contessa swelled to fill his world. Her raven black hair, which glistened. Her opalescent skin, luminescent in its marble-white perfection. Her eyes, so wide and expressive. They drank him in as he stumbled forward. It wasn't hard to imagine she was gazing out of her world, into his . . . into *him* . . .

He stumbled. Fell forward, and without thinking, stuck out his right hand—still clutching the glass of whiskey—to break his fall. He succeeded, only going down to one knee. But the glass shattered in his hand.

Pain throbbed dimly in the meat of his palm. He held up a shaking hand. No glass in his flesh, but a slice in the pad of his thumb pulsed red in a slow, wet ooze. He squeezed his hand into a fist. The blood pulsed more freely. Running down his wrist, and onto the floor. It was a bad cut. Most likely would require stitches. He should get up. Go to the bathroom. Clean and bandage it. Maybe even drive himself to Clifton Heights Hospital. Something like that. He should get up, he should . . .

He looked up. Contessa Victoria Williams loomed over him. Clad in a white gown, her slim curves shadowed through filmy fabric. Her black hair flew around her head, and her eyes—filled with yearning—gazed at him. Her face an expression of loss, need, and promise.

He shook his head, suddenly dizzy. Too much to drink, or rapid blood loss. Maybe both. But Contessa *wasn't* standing above him. He'd apparently crawled close to the flat-screen. As he looked up again through narrowed eyes, he dimly recognized the scene as the one in which Contessa appears for the first time as Arglwyddes from a hazy mist summoned by the hapless museum clerk. If his whiskey-blurred memory served him right, the clerk cut his hand on a sharp edge of her sigil and bled on it. Because, of course, there was power in the blood . . .

Darkness crept into his vision. Feeling feverish and faint, Earl raised a bleeding hand to the so-close and impossibly far away image of Contessa, before the dark rushed in and claimed him.

November 1st

Sheriff Chris Baker sat back in his chair, poker-face still solidly in place. In some ways, it bothered him that such a well-oiled expression of casual indifference came so easily to him. He'd had plenty of opportunities perfecting it, of course.

"Chosen? Chosen for *what*, exactly? And what chose you, Earl? Who?"

Earl's eyes flashed. He opened his mouth, sneering, as if about to express his contempt. A shadow passed over his expression, however, as the manic light in his eyes dimmed. The sharpness in his features softened as he slumped in his chair, gazing numbly into his blood-stained hands, shackled to the metal table. Looking confused and disoriented, he mumbled, "I . . . I don't . . . "

Earl shook his head. Closed his eyes, and said with a sigh, "You wouldn't understand."

"Try me. *Help* me understand. Like I said, there's a lot of discrepancy about what happened last night, and who did what. *Anything* you can add would be extremely helpful, and could only help you in the long run."

That wasn't necessarily true, of course, depending on what Earl said. But the eye-witness reports were so contradictory, so paradoxical . . . anything Earl said could shed light on what was possibly the biggest clusterfuck in Clifton Heights' recent Halloween history. Considering this town, that was saying something.

Earl sighed again, sounding like a love-lorn teenager, and not the central person of interest in a bloody explosion of nightmarish

Halloween-night violence. "Have you ever met someone, Sheriff Baker, who *completed* you? Who was like the missing piece your soul had longed for all your life? Your other half?"

Even after being a widower all these years, such a question always twisted Chris' guts. "Yes. I have."

Earl finally opened his eyes and gazed at Chris with a somber, sympathetic expression, one which was more recognizable as the mild-mannered librarian clerk everyone in town knew. "Now . . . imagine if you . . . if you'd *rejected* that other half. Spurned it. Turned your back on it, and chose another. Imagine, if you can, the dread recompense your other half would visit upon you . . . "

8.

Wednesday, October 5th

Earl woke with a start and sat up. It took several minutes to recognize his surroundings. He was in his bedroom. Sitting up in bed. He wore only a white t-shirt and boxer shorts. That didn't seem right, for some reason. He should still be wearing yesterday's clothes . . . shouldn't he?

But why?

He closed his eyes and rubbed his face. His head felt heavy and fuzzy. Not exactly hungover, but sluggish. Almost drugged. Like a narcotic fog still drifted in his brain, lulling his thoughts into a lethargic crawl. He concentrated, trying to piece together what happened the night before.

He remembered his humiliation at the hands of Bob Phillips. The casual dismissal of Contessa Victoria Williams. Being brushed aside by the Town Board Chairman. As if he was a fly, nothing more. The rest of the workday was a blur of cruel disappointment.

He'd gone home. Skipped dinner, went straight to his theater to watch *Daughter of the Mists*. He'd had too much to drink. At some point, driven by a strange rage and an equally strange despair, he stumbled upright from his recliner. Lurched forward, tripped, fell down on his hand . . .

His hand.

The one holding his glass of whiskey. The glass which had shattered and cut his hand . . .

Slowly, he raised his hand. Opened it, and examined his palm. His confusion only deepened when he saw nothing but unblemished skin. He probed the meat near the thumb, and felt nothing. No pain. Not the slightest trace of a scar, even.

How could that be?

He closed his hand into a fist. Squeezed it, and still felt nothing. He'd drank too much the night before. Was it possible he'd gotten so drunk he'd imagined falling and breaking the glass? Could he have actually stumbled to his bedroom, undressed, and gone to sleep, drunk? There was only one way to find out.

Earl eased out of bed, as if expecting a pounding headache or heaving stomach. Neither appeared, so he quickened his pace, getting to his study in minutes. Two things stopped him short, however. One: the door was ajar. Earl closed all the doors in the house at night. *Always.*

The second thing?

Pale light flickered under the door.

A numb kind of terror gripped him. Foolish, because he'd obviously not only forgotten to close the door to his theater, but he'd also left the television on. He had nothing to fear. Completely understandable given his mental state the night before, and how much whiskey he'd consumed.

Even so. He couldn't push down thoughts of something *waiting* for him beyond the door. What, he didn't know. Something undefinable, alien. Something both beautiful and terrible.

He swallowed down a tight throat. Shored up what little mettle he possessed. Reached out, pressed his hand flat against the door, and pushed it open. Before his resolve could fail him, he stepped into his theater.

The lights were off. The flickering glow indeed came from the television. On it, Contessa Victoria Williams stood in her ethereal beauty against a velvet dark night. He recognized the scene immediately. From the first time the hapless museum curator summoned her. He'd apparently paused the scene last night. Odd the television hadn't shut off like it was supposed to after five minutes. Nothing terribly strange, of course. Maybe the 'sleep' settings were off.

He stared at Contessa for several seconds, or maybe minutes. He lost track. Eventually, he roused himself from his stupor and grabbed the remote from next to his recliner. He shut the DVD off and shut the television off, also.

It seemed silly. But as he left to get ready for work, he couldn't help but struggle with a sense of shame. As if banishing her image from his television's screen was akin to betrayal.

9.

After a perfunctory breakfast of grapefruit and toast, Earl walked to work. October's charms were still lost on him. The gold, orange, and red tapestry in the trees; the crisp air, the houses decorated for Halloween. He saw none of it. Hands in his pockets, eyes downward, two things dominated his mind, making it impossible to think about anything else.

First, the Town Board's rejection of Contessa Victoria Williams, and their implication that his beloved classic monster movies were *boring*. It cut straight to his very being. Earl had never been one to think much about his life's purpose. He'd always moved from one day to the next. Taking what enjoyment he could out of each moment, and not thinking about the future. Looking ahead meant contemplating one's ultimate worth against the grand scheme of things. Earl long ago had decided that way led to madness.

However, if he was honest with himself, the annual Halloween FrightFest had *become* his purpose. In a rare moment of boldness, ten years ago he'd proposed a revival of the annual Film FrightFest to the Town Board. He offered his expertise in "classic monster movies." Abruptly, Earl Flanagan, a veritable ghost in his own town, came to annual prominence. He'd not only become responsible for the FrightFest's movie selections, but also responsible for obtaining said films, setting everything up in the days before, and *running* the FightFest. *Himself.* Welcoming everyone to the event. Introducing each movie. Offering closing comments, and wishing everyone a Happy Halloween.

Amazingly, it got easier with every year. As time passed, his short speech about the nobility and suffering of the classic movie monsters felt less rehearsed and more heartfelt. About how classic monsters existed apart from society, not through any fault of their own, but because cruel fate had exiled them to loneliness. Always misunderstood, and hated by humanity. He kept his remarks brief and pointed, resisting the urge to rant against the proliferation of the mindless physical ruination and gratuitous bloodshed in "contemporary horror movies," focusing instead on the elegance of the classic monsters, and their tragic lot.

In the middle of Black Creek Bridge, Earl stopped. He breathed, realizing with some shock how deeply he'd immersed himself in the past. He shook his head and approached the bridge's edge, leaned against folded arms on the railing, and looked down the gurgling length of Black Creek.

In a moment of clarity, he grudgingly admitted the Town Board's assessment wasn't inaccurate. He *had* noticed attendance dropping. Lately, he'd also noticed more restlessness during his short speeches. More youths slipping out in between films, sometimes *during* films. Raedeker Park's amphitheater wasn't as full as in years past.

Earl thumped the railing with his fist. Bob Phillips and the Town Board were right. No one really wanted to watch the classic monsters anymore. Maybe the early years of FrightFest had been flukes. Folks hadn't come to watch the noble suffering of exiled creatures. They'd been curious, nothing more. Black and white films with little bloodshed, scant sexual innuendo and no nudity had been novelties. That's all.

Earl turned away from the railing and trudged off the bridge, onto the other side of Black Creek. He didn't want to think about it anymore, but the only other thing to think about, he didn't want to ponder, either . . .

Last night.

Getting so drunk bothered him. As a man who avoided any kind of excess, his indulgence seemed out of character. Granted, he'd been reeling from the Town Board's betrayal. Enraged at it, really.

Even so, something about the whole thing nagged at him, deep inside. He'd never lost track of time like that. Never once experienced such a loss of memory. He'd absolutely no recollection of what happened. It made him feel not only terribly vulnerable, but also *violated*, in a way.

Violated?

By whom?

Himself?

Earl slowed. He opened his right hand, held it up, and examined it more closely than he had this morning. If he tilted it just right, in the morning light . . . did he see a faint line running across the meat of his palm? Slightly raised and a little uneven? Almost like the healed scar of a wound from a shard of glass?

As he stared at the faint line, he realized he hadn't checked the floor for blood or glass. He hadn't seen anything noticeable when he turned off the television, but he hadn't really gotten down and looked, either. What if someone had swept up the glass and cleaned the blood . . .

But who? Him? Unconsciously? If he looked into the trash, would he find the shattered remains of a glass tumbler, smelling of whiskey?

Earl squeezed his hand into a fist and stuck it into his jacket pocket as he crossed Main Street and walked briskly up the library's front steps. He tried to shake off such silly thoughts. Ridiculous, all of it.

He lived in the real world. Much as he loved the unexplained mysteries of his movies, another part of him knew those fictions couldn't exist in real life. The everyday world consisted of routines, duties, obligations, responsibilities, and the occasional indulgences and pastimes. Pastimes like his movies. That was the natural order of things. As unexciting, monotonous, and occasionally stifling as it was, the natural order must be preserved.

As he opened the front door of Bassler Memorial Library, he realized—with a sharp sense of dismay—the unexplained didn't feel nearly as romantic or as magical as his movies made it out to be. His hazy memories of last night and the scar-not-scar on his hand didn't feel magical or romantic. He didn't feel enthralled. He felt sick, weak, and insignificant in the face of something incomprehensibly large and pitiless to everything he was.

10.

The day's routine eventually blunted the weirdness of last night, easing the sting of the Town Board's betrayal. Business at the library was brisker than usual; but it always perked up in the weeks before Halloween. Unfortunately, not because people were patronizing the sadly neglected horror section of the Fiction bookshelves, but because they were renting horror movies from the library's movie section. And of course, none of them were the classic monster movies he himself had personally donated to the library, but rather the schlock that modern-day Hollywood considered horror.

Still, Earl managed to stay busy enough to keep disturbing memories at bay. In between customers, he worked on his various columns with renewed vigor. The writer's block from the day before had dissipated. By lunch break, he'd completed two of his three columns. He felt so good about them, during his lunch, he began an essay about Contessa's portrayal of Arglwyddes on the computer in the break room.

In a rare stroke of authenticity, he began the essay with a recounting of the Town Board's dismissal of his FrightFest selections. He even put into words his strange experience the night before. The heavy drinking, the odd moment when it seemed as if Contessa herself loomed benevolently over him. The hallucination of cutting his hand, then finding himself in bed the next morning, with only the barest sign of what *might* be a faint scar on his palm.

It was as if, Earl typed with a flourish right before returning to work, *in my moment of desperation and grief, I'd summoned Contessa as the Druid goddess Arglwyddes, to bless me with her otherworldly power.*

Earl stared at the words he'd written. He'd never fooled himself about his writing ability. He accepted it as being technically proficient, nothing more. In fact, he realized his columns probably sounded dry, but then again, *he* was dry. His writing style fit his personality.

This was different. He'd no idea where it was headed, and didn't know what an objective reader might think. He'd never thought his writing could be emotionally moving. It never moved him; how could it move anyone else? This, however. It made his gut clench. Tightened his throat. God help him, he almost thought it sounded . . . *poignant.*

He glanced at his smart phone. His lunch break had ended ten minutes ago. He saved the essay to his thumb drive, removed it from the desktop and pocketed it, and closed down Open Office. He stood, his heart glowing pleasantly as he replayed the final line of his essay in his head. Last night's weirdness and the Town Board's treachery, seemed, for the moment, distant and unimportant.

11.

His glow lasted until the end of the day. After he'd completed his end-of-shift rounds, replacing books and magazines left on tables and in the reading-area recliners, he decided to check his email on the break room computer before leaving. Still high on the personal essay he'd started at lunch, he'd managed to finish all three of his articles by the end of the work day, and had emailed them to his various editors.

Normally his articles were received and published with no feedback. For some reason, however, he felt the need to check. A strange anxiety spiked in him as he saw the response from **editor@celluloid.com.** When he clicked the email and read the response, the world swayed under his feet:

"Hey, Earl. This sucks, and I'm sorry for the screw up. Someone was supposed to email you. Unfortunately, due to budget changes and a drop in circulation over the past month, The Celluloid had to make some tough decisions about content. We all love your column, but unfortunately can't run it anymore. Need more ad space to keep us afloat. Again, sorry you had to hear like this. Darryl probably forgot to email. He's such an idiot."

Earl stared at the email for several seconds. Re-read it, understanding the words as English, but for some reason unable to process them. The email couldn't be saying what he thought it was. Could it? It wasn't possible that the editors of *The Celluloid* had done almost the exact same thing the Town Board had . . . was it?

An icy ball of dread settled in his stomach. He backed out of the message and clicked on the next in line, from **submissions@classicfrights.com**. For several seconds he stared at the message but refused to comprehend it. As if, by doing so, he might forestall fate. In the end, however, he gave in.

"Mr. Flanagan—over the past year, the site traffic of Classic

Frights has dipped considerably, causing several of our sponsors to reconsider their arrangements with us. Because of this, the publisher of Classic Frights has asked us to make some changes in our content. After long consideration, we've made the tough decision not to renew your column. Thank you for your commitment to us, and your diligence. We wish you the best of luck."

Earl stared at the message. A numb sensation spread from his center, all throughout him. His hand twitched slightly. Then, he clicked back to his inbox, and selected the final new email, from **webbfilmography@mailbox.com.** This email was shorter, more abrupt, also more impersonal than the others:

"Dear contributor: due to significant department budget cuts, a dwindling readership, and fewer staff volunteers, the Cinema Studies Department of Webb Community College will be discontinuing Webb Filmography. Thank you for your dedication, and best of luck."

Earl felt a detached conflict over the final email. He could choose to believe his column wasn't rejected in particular. Webb Filmography had fallen under the ax of Budgetary Fate, a situation out of his hands. Regardless, he still felt (irrationally) as if somehow his column about classic monster films was to blame for the Filmography's dwindling readership. As if his dedication to them had doomed the circular to oblivion.

The door to the break-room cracked open. "Earl," Ms. Bassler said from the doorway, "Kassie Frontera has to go out of town this weekend to visit family. Would you be able to run the front desk Saturday morning, until noon?"

Earl swallowed and summoned what he hoped was a neutral smile. Looked over his shoulder and said, "Sure, Lida. That'll be fine."

Ms. Bassler smiled in return. "Thank you, Earl. I don't know if I say it often enough; but the fact is, I don't know what I'd do without you. Have a good evening."

She bustled away and let the door close behind her. Earl turned, exited out of his email account, closed the browser, and pushed away from the computer. He went to the refrigerator, collected his lunch box, and grabbed his jacket from the row of hooks next to it. He was about to walk out the door when he saw them, sitting on a table against the wall, near the door.

The library often discarded items which hadn't been checked out in years. Lida never threw anything out, however. She held monthly sales of used books and movies under the guise of "raising funds," but her real purpose was to find new homes for their discarded items. Before she did this, however, she always offered her staff first crack, for free.

This month, a row of paperbacks, hardcovers, and several piles of audio-cassette and CD audio-books littered the table. As well as a stack of DVD and Blu-Rays. Earl recognized the covers immediately. With a slightly trembling hand, he reached out and sorted through the fifteen classic monster movies he himself had purchased for the library almost five years ago. At the time, he'd seen it as just another small part of his quest to keep the noble monsters of yesteryear alive.

He shakily opened each case. They'd never been checked out. He saw the truth; his gesture was nothing but an exercise in futile vanity. Even worse? Only Lida had the authority to discard items. She'd not only chosen to discard these, but had casually placed them on the discard table, with very little consideration as to how it would affect him.

Earl snapped the last DVD case shut.

He gathered them up. Feeling a bizarre and somewhat terrifying synchronicity in the act—discards collected by a walking Discard—Earl slipped out of the break room, and out of the library.

12.

Later, Earl was never sure if he'd *intended* on visiting Cutting's Liquor on Acer Street, or if he'd noticed it simply because it sat across from Handy's Pawn and Thrift, just across the way from the library. In the end it didn't matter. After going to Handy's, approaching the front counter and exchanging pleasantries with the shopkeeper (possibly the only person in town besides Ms. Bassler who greeted him warmly by name), he offered the shopkeeper most of the discarded movies. Having enjoyed many visits to the eclectic junk store and several wonderful discussions with the shopkeeper about classic horror cinema, Earl knew that, all else failing, the shopkeeper could find a buyer for the movies online.

The shopkeeper accepted the movies with a sad sort of smile, nodding reverently. He didn't inquire, but he seemed to know, without Earl saying a thing. He solemnly promised Earl he'd find new homes for them.

In the stack had been the three Contessa Victoria movies he'd planned on showing at FrightFest. He kept those, slipping them into his jacket pocket as he crossed the street to Cuttings's. Once inside, he proceeded straight to the bourbon section and bought a $25 bottle of Booker's.

Now, as he sat on the small promontory on Clifton Lake's east shore, intermittently sipping straight from the bottle, he thought it sad—and oddly amusing—that he'd expected the clerk to look at him in shock for buying a bottle of bourbon at five o'clock on a Wednesday night. As if the clerk would even know who he was. Or care.

Of course, the clerk rang up his sale with empty eyes and a slack face, showing neither shock nor recognition. Why would he? Even if he was a regular attendee of FrightFest, it hardly seemed likely he'd ever paid attention to who announced movies people apparently found so terribly dull. Earl shook his head, moderately bemused at the thought.

He raised the bottle to his lips and drank. It burned less with each sip, and the bourbon eased down his throat to settle into a numbing glow in his belly.

He'd called a taxi to bring him out to Clifton Lake, instead of making what would've proven to be a twenty-minute walk. Again, part of him expected the cab driver to give him and his brown paper bag a side-eye. However, the Yellow Cab driver simply stared into his rear-view mirror blankly and asked in a deadpan monotone, "Where to?"

Earl told him. Ten minutes later, after he'd paid his fare, the cab driver left without a glance.

It was a short walk on a narrow trail which followed the shoreline, to the promontory he now sat on. He knew it well. The only activity he and his father had ever shared was Saturday morning fishing. It didn't matter that Earl had no interest in fishing. As far back as he could remember, Paul Flanagan—a staid man who for thirty years held down a steady if unimpressive position as the General Manager of the Webb County Credit Union in Old Forge - took his only son fishing every Saturday morning. Until he was old enough to fish himself, Earl would sit quietly on the promontory next to his father, either reading his latest picture book, or staring quietly at the water. When old enough to fish, he would dutifully bait his hook and cast his line, never exactly taking pleasure in the activity, but not hating it, either.

Earl snorted at the memory. That's how it started, he realized. His dutiful compliance. Somehow he'd sensed it would've been futile to protest those Saturday morning fishing trips, because Fathers Took Their Boys Fishing, and that's all there was to it. He'd acquiesced and gone along.

He'd like to say it was because, deep inside, some part of him understood how happy it made his father. He didn't think that was the case. Oddly enough, he didn't recall his father expressing much joy in the act at all. More of a dutiful obligation to some ghostly memory most likely foisted upon him by *his* father, Earl's grandfather. A distant man Earl had never gotten to know because a heart attack had claimed his life before Earl was born.

No, the simplest answer was he'd gone fishing every Saturday with his father because he'd learned early on it was easier to go along. He'd adopted said philosophy as a way of life. Before this week, he'd always believed it had served him well. Before the Town Board and Bob Phillips showed him the truth: He was a pushover. A doormat. A speed-bump of little consequence, nothing more.

He took a bigger sip of bourbon, which burned more than the previous sips. It made him dizzy as the liquor filled his empty stomach with its blazing heat. The lake and its far shoreline began to waver. His stomach lurched slightly, so he closed his eyes in an effort to regain some hold on his suddenly shaky equilibrium.

In the darkness, he saw her.

Arglwyddes y Cors.

Daughter of the Mists. Striding out of ethereal fog, tendrils of which clung to her like a second skin. Black hair somehow shining brighter than the night. Large, luminous eyes glowing against pale skin. She was reaching for him. Bright red lips murmuring something loving. Something needful, yet mournful, also.

So powerful was the image that when Earl opened his eyes, for a brief instant, he imagined Contessa Victoria Williams as Arglwyddes y Cors, striding across the surface of Clifton Lake in an oddly messiah-like fashion, her white gown as insubstantial as the mists from which she came. He blinked once. The image vanished, leaving nothing but quiet waters and the red and orange leaves of the west shoreline.

At that moment, crushing despair descended upon him. Its weight felt unbearable. Earl Flanagan, a man who'd always prided himself on a life of moderation, felt as if a yawning black pit of emptiness had opened up at his feet. A pit he longed to cast himself into, because really. Who'd notice? Who'd care if he no longer drifted ghost-like through this life? Would anyone miss him?

Lida Bassler would, for a while, though he didn't think she'd be surprised. If asked, she'd say he was a quiet worker who always did his job, showed up on time, and treated her and library patrons with respect. But then she'd smile sadly, and say something like, "Still waters run deep," insinuating she'd always wondered how "happy" he really was.

His parents - down in their retirement mobile home in Boca Raton, Florida - would merely shake their heads sadly in their own reserved way, then go on with their retired lives. Most likely they'd express little surprise. Maybe say something along the lines of, "He was always such a quiet boy. Had no idea what was going on inside that head of his."

Of course, Mom and Dad had never made much of an effort to learn, had they? Just the fact that Dad took him fishing every Saturday during the Spring, Summer and Fall without ever asking him if he wanted to spoke volumes.

Mom's birthday and Christmas gifts were always functional. Clothes. Jackets. New shoes. School supplies. Even after he'd developed a love of the classic movie monsters, his gifts had always been what Mom deemed was necessary, not what he liked. So he'd come to accept it as a way of life. All you ever got was what someone thought you needed, not what you wanted.

Earl took a deep swig of bourbon. Closed his eyes, his face screwing up as his mouth and throat burned. As the glow faded, he shakily set the bottle down next to him. He picked up the DVDs he'd donated to the library. Opened the one on top, which he'd watched last night. His favorite. *Daughter of the Mists.*

It had been discarded, like him. Had he not rescued this and the others, they would've been jumbled into the wares for the library's next used book and movie sale. Maybe they would've been purchased. Most likely not. They'd get carted to the thrift store Lida's cousin owned in Booneville, to sit and rot on shelves next to DVDs and VHS tapes of *Mrs. Doubtfire, Driving Miss Daisy,* and *In the Heat of the Night.*

Discarded. Left to rot.

Just like him.

Earl snapped the DVD case shut. With a flick of his wrist, he impulsively tossed it out into the water. It hit with a thin splash, and floated for a moment. Tottered on its side, then sank. The other two followed quickly, consigned to the same watery fate.

He sat very still. Staring at the rippling water which had accepted his offerings so quickly. He'd no idea what time it was, or how much time had passed since he'd come here. He'd no desire to check his phone and find out. The sky had darkened, so he assumed six-thirty, seven o'clock.

A light fog was rising from Clifton Lake. A little odd, because fog usually came in the morning, though evening fog wasn't unheard of. It was just . . . uncommon.

Earl grabbed hold of the bourbon. It felt slick to the touch. He tightened his grip, guided the bottle to his mouth, and upended it, finishing the rest of it in one furious gulp which scorched his throat.

It almost proved too much. His throat spasmed. He lurched forward, coughing. Spittle flecked his lips and he drooled. For a moment, he felt certain he was going to vomit.

He closed his eyes and breathed slowly. Coughed once more. Gradually, the twitches in his stomach calmed. He raised his free hand and rubbed his face, which felt numb. His lips and his *teeth* buzzed. Wheels turned sluggishly in his head. He'd just downed a whole bottle in . . . an hour? Forty-five minutes? He didn't have much time left before he passed out.

Then he heard it.

Floating through the air like a distant melody carried by the wind. His name. Just his name, but sung as a haunting lyric, with a soulful yearning.

He looked out over Clifton Lake, and saw her. Gliding from the mists. Walking on water.

Arglwyddes y Cors.

Daughter of the Mists.

Tendrils of fog swirled around her, almost indistinguishable from her sheer, flowing white dress. Her green eyes luminous, full of great need. Her red lips parted in a song composed of only one lyric. His name. She strode across the water toward him, her glistening black hair (so striking against her alabaster skin) blown into a halo around her face.

For a moment, part of him felt fear. Another face lingered beneath the beautiful facade. Something vulpine and hungry, hair whipping and hissing like Medusa's head full of snakes. He blinked, and only the beauty remained. Hands reaching out, beckoning.

Her need spoke to him. Her yearning touched him in a place which had laid dormant all his life. Arousal flickered through him. He wasn't surprised in the slightest to feel himself stiffen in his pants, as her lovely voice caressed the deepest parts of him.

She wanted him.

Needed him.

And there was only one way she could have him.

With a sudden and violent movement, Earl slammed the empty bourbon bottle against the promontory. It shattered, leaving only the stem and its jagged edge. With a forcefulness which seemed to come from *outside* of him, he dragged the stem's jagged edge along the inside of his right forearm. He gasped as bright burning pain radiated from where glass teeth bit into his skin.

He clenched his jaw, however, and ground those jagged edges deeper as he stared at the Arglwyddes y Cors. She stretched out her arms, smiling, exposing white teeth which suddenly seemed far too sharp in a mouth which also seemed to open far too wide. A sliver of dismay pierced him, as her mouth stretched even wider . . . wide enough, almost, to swallow his head.

Still, those swirling green eyes drew him in. He ground the jagged end of the bottle's stem into his forearm even harder, feeling the jagged glass dig into flesh. Wet warmth ran down his wrist, but he didn't look. All he could do was fall forward into her swirling green gaze.

She beckoned to him again.

He nodded. Leaned forward, and slid off the promontory into the water, which came up to his waist. Stumbling on the algae-slicked rocks littering the bottom, Earl Flanagan slowly walked deeper into Clifton Lake, unmindful of the cold and the wet, mindful only of her need, and her yearning. He walked until the water passed his chin, his face, and his neck, and there was nothing but blackness, and her shimmering form.

13.

"Omigod! Holy shit! Are you okay? Hey . . . you with me?"

Earl heard the words distantly, as if they were spoken from far away. He felt numb and disconnected but sensed, somehow, he was lying on his back. He couldn't *feel* it, however. Couldn't tell what he was lying on, or where.

"Hey. Hey, give me a sign here. Shit. HELLO!"

There.

He felt a sensation. Something dull. Like . . . leather striking leather? No. A hand. A hand slapping the side of his face. It felt muffled. Like he'd been doped with pain medication. He felt like a protective layer of plastic enclosed him completely, shielding him from the world.

Another dull blow. This time it definitely felt like fingers on his face. Even so, he felt no pain, or anything else. Now, he thought, two hands cupped his face, and shook it.

"Hey! Hey, you with me? Oh, shit, Danielle, you *idiot*, check his fucking . . ."

Two fingers pressed against his neck. Checking for his pulse, no doubt. As if the thought summoned it into existence, he felt his heartbeat, then. In his ears, and against those pressing fingers. Slow, sluggish, lethargic . . . but still there.

Not dead, then.

Not yet.

"Okay. Okay. Got a pulse. Now . . ."

A sliver of light. At the same time, Earl experienced the very strange sensation of something—a fingertip? - peeling back his eyelid. Why couldn't he open his eyes? He wanted to. Wanted to speak. *Say* something, but he couldn't.

A ghostly oval swam into view through that slit. A face. Wisps of raven black hair floating around it. Wide green eyes set against alabaster skin, a too-wide mouth, ringed with grime-crusted, razor-like teeth . . .

With a gasp, Earl arched his back, then flopped back onto wet sand. He jerked, shivered, saw that frightfully wide maw once more, and sat up with a cry. The motion instantly made him sick. Before he could stop himself, he bent his head to one side and vomited water and bourbon into the sand in several lurching heaves.

"Whoa! Relax! It's okay. It's okay."

A cool hand held the back of his head. The other patted his back. "Breathe. Slow down. You probably swallowed half the damn lake. Lucky you didn't drown."

Earl closed his eyes and tried to slow his gasping breaths and pounding heart. His thoughts felt muddy and jumbled. He dimly remembered sitting on the promontory where his father used to take him fishing, methodically drinking an entire bottle of bourbon. A grave mistake, he understood now, given his usually moderate drinking habits. He'd been depressed, gripped by despair, because . . .

He blinked, thinking hard.

The pamphlet.

Canceled movies. His discontinued columns. Then, the final blow. Lida Bassler discarding movies he'd donated, like so much garbage. He'd reached the end of his rope, surely. Had he been about to . . . to . . . ?

A sudden urgency gripped him. He frantically examined the inside of his right forearm, expecting to see a jagged mess of slashed flesh oozing blood. He saw, however, nothing but unblemished skin.

like this morning.

No sign of the damage he remembered doing with the jagged end of the bourbon bottle he'd broken against the promontory . . .

The promontory.

Across the lake from where he lay, now.

"Look, I don't mean to pester you after what looks like a *really* bad accident . . . but what the hell happened?"

Earl looked over Clifton Lake to the promontory, which was only a distant speck. He'd been sitting on the shore *across* the lake. How the hell had he gotten all the way to the public beach on the other end?

"Mister?"

Earl shivered and looked back at the person who'd found him. He regarded her fully for the first time. Her hair was tucked under a baseball cap. Her face looked plain and unmarked, but with a certain girlishness which suited her. Her eyes glimmered an inquisitive, soft brown. He couldn't tell how tall she was, squatting next to him, but he thought she might be near his height. She wore running shoes, tights, and a windbreaker over what looked like an Under-Armour running shirt. Wireless buds poked from her ears.

"I . . . " Earl licked his lips. Glanced across the lake, his mind churning. What could he say? How could he explain what happened to this stranger, when even *he* wasn't sure?

"I . . . I rented a boat," he lied slowly, hoping she'd put his hesitation down to shock, "was feeling poorly about some things. Decided to row around the lake. Clear my head."

He glanced at her, saw nothing but concern in her eyes, then dropped his gaze. "I'm not going to lie. I'd been drinking. A lot."

At least *that* was true.

"I dropped my bottle overboard. I reached over to grab it . . . "

He shuddered. Not because of his horror at the fabricated memory, but at the realization he was lying through his teeth, and lying *well*. Like it was a latent talent which had been hiding inside, all this time.

He looked up at her, silently pleading her to accept his story. He assumed the confused and fearful expression of someone who found memories too painful, and didn't want to relive them. "I don't know what happened after that."

She laced her fingers together, elbows sitting on her knees as she squatted before him. A small, demure smile played on her lips. "I bet you're embarrassed as hell. Probably feeling a whole mile of stupid right now. But I used to work as an EMT for the town. You'd be amazed how many folks have taken a similar tumble over the years. You're not alone, trust me."

Earl smiled weakly, not because he felt sheepish, but because he still couldn't resurrect memories of what had happened after he went into the water. "If you say so."

She nodded, smiling wider, looking almost impish. And, Earl realized with a burst of surprise, attractive, also. "I do. You're sitting on your ass in wet sand, soaked to the bone, but you're also alive. That should trump any embarrassment, in my book. We've all done stupid things when drunk. At least you're still around to feel crappy about it."

She extended a hand. "Danielle. Danielle Lathrop."

He accepted the handshake, and again felt surprise at how firm it was, how assertive her grip felt . . . and how attractive he found that. "Earl. Earl Flanagan."

She eyed him with an inquisitive air. "Earl Flanagan. Why do I know that name?"

He shrugged. "I work at the library. Desk clerk."

She smiled again and shook her head. "Naw. I'm not much of a reader."

It seemed unlikely, however . . . "Well, I've run the Halloween FrightFest at Raedeker Park for the past ten years."

She snapped her fingers and pointed at him, eyes wide in bemused amazement. "That's it! You're in charge of those cool black and white movies they show every year. I *love* those."

An unexpected warmth filled Earl, chasing away the chill damp he felt crawling on his skin. "Well, thank you. Sometimes, these past few years, I've felt like . . . well, I've wondered if maybe people found them . . . boring."

Danielle beamed. "No way. The classics never go out of style."

He smiled in return. They sat like that for several minutes, grinning like idiots at each other, until she finally broke the silence as she stood. "So. Are you going to be okay? You need me to call anyone?"

Earl got to his feet also. Slowly, feeling achy and sore. He shook his head. "There's no one to call."

A shadow crossed Danielle's face. He realized he'd sounded much more depressed than he'd intended. "I mean," he added quickly, forcing a smile he didn't quite feel, "I live alone. My parents retired to Florida years ago. And I . . . I don't get out much. Don't have much in the way of a social circle, or anyone to call, really. It's fine," he added, not liking the look of sympathy he saw glimmering in her eyes, because it threatened to take him back to how he'd felt on the promontory, as he'd been drinking himself into oblivion. "I'm a solitary person, not a lonely one. Trust me."

For the most part, that was true. His attack of depression had come from the dismissal of his purpose, not from feeling lonely. However, even in the brevity of this encounter, Earl thought that, when he said goodbye to Danielle, he might know what loneliness felt like, after all.

Danielle nodded slowly, not looking completely convinced, but apparently deciding not to push the matter. "I can respect that. Don't get out much myself. This," she gestured along the beach, "is all the social activity I get. I work part-time in Old Forge at The

Adirondack Museum as a tour guide, and I spend all my free time behind a camera, so . . . ”

Something flickered to life in Earl. “You’re a photographer?”

Danielle nodded, looking sheepish, as if she wished she hadn’t brought it up. For some reason, Earl found that endearing. “Yes. Freelance. I shoot for some local newspapers, a few regional magazines and websites, and two national periodicals. Mostly scenic stuff. Classic Adirondack tourism shots.”

He sensed something in her which he recognized. A feeling which spoke to him. “But that’s not what you prefer to shoot. Is it?”

She smiled, looking a little embarrassed. “You’ll think it’s weird.”

He snorted and laughed. It came out sounding rusty; like a gear seldom used. “You just found me unconscious on the beach after I drank too much and almost drowned. I can handle it.”

She laughed. It sounded bright, unrestrained, and carefree. Earl couldn’t remember ever hearing anyone sound so delightful. “Point taken. Okay. I love to shoot abandoned ruins. Old, empty houses. Like Old Bassler House? The abandoned La Pierre place, out by the tracks? The old factory along Black River, near White Lake? That’s what I like to shoot. And in black and white. There’s something more . . . I don’t know what the word is . . . ”

“Elegant,” Earl said softly, knowing exactly what she meant, of course. “Stately. Black and white lends more gravitas.”

Something shimmered in Danielle’s eyes. “Yes,” she whispered.

A heartbeat passed. Despite the damp clothes sticking to his skin, despite the strange circumstances which had led him to this point, Earl felt a subtle warmth inside. It felt good talking with Danielle. Good and warm. God help him, he felt the faint stirrings of . . .

Something over her shoulder caught his eye.

Markings in the sand.

His breath caught in his throat. A bone-shivering cold doused him. He couldn’t repress a shudder, but at least he had a good explanation. He forced a smile and said, “Well. It’s getting late, and I’m getting cold. Should be getting home.”

Danielle frowned slightly, looking concerned again. “Are you sure you don’t need a ride? You’re not going to walk home in those wet clothes?”

For a brief moment, the thought of riding with Danielle filled

Earl with that pleasant warmth again. But his eyes flickered over her shoulder to those markings in the sand. It took all his effort not to break out shivering. "No, that's fine. I don't live far from here," he lied. "I don't want to get your car wet."

She tipped her head, lips pursed. Her expression suddenly coy, and hard to read. "It's no trouble. Really."

Again, a flicker of warmth, of desire . . . but he glanced once more at the sand, then nervously started to back away. "Thank you anyway," he said in a jovial tone he knew sounded forced. "I'll be fine. And thank you for . . . for helping me. It means a lot. Oh . . ." he hesitated, and then added, before turning to walk away, "stop by the library sometime! I work days."

Without waiting for a response (which he knew was rude, but he could no longer help himself) he turned and walked away. He knew it looked like he was retreating or running away, and he didn't want her to think that's what he was doing, though he knew he was.

From what?

Markings in the sand.

Markings which looked like narrow, feminine, bare footprints leading from the water to where he'd been laying in the sand. Then circling back to the water, from which they came.

14.

It took half an hour for Earl to walk through town, past the library, and to his home on Ford Street. As was his usual luck, he encountered no one. By the time he turned the key in his front door, his joints ached from the damp clothes, and he was actively shivering.

But he hadn't thought about being cold and the wet. He also (sadly) hadn't thought about Danielle Lathrop. All he could think about was those footprints. Bare-feet. Narrow, and though he was no expert, clearly feminine. Leading from Clifton Lake to where Danielle had found him lying on the sand, then returning to the waters. But they *couldn't* have been footprints.

Couldn't have been.

Earl immediately went to the bathroom. Turned on the shower and waited until steam filled the room. He stripped his damp clothes off and stepped under scalding hot sprays which warmed his chilled skin. He stayed under the shower for a long time, trying to wash away the memory of his passive-aggressive suicide attempt, and the impossibility of what had happened.

He'd had too much to drink. Hallucinated gouging his wrist open, and somehow fell into the lake, only to wash up on the *opposite* side, onto the public beach. He stood under the shower-head, pelted by hot sprays, trying to wash it all away, and only partially succeeding.

15.

Earl stood in his theater before the silent and dark flat screen television. He'd been standing there ever since he'd gotten out of the shower, toweled off, and dressed in a dry sweatshirt and sweatpants. He'd thought about watching one of his Contessa Victoria Williams movies to unwind—inclined toward *Daughter of the Mists,* of course—but for some reason, he hadn't put the movie into the DVD player, much less turned the television on.

Why?

Because he didn't want to see Contessa right now. Especially in her role as the Arglwyddes y Cors. Fragmented images kept flitting through his mind of a lady dressed in white. Black hair framing alabaster skin. Striding across Clifton Lake, beckoning to him. Of him sinking beneath the waters, and something swimming up from its depths toward him, drawing him close, embracing him, putting its mouth . . .

ringed with too many razor sharp teeth

. . . to his, and *breathing* into him. Breathing *for* him. As if they were connected. Sharing air, sharing lungs . . . sharing each other, as *one creature.*

He took his hands out of his pocket and covered his face. Rubbed his eye sockets with the heels of his palms, as if he could brush away the strange images in his head. They faded slightly, but still flickered there, regardless.

He stood like that for several more minutes, until a heavy exhaustion fell over him. He turned and left his theater. Shut the light off, closed the door, and went straight to bed, where he fell into a deep sleep.

16.

Earl floats in a blue-green, watery world. When he looks down, he sees not the lake bottom, but a dusty murk, out of which waved brownish—green fronds of something vaguely plant-like. When he looks up, he sees nothing. Just more water, with the barest glint of sunlight filtering down through the depths.

Earl

He thrashes his arms and tries to spin, but the best he manages is a lazy circle. He sees nothing behind him, just more water. It occurs to him, as he dangles in the blue-green abyss, that he isn't holding his breath. He isn't breathing, either. He's just *there*.

Earl

come

He faces forward again. In the distance, he sees a flicker of white. Something swimming toward him. Not a fish, or an animal. A person.

A *woman*.

Wearing a white dress which billows around her. Raven black hair streams in all directions from her head. A shiver runs through him as, once again, the name *Medusa* springs to mind. Even so, he feels an all-consuming desire loom in his chest. She's swimming closer. Will soon be close enough to touch. How he longs for that. How he longs for *her*.

Earl

come

be one with me

my love

do not reject me

please

Earl reaches for her. The woman's features become clearer. Her brilliant green eyes. High, proud cheekbones. Regal gaze. It's *her*. Without a shadow of a doubt, he knows it's her, and not that flimsy shade played by an unknown actress who died in obscurity, but the real thing. The *real* goddess.

Arglwyddes y Cors.

She comes within five feet. Reaches out, and touches her

fingertips to his. Her features light up with hunger and desire, eyes bright and alive. She intertwines her fingers with his, and the contact sends electric thrills through him.

She pulls him closer. Opens a mouth—ringed with impossibly sharp teeth—and lunges for his neck.

He screams, but nothing comes out, as water fills his mouth and throat. He thrashes in pain and manic fear, but something else pulses through him as those impossibly sharp teeth dig into his flesh . . .

Longing. Desire, and arousal.

Acceptance.

November 1st

"When you talk about someone *completing* you, Earl, making you feel whole . . . are you referring to Danielle Lathrop? I'm aware that you two had been seeing each other the past few weeks."

An expression of profound sadness and regret crossed Earl's face. He looked down into his blood-stained hands, which slowly clenched and unclenched, and said, "Danielle is a wonderful young woman. I've never met anyone like her, ever. Never met anyone who shares my love of elegance, of classical beauty . . . "

He trailed off, staring into his twisting hands. Sensing there was more to come, Chris remained silent, waiting Earl out. Five minutes later, the former librarian clerk said, "I truly enjoyed every minute I spent with Danielle. I really did, and I'm so thankful for our time together."

Chris leaned forward slightly, keeping his mask in place. "But."

Earl's shoulders sagged, as the air left him in a defeated sigh. "Have you ever assembled puzzles, Sheriff Baker? When you near the end, close to the picture's reveal, there's always this *one* piece which *looks* like it will fit where you want it to."

He raised bleary, sorrowful eyes to meet Chris' gaze. "It's not the best analogy, I know. But still. Danielle is a wonderful, warm, caring woman who loves the things I do. She *looks* like the right fit. I tried to make her fit, but in the end . . . "

He shrugged and looked away. "She didn't fit where I needed her to, and I couldn't *make* her fit, regardless of how hard I tried."

Silence fell.

Earl looked down into his hands, his gaze going very far away again. Chris let him sit there for several more minutes, before saying softly, "Interesting you refer to Danielle in the present tense.

"Considering she's dead."

17.

Thursday, October 6th
11 AM

Earl sat at the kitchen table, typing on his laptop, recounting the vivid nightmare he'd suffered last night. As he wrote, he experienced the confusing medley of emotions anew. Excitement, awe and arousal, clashing with terror.

He didn't know what it meant. Even so, he felt compelled to type it down. Something told him it was important that he chronicle everything which was happening. Why remained a mystery. Was he writing a book? A memoir? If so, it was destined for a box in the closet, because it was a memoir about an insignificant man. A manifesto no one would ever read. He knew nothing about publishing, and even less about self-publishing. The whole thing was a foolish endeavor.

Still, he'd called in sick for the first time in four years to stay home and write. He told himself it was to recover from last night's traumatic events, but he felt fine. Better than fine, actually. He felt healthy, fit, energized, and motivated. He felt better than he'd felt in years. Perhaps . . . ever?

Which was odd. FrightFest had been perverted. His columns canceled. Even Lida had rejected him by discarding the movies he'd donated to the library. He'd tried to commit suicide last night. How could he possibly feel so *good*?

Was it the mystery blossoming in his life? The dreams of Arglwyddes y Cors, which had been enthralling, arousing, *and* terrifying? The female footprints on the beach last night. He also couldn't deny his thoughts about Danielle. Maybe he'd misread her, but he thought something had sparked between them. Something he wanted to pursue.

This produced another confusing—and oddly amusing—conflict. The difference in his feelings about the dreams of Arglwyddes y Cors, and how he felt about Danielle. The former was intoxicating, enthralling, all-consuming. But his feelings for Danielle, a woman he'd just met, were different. Calmer, gentler. *Innocent* seemed trite and cliche, but he couldn't think of any other way to describe it. While a deep part of him desired *and* feared Arglwyddes y Cors, Danielle made him feel safe. Protected.

He spent the morning writing his thoughts, pausing only briefly to renew his coffee and visit the bathroom. His enthusiasm surprised him. He'd always enjoyed writing his columns, but after a dutiful fashion. He'd viewed them as tasks which needed completion. Once he'd finished them and emailed them off, he felt productive, nothing more. Writing the events of the last few days filled him with a sense of *completion* he'd never known before. In fact, so immersed was he in the act, that he didn't consciously register the wall phone ringing in the kitchen until it started up the second time.

18.

"Hello?"

"Earl? This is Bob Phillips. I called the library. They said you'd taken a sick day. Is everything all right? Was wondering if you had a few minutes to chat."

Earl turned slowly and looked out the kitchen window overlooking his modest backyard. The sound of Bob's voice made his stomach churn. Clearly, he hadn't gotten over the Town Board's decision to dismiss his FrightFest selections. "I'm fine," he said evenly, striving to keep the bitterness out of his voice, but at the same time, feeling no need to pretend amiability. "I dropped my cell phone into Black Creek and haven't gotten a new one yet. What do you want?"

Phillips paused, made a noise which sounded like he was clearing his throat. When he spoke, to Earl's mild shock, the chairman of the Town Board—one of Clifton Height's "pillars"— sounded meek and unsure. *"It's just that . . . well, to be very honest, I think maybe the Board was a bit hasty in its decision against the movies you proposed for this year's FrightFest."*

Earl continued staring out the window. He didn't respond for several seconds, trying to process Phillips' words.

"Earl? Are you still there?"

Odd, how nervous Phillips sounded.

"Yes, I'm here. I'm sorry, not sure I follow. Are you saying . . . you want to re-instate my selections for FrightFest?"

"*Well, yes. We never should have made those changes without letting you know properly. And I never should've passed that off to someone like Norman, who we all know is a terrible communicator. It should've come from me. You deserve more . . . respect than that.*"

Earl's mind struggled to make sense of what was happening. "So what are you saying?" He was having a hard time reigning in his emotions. The whole situation felt unreal, which put him on edge. "Are you saying that . . . "

"*Yes! Absolutely. If you're still willing to screen those Contessa Victoria Williams movies for FrightFest, I believe you should.*" Phillips sounded oddly desperate for Earl to say *yes*, for some reason. "*We were wrong to dismiss you so casually. Restitution must be made for wrongs done to you.*"

Earl frowned slightly at the phrase. Not only did it seem oddly formal, but something about it rang familiar. He'd heard it somewhere before. However, his slight uneasiness quickly faded as realization sank in.

Phillips was returning his purpose. Letting him fulfill the role he was meant to play. Even better, not only was he championing the elegant and tragic monster in an age of post-modern chainsaw maniacs, but also, he was holding up a tragic monster who deserved far more recognition.

Of course, the pamphlets advertising those *other* movies had already been distributed. They might face some criticism for changing the lineup when so many people had already bought tickets for a slasher fest. But Earl didn't care. Fate had finally turned in his favor. It had returned his life's mission.

"You have my deepest gratitude," he said to Phillips as he turned away from the window. "I can't say how much this means to me. Thank you."

"*You're very welcome,*" Phillips said, sounding enormously relieved. Almost too relieved, considering the circumstances. "*One last thing.*"

"Yes?"

"*This is going to be . . . an executive decision on my part. The Board hasn't voted on this, I've simply gone ahead and approved your movies for FrightFest. There might be lingering_resistance regarding my decision. Don't worry about it. If anyone on the Board opposes, they'll fall in line. I have no doubt."*

Phillips hung up without waiting for Earl's response. Earl stared at the phone for several seconds, until it started beeping at him. He hung it up, returned to the table, sat down, and slowly returned to his writing.

On the surface, he felt happy. He would get to reveal Contessa Victoria Williams to the moviegoers of Clifton Heights, after all. On a deeper level, however, he mulled over Phillips' odd statements. "Restitution must be made for wrongs done to you." "Any Board member opposing his decision would "fall in line." Something seemed ominous about both, though Earl couldn't put his finger on why.

19.

Earl spent the rest of the day writing. His essay had grown to almost five thousand words. It was far too long for a blog post, and he had no idea where it was ultimately going, or what he'd do with it when he finished. That didn't concern him, however. For whatever reasons, writing about these last few days and their strange events felt more fulfilling than anything he'd ever written before, so he embraced it.

For dinner, he celebrated by ordering a delivery of Drunken Noodles from the new Tai place on Main Street, right next to *Chin's Pizza & Wings*. He also decided to eat in his theater, while once again watching *Daughter of the Mists*. He poured himself only two fingers of Chivas Regal this time, on the rocks. He wanted to enjoy his viewing experience, instead of getting drunk again.

A third of the way into the movie, Earl experienced an odd revelation. The hapless museum clerk—as Earl had seen countless times before - cut his hand on a sharp edge of Arglwyddes's totem while unpacking it in the storage room. Hissing in pain and annoyance, he dropped the totem on the examination table and spun to find a towel or rag to stanch the bleeding. In turning, he missed the totem's faint, hazy glow. So intent on cleaning his hand, he didn't notice the mists spreading from the bloody totem.

The hand temporarily bandaged by a rag, the clerk turned back to the smoking totem, and stumbled back in fear. The image of a striking woman with straight black hair and piercing eyes slowly coalesced from the mists. Tall, regal, with high cheekbones and a haughty demeanor, for a brief moment the film's early special effects achieved greatness as the druid goddess' flowing white dress seemed to form from the mists itself.

The clerk stood rooted to his spot, clutching his wounded hand and staring at the

Arglwyddes y Cors as she strode imperiously toward him. Stammering, in a high, squeaky voice, the clerk managed, "*Who . . . who are you?*"

The Arglwyddes y Cors smiled demurely and coyly—as she always did, at that moment—and stepped closer to the clerk. She reached out and clasped the clerk's injured hand with hers. Pulled it to her, and said in a luxurious voice, "*I am Arglwyddes y Cors. The Daughter of the Mists. You have summoned me, and I have come. Restitution must be made for the wrongs heaped upon you by lesser men. I am that restitution.*"

She pulled the clerk into a ravishing embrace and kissed him passionately as she pressed his injured hand to her breasts. When they finally parted, (the clerk looking dazed and confused; the Arglwyddes y Cors looking *satisfied*), the rag fell away from the clerk's hand. A close-up revealed the hand miraculously healed.

Earl paused the scene. He stared at the healed hand, unable to stop himself from thinking about *his* hand the other morning. That, and before she'd kissed the clerk, the Arglwyddes y Cors had said something so familiar it sent chills running through him.

He rewound the scene to just before the kiss. Hit pause, and stared at Contessa's imposing figure. At her proud features, piercing eyes, and the elegant, arrogant grace which radiated from her. After several minutes, he reluctantly hit play.

"*Restitution must be made for the wrongs heaped upon you by lesser men. I am that restitution.*"

He paused the movie again, struck by a dull shock. Bob Phillips' parting words on the phone were very similar to the Arglwyddes y Cors's petition. "Restitution must be made for wrongs done to you."

Earl couldn't explain the similarity. Had Phillips watched *Daughter in the Mists*? Is that why he'd changed his mind? If Phillips had watched it . . . why use such a similar phrase?

For some reason, Earl's appetite fled, as did his enjoyment of

Contessa's film. A curious lethargy fell over him. Using the remote, he shut off the DVD and television. Drained the rest of his whiskey, and set about going to bed. Still thinking, the whole while, about Phillips' inexplicably odd use of the phrase.

20.

He is a hunter. He stalks his prey through the mists, and the wetlands east of Clifton Heights. The swamps. He's chasing something through low-lying water plants and shrubs. Chasing *someone* who stumbles and screams their way through stagnant water, peat moss, and other aquatic plants.

He glides after his prey, walking on water, a deadly messiah. Deep rage fills him. His heart thrums with a lust for revenge. As his victim trips over a fallen branch and sprawls face-first into pooling water, delight soars inside. Words whisper in his mind, heart, and soul:

"Restitution must be made."

He seeks restitution. He will *take* it, for the wrongs committed upon him.

His prey scrambles upright. Staggers forward, desperately grabbing at stunted pines, trying to pull itself ahead faster, as the mud sucks it down.

A great need fills him. A bottomless and insatiable appetite. With a roar he leaps forward, an engine of hunger.

His prey looks back, face contorted in abject terror. It throws its hands up to ward off his attack . . . too late. He lands on his prey's shoulders, driving them both down into the water and mud. There is a short struggle, until the prey's neck is laid bare.

He roars again. Jaws snapping, teeth clicking. Like a snake he strikes. His mouth is filled with the sweet taste of flesh and the coppery tang of blood. His body lurches and bucks with a hot, orgasmic release as he feeds at last, after so long . . .

November 1st

"Danielle Lathrop is dead."

Earl's eyes widened, his mouth opening slightly. Almost as if he was about to protest, claiming Lathrop still among the living. He seemed to collect himself, however, and sagged back into his chair, gazing into his hands once more. "I know. I didn't want that to happen. Never meant for any of this to happen, you have to believe me. I didn't want her dead, and I didn't kill Danielle."

Chris leaned further over the table and spread his hands, letting a little more of his true emotions show. "Here's the thing, Earl. I want to believe you. I *really* do, and this is what I'm trying to ferret out. Some of the survivors of last night can't remember what happened. Others adamantly maintain you *didn't* kill Danielle, while others say you did . . . horrible things to her. And, only your fingerprints are on her . . . body. Also, there's the question of your activities in the weeks leading up to FrightFest."

Earl continued staring into his hands dully. "I'm . . . not sure what you mean . . . "

But he did know, Chris thought. Earl Flanagan knew very well what he meant. Which debated the question: did *Chris* really want to know?

21.

Friday, October 7th

Earl woke the next morning plagued with the vague memory of strange dreams. However, try as he might, he couldn't recall what they were. Regardless, he felt incredibly well-rested. He felt better than he had in a long time. As he readied for work, he idly wondered why he felt so good. So fit and strong. He supposed it was Phillips reinstating Contessa's films for FrightFeast. However, it felt like more. He felt complete. Vindicated. Whole. Filled with a sense of belonging.

In any case, as he walked quickly to work, the air tasted crisper. The tapestries of reds, oranges, and yellows in the trees looked more vibrant. In his burst of energy he'd set out for the library early, so after he crossed Black Creek Bridge, instead of going straight into the library, he walked past it and down Main Street, just to enjoy the morning.

He noted with satisfaction many stores had started decorating for Halloween. Windows lined with yellow, orange and red lights.

Ropes of black and orange tinsel. Cardboard cut-outs of skeletons and black cats hung in windows. He took special pleasure from the window display in Brown's Pharmacy, which featured elegant cutouts of Frankenstein's monster, the Werewolf, Bela Lugosi's Dracula, and even the Bride of Frankenstein.

When Earl arrived at the library, Lida approached him and said, "Earl, I'm glad you're feeling better. I feel terrible. Hopefully *I* wasn't the cause for your sickness."

Earl tipped his head, smiling, confused. "What do you mean?"

Lida's hands twisted in front of her, eyes glimmering. "The movies you donated to the library several years ago? I'd taken them off the shelf because I was going to check them out for a friend of mine. Was going to give them to her last night, but I couldn't find them. When I talked to Cathy, she said she'd put them in the discard pile, because she thought that's what I'd meant them for. When I checked and saw they were gone, I was afraid you'd seen them there, and thought that perhaps . . . "

A warm glow blossomed inside. Of course. Lida would *never* have discarded the movies he'd donated. Even if no one had ever checked them out. She loved them as much as he did. How could he have ever thought she'd throw them out?

Of course, he'd donated most of the movies to the thrift store, and in his drunken mania two nights ago, tossed the rest of them into Clifton Lake, but that wasn't a problem. He owned multiple copies of all his movies. He could give her new copies of those same ones. He smiled and tipped his head. "No worries, Lida. I'm just happy you wanted to recommend them to others. I'll go home and get them on my lunch break."

She waved a hand, looking relieved. "Tomorrow will be fine, Earl. I'm just glad we cleared this up, and that you're feeling better. By the way," she smiled impishly, "a young woman stopped in yesterday, asking for you. A *striking* young woman, I must say. A classic beauty. Bravo for you, my boy. Begging my pardon if I'm overstepping . . . but it's about time."

The warm glow inside intensified. Danielle had stopped to see him yesterday? It was the only explanation, because she'd be the only young woman asking to see him. He simply nodded, and went to the front desk, amazed at how quickly a man's fortunes could change.

22.

It proved to be a busy morning, but not so busy that Earl wasn't able to work on his essay. The longer it got, the more excited he felt about it, but was also equally unsure what to do with it. Self-publish? He had no idea where to start, and felt certain no one would want to read it, save perhaps Lida.

During his lunch, when he checked his email on the break room PC, he was delightfully surprised to find two new messages. One from Classicfrights.com, the other his alumni newsletter, both informing him that after long deliberation, his columns had been reinstated. When could they expect his next installments?

He emailed both immediately, saying he'd email the latest columns by week's end. On a whim, he also inquired with Classicfrights.com about writing a new column for them, recounting his experience with FrightFest this year. He was amazed when he received an almost immediate response saying yes, certainly.

The afternoon flew by. The foot-traffic tapered off, but this gave Earl more time to work on his essay. Lida (perhaps still feeling guilty for the misunderstanding) seemed content to let him work on his essay undisturbed. He expanded the narrative, deciding to share everything. Even the fantastical bits about dreaming of Contessa, and his near brush with death at Clifton Lake. Maybe the editors at Classicfrights.com would go for it. Maybe they wouldn't. Either way, he wanted to find out.

The day was nearing its end when he heard a soft, "Excuse me? Earl?" He looked up, slightly startled, to see the tentatively smiling face of Danielle Lathrop.

"Danielle. It's very nice to see you." He smiled and folded his hands on the counter, suddenly nervous and unsure what to do with them. "What brings you to the library?"

Danielle smiled sheepishly. "Well, I don't mean to remind you of an uncomfortable memory . . . but I was wondering how you were doing after the other night."

"Ah." He nodded, strangely not feeling as uncomfortable as she'd obviously thought he might. "I'm okay, actually. Took the day off yesterday, as I'm sure you figured. Slept in, rested up, did some writing . . . " he shrugged. "Really, I felt very good by the day's end."

She smiled, looking genuinely relieved. "I'm glad. I'm not going to lie. You gave me a scare. I still can't believe you went home on your own."

He waved. "I made it just fine."

She smiled wider, her eyes sparkling. "That's good." She nodded toward the PC. "What were you typing? You didn't look up once as I walked over."

He nodded, feeling his cheeks warm, but the sensation felt oddly pleasurable. "I write several columns about the classic monster movies. I was just finishing those up."

A slight lie, of course. He was really working on his essay, but he wasn't ready to talk about it. That, and he'd just finished writing about Danielle's role. He wasn't sure how she'd take being the subject of his writing.

"Interesting. I'd love to read one of them. Like I said the other night, I adore the black and white monster movies." She paused, looking thoughtful. "They're more tragic, y'know? They end up being dangerous, and some of them even evil. But it's almost like those old movies wanted us to understand how easy it would be for *us* to become a monster."

She snorted and shook her head. "That probably made no sense. Especially to a film buff like you."

On the contrary, Earl found it hard to speak. It was one thing for Lida to share his love of classic movie monsters. Another thing entirely for someone so young and attractive (someone possibly *interested* in him), to feel likewise.

"Would you like to get lunch sometime," he found himself saying, his mouth moving of its own accord. "Maybe coffee?"

Danielle smiled. "I'd like that." She opened her purse and pulled out a white cardboard rectangle. She placed it on the counter, grabbed a pen, flipped it over, and started writing on it. "This is my freelance photography business card. But this," she said as she finished writing and handed the card to him, "is my personal number. Call me. We'll see what our schedules look like."

Earl accepted the card reverently. "Hopefully this doesn't make me sound too pitiful, but I'm fairly certain my social calendar is free."

She apparently didn't think so, because she smiled and said, "My social calendar is usually pretty free, too. I just have to check and see if I have any shoots coming up. I keep everything scheduled on my wall calendar at home. I'm not much of a digital-age girl, I'm afraid."

It was melodramatic to the extreme, but Earl thought he was falling in love on the spot. "Neither am I. Match made in heaven, maybe."

He'd thought perhaps the last bit was too much, and expected her demeanor to turn awkward. It didn't. She smiled wider and said, "Maybe. Talk to you soon."

She turned and left the library.

Earl watched her go. It wasn't a completely cliche departure. She didn't cast a longing glance over her shoulder as she pushed out the doors. Still, as far as cinematic encounters went, this one rated pretty highly.

He puffed out an amazed breath as he took out his wallet and secured the business card inside. He was just replacing his wallet when Lida sidled up to him, giving him a shocked yet pleased look. "Well, well, Earl. Aren't you just the man about town these days?"

He smiled, slightly abashed, but feeling very pleased with himself, regardless. "Hardly. I don't think one girl visiting me at work qualifies me as Lothario."

Lida, still smiling, looked slightly confused. "Honey. That's the *second* woman who's come looking for you in the past two days."

Earl frowned. "Wasn't Danielle the one who came yesterday?"

Lida shook her head, grinning now, as if tickled beyond measure. "Oh, no. Danielle is very cute in her own way, but the other woman was a very different sort. Tall, with good bearing. Almost regal. High cheekbones. She looked English. Almost aristocratic. With long, black hair, and the most striking green eyes."

Earl opened his mouth, but no sound came out. It sounded like she was describing . . . but it couldn't be. It was *impossible*.

"Also," Lida continued, "she wore a long white dress. Little outdated for these parts, but that's fine. She wore it so well. She looked *born* to wear it."

23.

Earl had just finished dinner and was about to spend a few more hours working on his essay when the doorbell rang. At first, a silly thought filled him with giddy pleasure. Danielle had stopped by unannounced on an impromptu visit (which, of course, didn't make sense, because he hadn't given her his address yet).

Also, even if he had, that didn't seem likely. One of the qualities he'd sensed in Danielle was a similar desire for orderliness. An impromptu visit didn't seem like her. She'd given him her number and asked him to call in a few days, to give her time to check her schedule. Though he didn't know for sure, he sensed that's what she'd prefer he do.

As he headed for the front door, another thought occurred. One slightly more disconcerting, but no less powerful. Perhaps it was the mystery woman who'd asked about him at the library? The one who looked regal in her out-of-date white dress and raven black hair?

He wasn't sure how he felt about that.

When he opened his front door and saw Sheriff Baker standing on the front step, campaign hat in hand, Earl's intrigue was replaced by confusion. What in the world was the sheriff doing on his doorstep?

"Evening, Earl. Mind if I come in for a bit?"

Oddly, Earl's initial instinct was to ask the sheriff if he had a warrant. Despite always liking Sheriff Baker (based on their few encounters), Earl felt oddly reluctant to allow him in.

He smiled, however, and said, "Absolutely, Sheriff. Come right in." He stepped aside and allowed Baker to enter, closing the door behind him. Another absurd thought. In so many of the classic monster movies he loved, this was the scene in which the local lawman visited someone responsible for raising an ancient evil. Why Earl thought that—especially when he'd nothing to hide—he didn't know.

"Can I get you something to drink? Take your coat?"

Sheriff Baker smiled and shook his head, looking grateful but slightly distracted. "No thanks, Earl. This won't take long. More a formality than anything else, but you know me. I like to do these things in person, instead of over the phone."

Earl nodded and crossed his arms, feeling a little relieved, yet still confused. "By all means. How can I help you?"

"When's the last time you spoke with Bob Phillips?"

The question took Earl aback. Oddly enough, his first thought was of the odd dream he'd had last night, which he couldn't quite remember.

"Earl?"

Earl gave himself a mental shake, slightly alarmed at how his attention had drifted. "Sorry, Sheriff. Haven't been feeling myself these past few days." A lie; because ironically, he'd never felt better. "Let me think. Oh, yes. Yesterday afternoon he called me. Wanted to talk about FrightFest."

He offered Sheriff Baker what he hoped looked like a genuine smile. "There was some miscommunication regarding the film selections this year. We were going over final details. He was approving my selections."

Baker nodded. "What time was this?"

Earl thought. "About one or two in the afternoon? Can't remember, honestly." He frowned, again troubled by the elusive nature of last night's dream. "Is everything all right?"

Baker shrugged. "Not sure. Got a call early this morning from Mary Phillips, Bob's wife. He never came home last night. So far, we haven't been able to find his car. The last person who saw him was his secretary. She said he left for the day around three in the afternoon. We traced his last call to you, around 2:30, actually. You were likely the last person who spoke to him. What'd you talk about, again?"

A cold spot had formed in Earl's stomach. He swallowed and tried to speak as evenly as possible, feeling (though it was ridiculous) as if he stood on the edge of incriminating himself. Of what, he'd no idea. "The selections for this year's FrightFest. We initially didn't see eye-to-eye on them, but last night we came to an understanding."

Baker nodded. "He sound agitated? Out of sorts, rushed, nervous? He say anything odd?"

It flashed through Earl's mind like quicksilver. There one instant, gone the next. Bob Phillips' odd parting: *Restitution must be made for wrongs done to you.* He shook his head, however, and lied. "No. I didn't notice anything strange at all. Everything seemed fine."

Baker nodded his head. "I figured as much. Just wanted to make sure." He replaced his campaign hat on his head. "I don't think it's likely, but if you hear from Phillips, you'll call me?"

Earl crossed his arms, hoping his concern for Phillips looked genuine, when really it was for himself. "You have my word."

Sheriff Baker touched the brim of his hat. "Thanks, Earl. I have my suspicions as to where Phillips has gone. Like I said, just needed to check this off my list. Have a good night."

Earl opened the door for Baker, barely restraining himself from shooing him out the door. "You too."

Baker stopped and smiled over his shoulder. "Glad Phillips went with your recommendations. Gotta love the classics."

Despite his best efforts, Earl's smile felt forced and thin. "Yes, you do."

Baker nodded, turned, and left.

Earl shut the door as the sheriff proceeded down the walk toward his cruiser. Stood there for several minutes, equal parts fear and *wonder* mixing inside.

Abruptly, like the night before, he felt desperately tired. Washed out and fatigued. He'd been intending on working more on his essay, but instead, he showered, changed clothes, and went to bed, where he dreamed, once more.

24.

Mists blanket the ground, oozing like something alive. Wispy tendrils whip and lash the air, then fade into nothingness. A white, pearlescent glow lights up the forest with its unearthly hues.

In it, he feeds. Face buried into flesh which stinks of copper and rot. Instead of finding the scent repugnant, it inflames him. Stokes the flames burning deep in his belly. Making him hungrier, urging him to gorge himself even more. The rubbery consistency of raw flesh against his sharp teeth and tongue, sliding down the back of his throat, should turn his stomach. Instead, it whips him into a frenzy as he spreads his jaws wider than should be possible to take ravenous, inhuman bites.

His sharp and elongated incisors clamp down and tug on a particularly stubborn chunk of flesh. He yanks, swings his head back and forth, but the scrap still won't come. Finally, a growl building in the back of his throat, he jerks his head back. The chunk of flesh comes free with a splattering of cold and thick blood. As his head pulls back and he gulps down the shredded flesh, he catches a glimpse of the face which belongs to his meal. Something in him stirs as he recognizes its features. The color of its hair, its expression of fear.

Suddenly, all his hunger dies in the face of unrelenting terror as he scrambles back in horror at the twisted face of Bob Phillips, his mouth contorted in a frozen scream . . .

November 1st

"Let's talk about Bob Phillips for a minute."

Chris' transition had the desired effect. Earl glanced up quickly, face tightening, lips pressed together, eyes narrowed. In the man's quick mood shift, Chris sensed not only a lingering resentment, but also a detached kind of guilt.

When Earl didn't say anything, however, Chris continued. "No one knows where he is. Still missing. None of his out-of-town friends have heard from him, and he hasn't drawn from any of his credit accounts, nor has he used his smartphone."

Earl looked away, seemingly unwilling to meet his gaze. "I thought you already knew what happened to him."

"We have a theory. One we can't corroborate, at all. We really don't know where he's gone."

Chris waited a heartbeat, then said, "He's not the only person who's gone missing the past few weeks. Is he?"

Earl said nothing; just glared into his hands, which Chris saw were clenching and unclenching again in a disturbing frenzy, his nails digging into his palms so hard, Chris wondered if they would draw blood.

25.

Saturday, October 8th
9 AM

As Earl dressed for work, he couldn't stop thinking about last night's horrible dream. He'd sat upright in bed around three in the morning, confused and disoriented. Fully expecting to find himself in the middle of the forest, with the cold damp earth beneath him, white mists clinging to the ground.

Instead, of course, he'd found nothing but sheets and blankets. His relief had felt silly. Where else had he expected to be?

He remembered swallowing carefully, also expecting to taste the coppery tang of blood. He'd tasted nothing but dry cotton-mouth. Experimentally, he'd probed his teeth with his tongue and found regular teeth. Not razor-sharp fangs, (which was also a ridiculous thought) clotted with chunks of flesh.

Shaking off those thoughts, he stood before his bedroom mirror. After giving his outfit one last check, he closed his eyes and rubbed his face with his hands. A dream. A nightmare. That's all. Sparked by what, he didn't know.

Or, maybe he did. The recent events regarding the cancellation of his movies. His moment of near-despair a few nights ago. Hitting rock-bottom? He was surprised he hadn't been having nightmares before now.

The gruesome nature of his dream? Him *feeding* on Bob Phillips? He understood why he'd been dreaming of enacting violence upon the Town Board chairman. Phillips had started everything, of course. Informing Earl so casually they'd dismissed his proposal for this year's FrightFest. Replacing Contessa Victoria Williams' movies with tripe slashers. His repressed anger at Phillips, certainly. Even though Phillips apparently reversed his decision . . .

restitution must be made for wrongs done to you

. . . Earl had no doubt something besides good will must've forced Phillips' hand. The self-involved chairman of the Town Board wouldn't have recanted his position out of concern for Earl's well-being. Whatever motivated his change of heart, Earl felt sure it must've been self-serving.

Earl uncovered his eyes and ran a hand through his hair. Truth be told, the only thing which really bothered him was the nature of his nightmare. It had all the elements of a cheap slasher film, the kind he abhorred. A bestial creature in a bloody scene. Feasting on the torn flesh of its enemy in the woods? Devouring the dead in a grotesque display of inhuman savagery? Rending flesh with snapping teeth and drinking blood with ghoulish delight? It just wasn't his style.

Earl sighed and examined himself in the mirror, finally satisfied he looked presentable. Normally he didn't care whether or not his clothing made him look "attractive." Today, however, he'd fretted over his orange knit sweater, with a white button-down shirt underneath. He worried it made him look "frumpy," realizing, (not for the first time), he looked a bit like Mr. Rogers. He'd formerly considered that a *good* thing. Mr. Rogers was one of the most squared-away personalities he knew. In the past, such a realization would've brought a sense of satisfaction.

Now, however, all he could do was worry. What if Danielle

stopped by the library again? Would this outfit appeal to her? Or would it make him look completely out of touch? Or, maybe she wouldn't take notice of what he wore at all.

Also, what of the *other* woman Ms. Bassler said had asked for him? The mysterious woman with black hair, in the flowing white dress. The one that (despite his best efforts) Earl kept picturing as Contessa Victoria Williams. It seemed a bit strange to feel just as concerned about what this mystery woman would think of his appearance. Yet there it was, regardless.

Earl pushed such thoughts aside. He should feel pleased, after all. First of all, he was alive, when he very easily could have died during his self-indulgent stunt the other night. Instead of dying, he'd met someone who seemed interested in him. Also, his beloved movies had been returned to FrightFest's roster. Two of his columns reinstated. Something was happening to him.

Something *big*.

Earl examined his appearance once more. Brushed his bangs with his fingers, and finally turned to leave for the work day. It occurred to him, on a subconscious level, that he didn't include the mysterious woman in white as one of his sudden fortunes. However, he pushed this thought aside, also.

26.

Thinking about calling Danielle after work, Earl almost missed the dirt-encrusted gold pen jammed into the ditch before Black Creek Bridge. He would've walked right by it if sunlight hadn't peaked through the morning clouds and reflected off it.

Earl's first instinct was to keep walking. It was a pen, after all. Most likely a cheap commemorative gift for "valuable years of service" or "employee of the month." He would know. He had several of them at home, received for his years at the library.

But something in his gut tugged at him. He stopped and stared at the half-buried pen for several minutes. It seemed ridiculous, but he recognized it. Something about its gold shimmer in the light.

He squatted and picked up a stick, thinking for some reason he shouldn't touch the pen, because he didn't want to leave his fingerprints on it. Why he thought this, Earl didn't know. With the branch he levered the pen out of the mud, revealing two initials, in black, ornate script.

BP.

BP, for Bob . . .

Earl stood. A weird kind of hysteria pulsed through him. He tossed the stick away into the woods and kicked the pen. It spun into the air, down the bridge abutment, and landed with a light splash into Black Creek. For a moment, he stared at where it disappeared into the water, then he pushed all thoughts of it out of his mind as he strode purposefully to work.

27.

Sunday, October 9th

"You know what I like about Halloween the most? I like the fall colors, of course. The leaves in the trees. The fields going over; the goldenrod. Makes for great photography. But what I *really* love about October and Halloween is more instinctual, I think. More childlike."

Earl smiled as they walked through the pumpkin patch at Kaminsky's Farm. Part of him hung on Danielle's every word. Another part simply took her in. Her wind-blown hair. Flushed cheeks, and bright eyes. Still another part refused to believe he was actually here. Choosing pumpkins with an attractive woman, when he hadn't picked a pumpkin - much less carved one—in years.

Visiting Kaminsky's was the first thing Danielle suggested when Earl called. At first he'd been a little taken aback. Adults picking pumpkins for jack o'lanterns? After thinking about it, however, he felt ridiculously pleased by the notion. So pleased, in fact, he hadn't thought about that gold plated pen he found yesterday morning, (engraved with the initials BP), at all.

"It's the mystery in the air," Danielle continued. "All the legends about walls between worlds growing thin." She flashed him a big smile. "Not sure if I believe in all that, of course. I'm kind of agnostic when it comes to the supernatural. Even so, it's the *possibility*. The mysterious *elegance* of it all."

Earl nodded. Danielle's smile widened and she looked ahead, scanning a brilliant orange sea of round, oval, oblong, and warped pumpkins, presumably looking for just the right one. She seemed the type of person who'd be extremely particular about the shape of her jack o'lantern. Earl thought that adorable.

"Of course you love the mystery and the elegance," he said, picking his way carefully through pumpkins of all sizes. "You love the classic movie monsters. The old monsters embodied mysterious elegance."

Instead of responding, Danielle pointed to the middle distance, at something he couldn't quite see. "Oh! Look! That one is *perfect!*" At first, slight annoyance rippled through him at her dismissal of his classic monsters, but then her bare hand grabbed his. His skin flushed into instant warmth at the contact. As she pulled him toward her coveted Halloween prize, satisfaction filled him . . . though, deep inside, a strange *guilt* burned.

As if he were being unfaithful to another.

28.

After storing her pumpkin (a nearly perfect, spherical specimen) into the trunk of her mid-size economy Nissan, Danielle managed to talk Earl into walking through Kaminsky's Corn Maze. Again, faint amusement glowed inside Earl. He hadn't walked through Kaminsky's Corn Maze since his father had dutifully allowed his twelve-year old son to drag him through it almost twenty-three years before.

Unexpectedly, he found himself pleasantly content to wander through the maze with her, chatting aimlessly about whatever came to mind. This probably had something to do with the feel of her hand pressed against his. The sheer delight he felt at the unaccustomed intimacy mostly overwhelmed the strange guilt burning deep inside.

Mostly.

Luckily, Danielle turned her questions toward him, which helped Earl distance himself from the odd, guilty feeling that he was cheating on someone. "So I told you why I love Halloween so much. Your turn."

He smiled and arched an eyebrow. "What makes you think I love Halloween?"

"Oh, c'mon!" She playfully bumped shoulders with him. The contact nearly unmoored him, emotionally. It was the type of gesture he'd seen countless of young, happy and laughing couples make. Walking along the Clifton Heights sidewalks at any given time of year. Heads close, hand in hand. Though there'd been a time when he'd believed he *wasn't* lonely, he now had to admit how much he'd envied those couples. Especially when he saw one playfully nudge the other with a shoulder, like Danielle had just done to him.

He smiled and shrugged. "Halloween is the time of year when my love for the classic monsters is most appropriate. It's also when I share that love with the rest of the town at FrightFest."

"Let me guess. As a kid you always dressed up as one of the Universal Monsters? Your favorites were . . . " Danielle held up a finger, affecting a deeply thoughtful expression. "Frankenstein, the Wolfman, and the Mummy."

She grinned, eyes bright and shining. Something stirred deep inside him, along with that strange sting of betrayal, which he pushed aside. "Am I right?"

He tipped his head as they rounded a corner. "Actually, I didn't discover the classic monsters until sixth grade. Before then, I wore whatever my mother chose for me. Indian, fireman, astronaut, cowboy. I never really cared, she never asked my opinion, and I never objected. Until," he conceded with a nod, "I asked to go as the Mummy, seventh grade year."

She poked him in the ribs. "I was right!" Normally he would've found such a gesture annoying. From her, it was anything but. "How'd your Mom react?"

He shrugged again. "I'd love to say that even though my choice horrified her, I adamantly stuck to my guns in a daring act of adolescent rebellion. Sadly, that wasn't the case. She merely asked, 'Are you sure?' When I said yes, she shrugged her shoulders. That's all."

Danielle wrinkled her nose. "That's anticlimactic."

Earl nodded. "I have to admit. I was hoping for more of a fight. Felt cheated, almost."

Danielle was about to say something when her phone rang. They stopped at an intersection in the corn maze as she dug into her pocket. She blew her bangs out of her eyes noisily, and frowned. "The life of a freelance photographer," she quipped. "Always pictures which need to be taken *yesterday*."

She glanced at her phone's screen and groaned. "Yep. My editor." She looked at him with regret. "Do you mind?"

He nodded and smiled. "No worries here."

She beamed gratitude. "Thank you!" She answered the phone, put it to her ear and said, "Hey, Pete. What's up?"

Earl stuck his hands into his pockets and took a few steps away, to give her some privacy.

November 1st

"Let's talk more about your relationship with Danielle."

Earl didn't respond immediately. Just looked down into his hands. Chris didn't say anything, content to wait him out again. Finally, after several minutes of silence, Earl whispered, "I'd rather not, if you please."

Chris sighed, struggling to retain his composure. "That may be, but county police is going to be here soon, and they're going to ask these questions not nearly as nicely as I am. Danielle Lathrop is dead. So are others, but what happened to Danielle. What someone *did* to her . . . "

Chris swallowed and trailed off, at an unusual loss for words. He'd thought himself hardened to the strangeness of Clifton Heights, but this month had been one of the worst in recent memory, *especially* how Danielle Lathrop died . . .

Chris swallowed again, tasting bile at the back of his throat. "Whoever did that to Danielle, they enjoyed it. Loved it. *Reveled* in it."

A heartbeat passed.

Earl Flanagan looked up and met Chris' gaze. His expression empty, eyes an icy cold blue. His hands no longer clenched each other, but rather lay on the table, folded, at rest. "They say that love is a harsh mistress, Sheriff Baker. Perhaps the harshest. And acts done in the name of love? Often brutal, and without inhibition."

"That was *not* love," Chris said evenly, surprised at the anger rising within him. "Not love. Not by sane standards, anyway."

A strange smile flickered on Earl's lips. "Eye of the Beholder, Sheriff. Eye of the Beholder."

29.

Saturday, October 22nd

Over the next two weeks, Bob Phillips' mysterious disappearance simmered, falling from public consumption but never quite fizzling out. He never came home. His car was never found. Suspicion of foul play had cooled considerably, however. His secretary eventually confessed Phillips' last visitor had been an "attractive" woman she didn't recognize, probably from "out of town."

Two days later, Martha Phillips admitted what many in town had suspected for a while but had never dared mention. Bob Phillips had cheated on her often over the years. As far as Martha knew, he'd been loyal recently. However, the testimony of Phillips' secretary was damning. It seemed likely Bob Phillips had finally run off with someone.

Strangely, Earl felt nothing about the missing Town Board chairman. He hadn't expected to feel grief, really, and he certainly hadn't expected to feel *happy*. But he didn't feel guilty, either, though he didn't know why he should. Thoughts of the gold pen he'd kicked into Black Creek lingered in the back of his mind. Of course, that could've been anyone's pen. Who knew how many people in town had the initials BP?

Instead of feeling bad, or pleased, or guilty about Phillips' disappearance, he felt nothing. He was too caught up in the relationship progressing between him and Danielle. They'd enjoyed their time together over the past few weeks. Their first outing, picking pumpkins at Kaminsky's Pumpkin Patch, and walking through the corn maze. Two nights later, dinner at The Skylark Diner. Lunch once during his break at the library. A visit to Raedeker Park Zoo, before it closed for the season.

She hadn't invited him over to her place yet (a duplex at Hyland Court), and he of course hadn't invited her to his. She'd seemed very comfortable with their outings so far, not showing any interest in his home. That, of course, served him well. In his mind, inviting her over inevitably meant inviting her into his theater. He wasn't sure he was ready for that. He didn't think for a minute she'd ridicule him, of course. Actually, he felt certain she'd be suitably impressed with his collection.

Something else had held him back. The strange sense of needing *permission* to admit an outsider into his sanctuary. Which was ridiculous. It was his room, in his home. Whose permission did he need?

He put it down to a basic nervousness about intimacy. It was the only logical answer. Regardless, she had seemed very content— happy, even—to meet him on neutral ground.

But it seemed as if Danielle was taking the first step of intimacy with this afternoon's outing. She hadn't invited him to her house, but she *had* invited him along on her photo-shoot for Webb County Online's feature on Webb County's Halloween-themed activities.

The shoot was in Clifton Heights, at Feldpausch Horror House, their very own "scare attraction" on Clinton Avenue. It was formerly the home of a kindly old widow named Christina Feldpausch, who'd worked as a nurse at Webb County Hospital before retiring at age 70. Mrs. Feldpausch had been a cornerstone of Clifton Heights' Halloween for many years, a must-stop destination on everyone's route (children and teens alike) because of her generous helpings, and homemade caramel-corn balls. She'd adored Halloween and her annual visitors, and dressed up every year; costuming as a witch, a fairy godmother, and even Maleficent, one year.

When she passed fifteen years ago, the town bought the property and turned it into their own haunted attraction, in honor of Ms. Feldpausch. For the first few years, Feldpausch Horror House (as it came to be known), offered little more than a mildly spooky Halloween tour through an old house, featuring cheap Halloween mannequins and home-made decorations, much like Frankenstein's House of Wax in Lake George.

However, as the years passed and as bombastic Halloween attractions such as Reaper's Revenge, Slaughterland USA, and Field of Screams became more popular, the Town Board Member in charge of Feldpausch House—Cynthia Woolridge—became determined to add a little bit every year. It would never be a Reaper's Revenge, but they were determined it would be more than a House of Wax.

Earl had to admit it certainly was. Though he had little frame of reference because he'd never attended a Halloween theme park, much less the "haunted house" the PTA had hosted in the Clifton Heights Elementary gymnasium when he was young. Even so, from the outside, Earl thought Feldpausch Horror House an impressive site.

The house had been maintained over the years, even restored in places, but the curators had obviously been busy over the past few weeks, preparing for Halloween night. Fake cobwebs covered the front porch railing and siding, and hung from window sashes, arches, cornices, and clung to the front doorframe. In the daylight, Earl thought it looked like the house had been painted with a particular type of stain which, under the right lights—floodlights he could see situated in the front year—would make the house appear weathered and rotten.

The front yard was in the process of being turned into a graveyard. Earl could see foam tombstones lying on the ground near the floodlights. He assumed when they were erected, they'd be situated in order to hide the lights. Grasping skeletal hands and screaming skulls lay scattered about, the kind which would be staked into the ground before tombstones, to depict the dead rising from their graves. Earl imagined the visual, (though not to his taste), would prove very effective after night had fallen.

What struck Earl as most impressive, however, was the detailed mannequin standing next to the front door. As Danielle snapped pictures of the in-progress graveyard and the cobwebbed exterior, he wandered up the walk to appraise it. He felt a foolish, surprised sort of joy.

Standing at the door, in a classic pose from the 1931 *Dracula*, with its cape draped over a raised forearm and its white, haughty yet slightly bestial face, was a magnificent reproduction of Bela Lugosi's Count. It stood life-size, and as Earl climbed the steps, he marveled at the very *solidity* of the mannequin. For a moment, he even wondered if it might leap for his throat.

"Wow. That's amazing."

Earl jerked slightly as Danielle came up behind him, snapping pictures. He fought down an odd irritation at her casual manner. Bela Lugosi's Count Dracula was not something to be snapped at with a camera like a tourist. It was something to be revered, and respected. Honored.

Earl frowned slightly, thinking such a notion was a bit ridiculous. He chided himself for feeling irritated at Danielle. She loved the classic monsters as much as he did. Why should he feel she was being disrespectful?

"It is," he replied, moving aside to give her a better angle. "It's extremely life-like. I have to be honest," he offered Danielle a smile, feeling guilty, now, for his flash of irritation, "I didn't expect Bela Lugosi's Dracula. I thought it would feature something more modern. Like an ax-wielding maniac, or something."

"We're changing our focus, this year," a soft, cultured voice said from the front doorway. "Casting our vision back, to the classics of old."

Earl turned toward the voice, and beheld a vision which struck him so forcibly, he felt sure he was staring open-mouthed. Standing in the doorway, wearing a white dress—but one of a modern cut, with a casual white blouse—was Contessa Victoria Williams.

He blinked. It *wasn't* Contessa, of course. The resemblance was uncanny, however. Straight, raven black hair, styled in contemporary fashion. Striking green eyes. High and proud cheekbones, aquiline nose. And full, red lips, which parted in a half-smile which seemed sensuous and amused, all at once.

If Danielle noticed the woman's impact on him, she didn't let on. In fact, she seemed immune to the aura wafting off the woman, smiling easily and sticking out her hand. "Hi! I'm Danielle Lathrop. Webb County Online, photo-journalist. I'm doing a piece on all the Halloween attractions in Webb County. Did my editor contact you, say I was coming over today?"

The woman (*not* Contessa), tipped her head. "Yes, he did. Thank you for coming. We're very excited for this year's Feldpausch Horror House. Especially with our new features."

She took Danielle's hand and shook it gently, almost like nobility, Earl thought. "My name is Connie Victor."

Danielle shook her hand, released it, and looked at her closely. "You're not local, are you?"

Connie Victor (*not* Contessa Victoria) shook her head. "No. I'm a professor of Golden Age Films at Utica College."

"Huh." Danielle crossed her arms, to Earl's surprise, looking moderately *suspicious*, of all things. "So how are you involved? I thought this was Cynthia Woolridge's gig."

"It usually is," Ms. Victor replied smoothly, "but Cynthia's been feeling poorly as of late." She spread her hands. "I'm afraid she tested positive for COVID two weeks ago. She's currently in quarantine, and her rheumatoid arthritis is causing complications.

We have some friends in common who put her into contact with me, because she wanted to do something different, but is feeling quite incapacitated this year."

She clasped her hands at her waist, and straightened. Though smiling genteelly, Earl couldn't help feeling she was daring Danielle to challenge her claim. "So here I am."

Danielle pursed her lips. She didn't look quite as suspicious anymore, but Earl could tell she still hadn't made up her mind. She nodded at the Bela Lugosi Dracula. "I'm guessing the 'something different' is classic movie monsters?"

All the challenge left Ms. Victor's face as she beamed in delight. "Yes. That's really how and why our mutual friends put us into contact. They know I specialize in Golden Age films, and also know I have a particular love for the classic monsters. Universal, and lesser knowns."

Ms. Victor turned her bright, penetrating green gaze upon Earl. "I hope I wasn't too forward in looking for you at the library a few weeks back. I'd just arrived in Clifton Heights, and I wanted to consult with the town expert on classic monsters before I began my work here."

Earl again had the distinct feeling he was staring, mouth wide enough to catch flies, but he couldn't help it. She wasn't Contessa Victoria Williams . . .

but their names are so similar
aren't they?

. . . he knew that, but even so. Something deep and primal inside him was reacting to those swirling green eyes, moist red lips and long, luxurious black hair. Though she wore nothing but a modern, simple white blouse top and white skirt, he kept imagining her as the Arglwyddes y Cors. Dressed in a sheer white gown which hinted at her curves and hidden places. Striding out of the mists toward him, hands outstretched. Ready to enfold him into her embrace, where he could press his face between her breasts, or nuzzle the base of her neck with his lips as he ran his hands all over her . . .

Danielle cleared her throat, sounding both amused and annoyed. With difficulty, he pushed aside the sudden and powerful fantasy and stammered, "That was you?"

Ms. Victor—*Connie* Victor, not Contessa—tipped her head. "Of course. If I was going to re-fashion Feldpausch Horror House into a House of Classic Horrors, the first person I'd want to contact would be Clifton Height's eminent expert on the classic, Golden Age monsters."

Earl cleared his throat, forcing himself not to gape again, although for a much different reason, this time. "You know of me? How?"

Ms. Victor smiled. "Well of course Cynthia raved about you and your annual FrightFest. How you've made it your mission to keep the old, elegant monsters alive. If I were going to try and do the same here at Feldpausch Horror House, I'd want your input, without a doubt."

"But," she raised a finger, looking for all the world like a blushing school girl about to admit a crush, "I must confess I've already known of you for quite some time. I follow your columns, in both Webb Filmography, and on ClassicFrights.com. I must say, I'm impressed with both the breadth of your knowledge, as well as your love and reverence of the old monsters."

Earl found that, ridiculously, he had to clear his throat for a third time. His mouth felt sticky and dry. "I honestly never thought anyone read my columns. I'm delighted you've enjoyed them."

A thought occurred to him, and he asked, knowing how this might sound to Danielle (the woman who, mere moments before, had been the sole focus of his attentions, and now seemed to be just *there*), and not caring, really. "Why didn't you come back to the library? It's been about two weeks or so."

Ms. Victor's face fell slightly. "I'm afraid with Cynthia in quarantine, this has been my sole focus the past few weeks. I haven't had much free time. Besides," she smiled, her face and eyes brightening up, "I realized I'd read enough of your columns to feel confident that what we'd planned would meet with your approval."

Ms. Victoria glanced at Danielle, who, Earl saw, still looked slightly askance at the woman. She smiled, then looked back to Earl. "I must say, it's rather fortuitous that you happened to be with Ms. Lathrop. I can now make my proposal to you face-to-face, before you hear it from the Town Board."

"Proposal? I'm not sure I understand."

Ms. Victor took a deep breath and clasped her hands together, looking almost nervous, of all things. As if fearing greatly his disapproval. "I've approached the Town Board and have asked them—considering our focus this year on the classic monsters—to consider moving your FrightFest to the backyard of Feldpausch Horror House."

Whatever it was Earl had thought she was going to propose, *that*, of all things, wasn't it. Before he could open his mouth to speak, however, she held up a hand and rushed on. "I know what you're thinking, because at first, the Board had the same reservations. Not enough room? The thing is, no one has cleared the backyard behind Feldpausch House since Ms. Feldpausch passed on. I hired landscapers to clear it out; they just finished a few days ago. You'll have ample room for seating, the screen, and projecting equipment."

Earl's mind whirled, struggling to process this completely unexpected occurrence. He opened his mouth—to say what, he wasn't sure—but before he could speak, Ms. Victor held up another hand. "Please, Mr. Flanagan. I'm not asking for a decision today. A Norman . . . Fuller, is it? . . . will be calling you soon with the official details of the proposal. I just wanted to take advantage of this wonderful opportunity to make my pitch to you in person. Considering your lineup, this year—*three* movies with the incomparable Contessa Victoria Williams—I think having your FrightFest here on Halloween night would be absolutely perfect. Almost kismet, when you think about it."

Earl stood in stunned silence, hoping he wasn't staring again, but not quite caring. It was too much to process. Moving FrightFest to another location simply seemed too large a thing to wrap his mind around. But even so. The idea that Ms. Victor *wanted* his FrightFest—an event which, two weeks ago, he'd thought of as raped and violated—at her attraction, *because* of its honorarium to the classic monsters . . .

Danielle seemed less than impressed, however. Rather than thawing, her attitude had gotten chillier as Ms. Victor had continued talking. A flash of insight made Earl wonder if Danielle felt jealous. This pleased him in a mean sort of way, which only made him feel worse. "Is Cynthia feeling up for a phone call? I'd love to get her take on all this for the feature. I think everyone was expecting her to simply *add* to the Feldpaush Horror House; not revamp it entirely."

Ms. Victor gave Danielle a sad look. "She really doesn't have the energy, right now. Even we've been out of touch. However, if she calls me for an update, I'll let her know you'd like to hear from her."

Danielle nodded and smiled tightly. "You do that."

"Now," Ms. Victor stepped aside and waved to the dark doorway of Feldpausch Horror House. "Would you like a tour? I promise, you won't be disappointed."

30.

The foyer had been crafted to resemble a seance parlor, with a round mahogany table covered with a black silk spread, an ornate crystal ball mounted in the middle of the table. "This," Ms. Victor pronounced with a slightly dramatic wave, "is where the tour will start. One of my students, studying theater at Utica, will be portraying Maleva the . . . "

" . . . gypsy, from *The Wolfman*, 1941," Earl continued with a slow smile, as he turned in a circle, taking in the lovingly crafted room, "played by Maria Ouspenskaya."

He turned back and met Ms. Victor's green-eyed gaze, once again feeling an oddly erotic thrill run through him at the bold way she returned it. "She informs Larry Talbot—played by Lon Chaney—that the wolf he killed while out walking at night was actually her son—played by Bela Lugosi—and now *he's* cursed to be a werewolf, also."

Ms. Victor—*Connie*, he thought to himself, he should think of her as Connie—pursed her lips in a satisfied smile. "I see my estimations about your expertise weren't mistaken."

Danielle snapped a few photos of the seance parlor. She quipped dryly, "I graduated from Utica. Didn't realize they had a theater program."

Ms. Victor—*Connie*—waved dismissively. "It's more of a club, really. They're looking to expand the curriculum the next semester. Several of them will be helping this year."

"Hmm," was Danielle's only response. "How does the Town Board feel about that? Bringing in folks from out of town?"

Connie smiled sweetly. Maybe too sweetly, but so enraptured was he by the way she looked at him, he didn't notice. "The Town Board was delighted. I assure you."

Danielle shrugged, but said nothing more.

"In any case, our actress playing Maleva will give tour groups a suitably atmospheric pronouncement of doom for anyone who enters. And now," she waved toward the hall leading away from the séance parlor, "we shall proceed."

They followed her down the hall. Toward its end, Connie stopped to open a narrow door-sized panel to their right which, had she not opened, lay so flush against the wall Earl never would've seen it. "This is where, in past years, a poorly trained actor would've burst out with a fake chainsaw, wearing a hockey mask. This year, however, a Utica student will offer an excellent portrayal of Lon Chaney's Wolfman."

She turned and gave another of her sweet smiles to Danielle. It occurred to Earl, then, that as jealous as Danielle might be of Connie's attentions (which seemed strange; why should she feel jealous?), Connie seemed to know this, and didn't shy away from it, at all. "You would prefer something to take pictures of, however." She gestured grandly into the next room. "You'll like what's next."

They entered a room decorated in Egyptian motif. In the corners stood very realistic, foam statues of Egyptian gods. In one corner, Osiris. In the others, Ra, Horus, and Set. Symbols reminiscent of hieroglyphics had been meticulously painted on the walls. The floor had been covered with a gritty type of paper, mimicking a tomb's sandstone floor. Scattered about the room were jars filled with, Earl assumed, fake rubies, gold coins, and other treasures Egyptian Pharaohs usually had buried with them.

Whatever her feelings about Connie, Danielle remained professional, avidly snapping pictures around the room. She stopped before the sarcophagus in the room's middle, pausing to stare. Earl shared her wonder. If you looked closely, it had been built out of cheap stained plywood, the cover fashioned from chicken-wire and papier-mâché. But in just the right lighting . . . it would look creepily authentic.

"This is . . . impressive," Danielle admitted, taking pictures from several different angles. "Who built it? Your theater students?"

"Many in the club are interested in set design and production, so yes. They've been hard at work, trust me. Also . . . " She raised a hand, "prepare yourself."

She stepped toward the sarcophagus, taking care to place her right foot in the middle of an obviously fake but quite ornate rug covered with hieroglyphics. She pressed her foot down . . .

The sarcophagus' lid flew open with a bang.

And upwards sprang a form, with linen-wrapped hands outstretched and reaching. Even with her warning, both Earl and Danielle leaped back, the latter with a bright yelp.

Adrenaline surged through Earl, setting his heart pounding. It was a jump scare. The kind he normally found cheap, obvious, and inelegant. And yet . . . a strange, wild kind of pleasure thrummed through him, along with his pumping heart and tingling veins. A kind of pleasure he'd never once experienced in watching any of his beloved classic horror movies. Was . . . this what fans of slasher movies sought?

Annoyed and conflicted in equal measure at his revelation, Earl instead focused on the prop which had sprung up from the sarcophagus. Sitting upright, hands rigidly outstretched, it was hard to believe he and Danielle had been so startled. However, like the Bela Lugosi mannequin standing at the front door, the mummy reaching for he and Danielle looked alarmingly . . . alive. Real. Though he knew it had to be an aftereffect of the adrenaline shock he'd received, Earl couldn't repress the feeling that if he turned, for just one moment . . .

Danielle snapped several more photos. "Looks pretty realistic," was all she said. Again, though Earl could've been mistaken, he thought it came out more as a challenge than anything else.

"Yes," Connie replied simply. "It does." She gestured toward a door at the far end of the room. "Shall we continue?"

31.

The next room had been designed to resemble Henry Frankenstein's castle laboratory from the original movie, featuring Boris Karloff as the monster. It wasn't an exact match, of course. Though the walls had been painted a slate gray, they were still very obviously wood, and not castle stone. As in the Egyptian tomb room, under regular light, the spiral tubes and banks of instruments were very obviously constructed of cardboard and cheap plywood, from wires and cast-offs found at a thrift store, or from a recycling bin.

But he could see how it would look, with the lights dimmed. With the LED lights on the banks of cardboard generators glowing, and with the static electricity ball (likely bought at a hobby store) sparking. And there, lying on a flat table (which, Earl could see, looked like an old high school cafeteria table covered with a tarp) near a bank of cardboard generators . . .

The monster. Lying under a white sheet, the only thing visible was a square, block-like head so reminiscent of Karloff's iteration. Eyes closed, pale skin, but the hair . . . the hair looked . . . *different* than Karloff's. More unruly. Wild. Almost . . . *real.*

Of course Karloff's monster wouldn't be complete without the neck bolts. Two wires ran from the bolts to something which looked far more real than the cardboard banks of generators. Earl peered closer, and realized—with an odd feeling—that it looked like a real generator.

Wary from their experience in the Egyptian tomb, Danielle glanced at Connie and asked, "Why don't you show me the gag *first*, this time?"

Connie nodded. She approached an old fashioned throw-switch on the wall above the very real-looking generator. Just like Colin Clive's Henry Frankenstein from the 1931 movie, Connie grabbed the switch, and with a flourish of her free hand toward the monster, threw it.

The very real-looking generator hummed. The air buzzed and crackled. Even though Earl assumed the sounds came from hidden wall-speakers, he fancied the hair on his arms stirred.

A shudder rippled through the gigantic body under the blanket, its chest heaving in spasmodic lurches. The generator's hum increased to a higher pitch, and the air crackled and snapped. The figure beneath the sheet—a clever animatronic—writhed now, bucking as if it wanted to rise from the table, but was held back by the straps crossing its barrel chest and tree-trunk legs.

One of the arms trembled under the blanket. Shifted, and began to reach out a large, misshapen, gray, blue-veined hand, its fingers longer than they should be . . .

The humming stopped abruptly, the whine cutting out to silence. The tension in the air eased, and the body under the blanket relaxed, the arm sagging back down to the table, the abnormally large hand curling and settling back under the white cloth.

Silence fell.

For several seconds, Earl just stood there. Staring at the form under the sheet, at a loss for words. Danielle squeezed his hand; it was only then that he realized she'd been clutching it with a death-grip the past few minutes.

"That was . . . impressive." Earl glanced at Danielle, and saw she no longer looked suspicious or jealous of Connie Victor, but was staring at the Frankenstein scene with a muted expression of awe. She nodded. "I'll say."

"And it's not even the *whole* exhibition."

He and Danielle turned to see Connie standing next to the old fashioned throw-switch, hands clasped before her, looking well-pleased. "There's more, but I don't want to spoil it for your readers." She faced Danielle with a cold—maybe even challenging—glance. "We want to help keep them in suspense . . . don't we?"

Danielle must've noticed the gauntlet thrown in Connie's tone, because her eyes narrowed. "Worried I can't keep my mouth shut?"

Connie tilted her head and smiled sweetly. "Not at all. But if you genuinely don't know what's ultimately supposed to happen here, your readers will sense that in your writing, and be all the more intrigued."

Danielle snorted. "Glad you have so much faith in my writing; thinking I apparently can't make it sound mysterious on my own."

"I meant no offense, of course."

The two women stared at each other for another heartbeat. Earl looked back and forth between them, abruptly and profoundly uneasy. Initially, he'd found some amusement in his suspicion the two women were sparring over him. Now, however, something cold and sharp had formed between them, and he didn't know what to make of it. Even stranger? Some deep part inside felt *pleased*.

Danielle broke the stalemate, smiling brightly. "I think I've got plenty of pictures inside. Don't want to spoil it for my readers, right?" She nodded back toward the front. "I'll just get a few more shots out front, if that's okay?"

Connie dipped her head graciously. "Feel free. Just don't mind the mess. We're not quite finished out there, yet."

Danielle's smile was so sugary-sweet, Earl's stomach clenched. "No worries. I won't shoot any of that stuff."

She glanced at Earl and said, "Want to grab a bite to eat after?"

Earl thought it was his imagination, but he thought maybe he caught a slightly desperate glint in Danielle's eyes, as if she fully expected him to turn her down in favor of remaining with Connie

Victor. He would've dismissed the notion as fancy . . . except for the very real temptation to do so.

He offered Danielle what he hoped was a reassuring smile and said, "Of course. The Skylark?"

Danielle's face visibly relaxed. She had been nervous, and now looked relieved. That relief proved short-lived, however, as Connie laid a hand on Earl's forearm and said—almost *purred*, "Would you mind if I chat with Earl a moment about my proposal regarding FrightFest? It won't take long, I promise."

Danielle's expression stiffened slightly. She glanced at Earl, and he tried to offer the same smile, but he saw she took no reassurance from it this time. She nodded, lips pressed together, and turned without another word to the front door.

"Follow me," Connie said, squeezing his forearm once before letting it go. "I want to show you the renovations we've made to the backyard, for the showing."

She turned and left. Earl found he'd no choice but to follow.

32.

He followed Connie in a daze as they wound through the twisting halls, which had clearly been altered over the years for the scare attraction's tours. Connie rattled on about some of the other classic monsters she planned to feature—The Phantom of the Opera, The Hunchback of Notre Dame, even the Creature from the Black Lagoon—but Earl had trouble following her words. His usually ordered emotions and thoughts were jumbled, knotted masses of confusion, arousal, and even . . . fear.

Connie Victor.

Contessa Victoria Williams.

Raven black hair. Alabaster skin. Brilliant green eyes.

Mouth wider than it should be, ringed with too many teeth.

Even more worrisome, Earl knew he'd made some missteps today with Danielle. She wasn't blind, or stupid. She had to have sensed how powerfully Connie's presence impacted him. Also, he thought following Connie back here was a mistake, one which most certainly would have ramifications, if he wasn't careful. And yet, he'd felt compelled to follow Connie. Almost as if he had no choice in the matter.

Finally, they exited onto a wide back porch which overlooked a hollow behind the home. Framed on all sides by tall Adirondack pine, it was deeper and wider than anyone would've guessed from the street view. Also, as Connie had said, the area looked freshly mowed and cleared of brush. Near the tree line, Earl saw an ax buried in a tree stump, which he supposed had been used to cut down small trees growing in the backyard.

"So, my proposal is this," Connie said in a very swift, business-like voice. "The projector equipment will fit on this porch. And . . . I have a surprise regarding that, if you don't mind." She offered him a suddenly coy look, one which made Earl squirm (not unpleasantly) inside. "I'll be providing the projector equipment. I've got something . . . special in mind. Something vintage."

Earl nodded, but before he could say anything, she continued. "Based on the numbers Norman Fuller has provided regarding ticket sales thus far, we should be able to easily accommodate a fairly large crowd. Chairs will be provided by the Town Board, but people will also have the option of watching the movie on a picnic blanket, or in their own chairs. This should offer plenty of over-flow for those who take the tour and decide to attend the screening at the last minute. The Town Board, of course, will offer the same movie screen you've used at Raedeker Park, so long as you give your approval."

"Certainly. What time will the showing start?"

"The same time it always has, eight PM sharp."

Earl folded his arms and gazed across the now-empty backyard, his detail-oriented mind finally kicking into gear to assess the situation. It helped that Connie was speaking factually, and had dialed down her . . . influence, a little. "Will tours still be running during the movies?"

"No. We'll announce the whole week prior to Halloween that on Halloween night, we're ending the tours early, so we can focus entirely on FrightFest."

Earl nodded slowly, warming to the idea. "Impressive." He glanced sidelong at Connie, and was struck by how she was . . . staring at him, and apparently had been for several minutes. Her large green eyes glistened, her full red lips parted slightly, and for a moment, he had trouble collecting his thoughts. Finally, he managed, "It's amazing you were able to convince the Town Board of all this. In the past, they've proven remarkably . . . close-minded."

Connie smiled, a strange look glimmering in her eyes. "I believe in your vision, Earl Flanagan. I believe in *you*. In cases such as these, I can be . . . quite persuasive."

"That's . . . " Earl licked his lips, swallowed, and continued. "That's very kind of you."

Connie didn't say anything for several minutes. She just looked at Earl, eyes wide, lips parted slightly. Then, in a surprisingly intimate gesture, she stepped toward him, and placed her hand gently on his chest. A hand which felt warm, soft, and inviting.

"They changed your viewing recommendations without telling you. They *lied*. Fuller didn't forget to inform you of the change. It wasn't a miscommunication. He'd been instructed not to tell you, in hopes you wouldn't find out until too late. And if you *did* find out—which the Fates made sure of—Bob Phillips felt confident, I'm sure, that you'd react one of two ways. Either knuckle under and go along, or quit."

Earl's mouth hung open, his head spinning, his chest practically *glowing* from the warmth he felt radiating from Connie's hand, through his shirt. "How . . . how do you . . . "

She stepped closer. Closer, in fact, than any woman had ever been, including Danielle. "You feel guilty about Bob Phillips being gone. Feel like you're responsible, somehow. You shouldn't. It is simple restitution made for the wrongs done to you."

Earl stared at her, speechless, mind spinning. Connie leaned even closer, put her lips to his ear, and whispered, "She is not worthy of your devotion. Only *I* am. The one responsible for your turn in fortune. The one responsible for your salvation."

She looked deep into his eyes. An erotic dizziness pulsed through Earl, setting every nerve on fire. "Reject me, and I'll show you the *true* face of an old monster."

She leaned in, pressed her lips to his, and kissed him, deeply. She grasped the back of his head with her other hand, her right hand still pressing against his chest. Conflicting emotions exploded inside Earl. A nearly all-consuming desire to not only embrace Connie, but to fling propriety away by pushing her to the ground, tearing her clothes off, and ravishing her right then and there. Also, panicked guilt that at any moment, Danielle might walk around the back corner of the house and discover them.

Mingling with these feelings was an undercurrent of terror, as the image of a mouth filled with too many teeth opened far too wide . . .

Abruptly, the kiss ended. Connie Victor pulled back, green eyes wide and shimmering, and whispered, "Remember. Reject me at your peril."

In an instant, she retreated several paces, resuming her business-like air, all trace of sensuality faded. Indeed, it was like she'd never stepped close to him at all, much less kissed him.

"So," she continued in matter-of-fact tones, "Norman Fuller should call you this evening to finalize all the details, if you'd like to accept my proposal. Please. Take the day to make your decision. Does this sound agreeable to you?"

Earl swallowed (tasting her still on his lips, and tongue), and nodded, feeling lightheaded, confused, guilty, aroused, and even a little scared, all at once.

"Very good." She nodded toward the house. "Let's not keep Ms. Lathrop waiting, shall we?"

She turned to re-enter the house, to lead him back out front. As before, Earl couldn't do anything else but follow.

33.

Lunch at The Skylark began as a scattered, numb affair. An unfamiliar and uncomfortable tension had settled between Danielle and Earl, and for the first time since he'd met her, their interactions felt forced and strained. Danielle seemed to sense this, and filled the empty spaces with prattle about the trials of working as a free-lance photographer, mostly complaining about the low pay, staff competition, and the unreasonable demands of most photo editors. Of course, she continued on, it was much better than her part-time job as a museum tour guide, a job she'd quit except she needed a regular paycheck . . .

Earl barely said three or four words for the first twenty minutes of their lunch. He tried to nod in all the right places, and grunt and offer half-hearted interjections where they seemed appropriate, but for the most part, he felt like he was drifting above her one-sided conversation with him, his mind untethered, consumed by the mysterious, fascinating, beautiful Connie Victor, or . . .

no

it's impossible

But she'd said the words, hadn't she? "Restitution made for the wrongs done to you." And she'd claimed to be the reason good things had happened to him the past few weeks, even saying she was responsible for his "salvation." Was she trying to say *she'd* been the one who'd dragged him from Clifton Lake?

narrow, feminine footprints in the sand

Impossible.

Also . . . had she *threatened* him? After that kiss (which he *still* felt tingling against his lips), when she'd said something about rejecting her at his peril, and she'd show him the true face of an old monster? What the hell had that meant?

" . . . I'm a little suspicious, I'm not going to lie."

Earl blinked and forced himself to focus on Danielle's worried expression, a look which quickly became annoyed when she realized he hadn't been paying attention. "I'm sorry," he managed, "I missed the last part. Was drifting a little."

Danielle's eyes narrowed. She didn't say it, but she didn't have to. The accusation was written on her face: *You're thinking about her, aren't you?*

Aloud, she said, "Something about this Connie Victor doesn't sit right with me. Cynthia Woolridge has been running Feldpausch Horror House since the beginning. She's become as much of a Halloween fixture as Widow Feldpausch was. I mean, I'm sure if she's got COVID she feels lousy, and I know her arthritis does kick up. Even so."

Just finished with her minestrone soup, Danielle laid her spoon in the bowl and fixed Earl with a probing look he couldn't quite decipher, and didn't quite like, at all. "What's the deal with moving FrightFest? Just because she thinks it's a good idea, you're ready to move the whole thing to a new location, this late in the month?"

Earl shifted in his chair, emotions warring inside. Even though he knew it was silly, he took offense at Danielle's accusatory tone. FrightFest was *his*. He'd do with it what he pleased. If he wanted FrightFest at Feldpausch House this year, so be it.

He felt guilty, also. Danielle was right. Connie Victor had snapped her fingers, and Earl was falling in line. And there was the kiss, as well. He'd yet to kiss Danielle (as much as he'd wanted to) and as pleasant as he imagined it would be . . . he didn't think there was *any way* it could match up to the kiss Connie had just given him. That made him feel, quite frankly, like an asshole.

Consequently, Earl responded more harshly than he intended. "Hold on. I haven't decided anything yet. It's not a bad idea at *all*. Maybe a change in venue is exactly what FrightFest needs, to inject it with new life." He paused, and then, almost as an afterthought, he flung at her, "I suppose *I'll* be the judge of what's good for FrightFest, thanks."

Danielle's eyes widened slightly, lips parted, clearly stung by his response. Earl immediately regretted his tone, but instead of softening him or motivating him to apologize, it only made him feel even surlier.

Danielle's expression hardened. Hurt as she was by Earl's tone, she wasn't about to drop the matter, apparently. "I still think something's off. She kept talking about students from Utica College helping her set up. Sure, the place looked under construction, but where was everyone? I didn't see any college students, did you?"

Earl shrugged. "Maybe she sent them on a break because she knew you were coming and didn't want them there, mucking up the photo-shoot."

"I dunno. Maybe." She rubbed her face, took a deep breath, and gave Earl a pleading look. "This is getting a little weird and tense. I didn't mean to imply anything bad. It's just odd . . . but the last two weeks have sorta been odd, I guess."

She did the unexpected, just then. She reached across the table, took his hands, and gripped them firmly. "I know how much FrightFest means to you. How much it hurt you when they changed the movies without consulting you, and how excited you were when Bob Phillips changed them back. Of course, if you think FrightFest should move to Feldpausch House, that's your call, and I'll support it."

Earl squeezed her hands back, feeling sheepish, embarrassed, and ashamed (and guilty, also, because of that kiss). How could he have spoken so curtly to Danielle? The last two weeks with her had been the most enjoyable weeks of his life.

"I'm sorry, too," Earl said softly. "I truly didn't mean to imply anything. You're right, the last two weeks have been strange, with Bob Phillips missing . . . "

Danielle looked at him oddly. "I thought everyone just figured he finally ran off with someone."

"Well, yes, of course," Earl stammered. That's the prevailing theory, but no one knows for sure, do they?"

chasing something in the swamp

a gold pen stuck in the mud with the initials B.P.

"It's all very odd. Sheriff Baker is a nice enough man, of course, but it's always a bit jarring when the sheriff visits your home, not only once, but twice."

Danielle smiled brightly, and squeezed his hand again. "Well, it's not like you're a suspect, right? Like anyone is going to believe *you* could ever commit a crime."

Earl smiled weakly, one word flickering in his mind, over and over.

restitution

Danielle withdrew her hands. "Anyway. I'm sorry if I acted weird this afternoon at Feldpausch House, and I didn't mean to accuse Ms. Victor of anything underhanded, I promise. Although."

A small, mischievous smile spread. "I think she was quite taken by you. Was maybe even flirting."

Remembering the heat of Connie's lips on his, and her hand cradling the back of his head, Earl felt his face flush with warmth, as guilt soured his stomach. "Really? I'm not good at . . . well, it's not like women flirt with me very often, so . . . "

Danielle's smile widened. "I gotta admit. It made me a little jealous."

A surprisingly pleasurable heat filled Earl. "I'm unused to receiving much attention from one woman, much less two at the same time. I apologize if I seemed flustered in Ms. Victor's presence. However . . . "

He paused, reached out, and took her hand again. "I've spent the past two weeks with *you,* Danielle. I like *you,* very much. As striking as Ms. Victor is . . . you're the one I want to spend time with, rest assured."

As the words left his mouth, Earl felt, with a small flush of satisfaction, that they were true.

Mostly.

Danielle fairly beamed at this, which only made Earl feel even warmer inside . . . except, of course, for that little cold spot in his heart, where the memory of Connie's rapturous kiss nestled, hissing, like a deadly snake lying in wait. Even so, he tamped that coldness down and gamely returned Danielle's smile.

She held up her Nikon. "Believe it or not, it's going to take the rest of the day and most the evening to sort through these pictures. Want to catch up for dinner, tomorrow night?"

A wild compulsion seized Earl. He leaned forward and said, "Yes. In fact . . . I'd like to have you over, to my place. For dinner. If you're interested, that is."

Danielle's eyes widened and her breath caught. "I'd love to," she said quickly. "What time?"

"6? I'll text my address before you leave."

Danielle nodded, smiling even wider. "6 is great. I can't wait."

Earl returned her smile, picked up his phone, (which he'd just bought to replace the one he'd ruined in Clifton Lake, something he didn't want to think about at all) and texted her his address. As they waited for their check, he and Danielle chatted about trivialities, their mood much lighter and more carefree than it had been in the beginning. Even so, that cold spot in Earl's heart festered, refusing to go away.

34.

When Earl returned home, he felt himself drawn to his laptop, and he immediately sat down at the kitchen table and continued his narrative. He spared no details, even writing about his fantastical thoughts about the eerie similarity between Connie Victor and Contessa Victoria Williams. Even so, no matter how strange and bizarre his notions, Earl wrote them down. Even her insinuation that she was responsible for his change in fortune, and the (impossible, of course) chance she might've been the one who'd saved him from drowning in Clifton Lake.

He wrote about his dreams, and the irrational guilt he felt about Bob Phillips' absence, and even the kiss. The rest of the afternoon passed in this fashion, until Earl came to, his slightly aching fingers resting on the laptop's keys, as if he was just waking up from a dream. His new cellphone was ringing, and Earl dreamily realized it had been ringing for some time. Shaking his head, he picked up the phone and answered it. "Hello?"

"*Earl, this is Norman Fuller. From the Town Board?*"

"Oh. Yes. Ms. Victor said you'd be calling. Is this about . . . "

"*. . . moving FrightFest to Feldpausch House. I trust Ms. Victor has gone over the details with you?*"

"Yes she has. I . . . I have to admit, I was skeptical when she first mentioned it to me. I didn't think there'd be enough room behind Feldpausch House, but seeing its backyard . . . well, it seems like it'll work fine."

"*Great. Then I can inform Ms. Victor you accept her proposal?*"

Earl frowned, again feeling—like that night with Bob Phillips—that Norman Fuller's speech sounded stilted and oddly formal. He sounded desperately afraid Earl would be offended with him, for some reason. "Yes, absolutely. She said the Town Board would provide the chairs and the movie screen, and that she was apparently providing the film equipment. Something 'vintage,' she said."

"*Yes, absolutely,*" Norman answered quickly, once again, as if afraid of offending Earl. "*Everything will be taken care of for you, and Ms. Victor has informed us of the projector arrangements. You won't have to do a thing, I assure you.*" A brief pause, and then, "*You'll tell Ms. Victor of your satisfaction? That restitution has been made?*"

Earl blinked, so taken aback by Norman's rushed, almost panicked tone that he almost missed that word, once again: *restitution*. He nodded numbly (forgetting for a moment he was on the phone) and then said, "Yes. Tell her that's all fine."

"*Thank you, Earl. Just so long as everything is the way you want.*" Another awkward pause, and then, "*Bob and I never should've changed your movies, Earl. That was a misstep on our part. We . . . crave your pardon.*"

Again, Norman's groveling tone knocked Earl off balance. All he could manage was, "Thank you, Norman. It's much appreciated, I assure you."

"*Goodnight, Earl.*" Before Earl could respond, Norman Fuller hung up.

Earl stared at the phone for several minutes, mind spinning, grappling with the strange fantasies they'd churned over the past few weeks. After another heartbeat, he set his phone down on the kitchen table, got up and walked away, because he didn't want to write anymore.

35.

After Norman Fuller's strange call, Earl didn't have much of an appetite. He decided to retire to his theater for a few glasses of whiskey, and one of his classic black and white creature features, though he decided against any of his Contessa Victoria films, opting instead for *Isle of the Dead,* with Boris Karloff, and Val Lewiston's *The Cat People.*

Neither film seemed to scratch his itch, however. He only made it halfway through *Isle,* and only past the first ten minutes of *Cat People.* He didn't know why, really. Both were fine films he'd enjoyed countless times before, but for some reason he couldn't focus. A thought kept nagging the back of his mind. A scrap of memory teasing the edge of his thoughts.

As he carefully returned *Cat People* to its case and its place on the shelf to the far right, the memory coalesced. *We crave your pardon.*

"Oh no," he whispered. "It can't be."

He quickly turned to the section of shelving which held his beloved Contessa Victoria's movies. He selected not *Daughter of the Mists,* but one of his other FrightFest selections, *Dark Priestess,* in which she played Ammit, the Egyptian soul-eater who punished the wicked. His finger fumbling, thinking *this is crazy, it's impossible, it can't be,* he withdrew the Blu-Ray from its case, walked shakily over to the Blu-Ray player, inserted the disc, grabbed the remote, and started paging through the scenes.

He found it in minutes. Clicked 'Select.' Then, as the image appeared on the screen, pressed 'pause,' freezing Contessa Victoria Williams (slightly past her prime in this film, but still beautiful) looming over a cowering Egyptian manservant (back then, played by a white man, of course) who was backpedaling in fear, face frozen in a rictus of terror, eyes wide and manic. Contessa wore strips of white rags (reminiscent of mummy wrappings, which made sense, because this film unfortunately was somewhat of a *Mummy* rip-off), and she reached hands which looked claw-like at the man, a malevolent look of anger twisting her features.

Earl breathed once, and pressed 'Play.' The movie's grandiose soundtrack of clashing cymbals and pounding drums filled the room, as well as the Egyptian servant's screeching voice . . .

"No! No! Priestess, I crave your pardon . . . !"
Earl paused the movie.
Was about to rewind and play it again, when his doorbell rang.

36.

As Earl opened his front door, he imagined several different visitors. Sheriff Baker, coming to ask more questions about Bob Phillips. Norman Fuller, here to make a strange confession of guilt, or to explain his odd manner over the phone. Connie Victor, attempting to make good on her passionate kiss from earlier in the day. Even a fantastical image of the Arglwyddes y Cors herself, in a scene straight from Earl's beloved movies, offering a Machiavellian pact to destroy his enemies and bring him even more fame and fortune.

He was pleasantly surprised to see Danielle Lathrop, standing on his doorstep, looking equal parts eager and nervous, twisting her hands anxiously.

"Danielle? It's . . . it's wonderful to see you. I thought you'd be tied up the rest of the night working on your photos?"

She spread her hands and smiled nervously. "I couldn't focus. My mind kept bouncing all over the place . . . hey, can I come in for a minute?"

"Certainly." He stepped aside and allowed her to enter, then shut the door behind her. He locked it, for some reason, heeding a vague survival instinct. As if some part of him thought locking the door would keep Danielle safe.

Danielle took several aimless steps into his home, then turned and said, looking even more nervous, "Look. I sorta lied earlier. I said I was a little jealous of Ms. Victor. I wasn't a *little* jealous, Earl. I was really, *really* jealous. *Insanely* jealous. Which is weird, because I don't get that way. At least, I never have."

Earl blinked, taken aback with a delighted surprise spiked with worry that maybe he'd caused more damage to their budding relationship this afternoon than he'd thought. "Danielle . . . I . . . I don't really know what to say . . ."

She stepped closer and placed a hand on his chest. As she continued, it wasn't lost on him that the gesture almost directly mimicked Connie's from earlier in the day. "It's just . . . I really,

really like you, Earl. A lot. I don't think I realized how much, until I thought you might be interested in someone else. It drove me crazy thinking about it, and I had to come over here tonight and tell you, in person, but now I feel a little stupid for doing so, and I don't want you to think I'm clingy or possessive or . . . "

Earl Flanagan, the mild-mannered man who, for his entire life had led a simple, balanced, mundane life, reached up, softly cupped both sides of Danielle's face, and kissed her. For a second Danielle stiffened, obviously surprised. But that second passed, and she relaxed—no, she *melted*—into him, returning his kiss with a surprising fervor, pressing her body to his. For the next several minutes, they eagerly devoured each others' breath, as Earl's heart pounded in his chest, and his skin burned and tingled where it touched Danielle's.

Seemingly an eternity later, they broke apart, both of them gasping slightly. In Danielle's eyes he saw a hunger he'd never seen directed at him before by any woman, and also, something else. A luminous, transcendent glow.

"Can I stay?" she rasped.

"Oh, yes," he whispered, drawing her close again. "Yes, *please.*"

37.

Earl is flying.

He didn't know how it was possible, but he is. Soaring through the chill night air, at one with the dark, wearing it like a second skin. He feels free, powerful, and more alive than he ever has. And even more?

He's *hungry.*

Below him, small like a toy, he sees the pickup truck fleeing along the lonely country interstate, swerving back and forth over the yellow line, careening around tight corners in its desperate, futile flight. A lusty glee surges through Earl as he dives toward the truck, a literal bird of prey swooping down upon its kill.

He lands feet-first in the truck's bed so hard the vehicle bucks on its shocks. Somehow he keeps his balance as he leaps fluidly forward and thrusts his hands (which look too narrow and feminine to be his, and tipped with hellish, jagged nails) through the cab's rear window, shattering the glass effortlessly.

Earl latches onto the driver's thick and doughy neck, digging his nails (sharplike talons) into springy flesh, drawing blood and a frenzied shriek from the driver, which chokes off into a gurgle as Earl bends the driver's neck back at a ninety degree angle. Something deep in that neck cracks, and Earl plunges his mouth to the driver's exposed jugular, teeth burying into flesh as hot blood spurts all over his face and the driver's truck swerves out of control . . .

38.

Earl jerked awake, sitting bolt upright in bed, as he struggled free from another nightmare which he couldn't quite recall. A dizzying sense of disorientation gripped him, as if he felt like he should be somewhere else, doing something else. He placed a hand on his sweat-slicked chest and breathed slowly and deeply, trying to still his heart.

Gradually, his confusion passed, and his heart relaxed. He was in his bedroom, as he should be. In bed, body aching slightly (in a vaguely pleasant way), after several bouts of lovemaking with . . .

He looked to his right, at Danielle's peacefully sleeping form, curled up under his covers. For a second, his heart threatened to speed up again. Maybe it was a trick of the shadows, him turning his head so quickly, but for the briefest of moments, it had looked like a menacing dark form was standing on Danielle's side of the bed, glaring down upon her with malevolent green eyes. Eyes which burned with hate, and jealousy.

But there wasn't anything there. Just darkness. It had been a trick his mind played on him, nothing more.

Earl slipped back under the covers and snuggled up next to Danielle's naked form, wrapping his arms around her, spooning her. She sighed and unconsciously settled into his arms, and the gesture filled Earl with a kind of warm contentment he'd never felt before, ever.

Even as he drifted back off to sleep, however, a vague worry still lingered just below his thoughts. Along with the sensation of being watched by green, burning, hateful eyes.

November 1ˢᵗ

Chris glanced at the interrogation room's wall clock, feeling time slipping away. Wouldn't be long until the county sheriff's deputies arrived, and even though he knew that (as usual) his attempts to understand yet another strange and horrifying occurrence in his town was futile, he felt compelled to try. It was his *job*, after all.

"Earl, we haven't got much time, and I still have lots of unanswered questions, things which need explaining. Working in this town, I'm used to that . . . but even so. The more I know what happened, maybe I can . . . "

Earl raised wide, haunted, and hopeless eyes to meet his gaze. "Help me? Sheriff Baker, your unflagging determination is admirable. Also, a survival instinct in this town, I'm sure. Regardless, futile in my case."

"Humor me."

Earl sighed, and he folded now-still and passive hands amid their shackles. "Very well. Do your duty and ask away."

"Who was Connie Victor? Only a handful of people actually met her face to face. You, Lida Bassler briefly, and also according to you, Danielle Lathrop and Norman Fuller. No one knows anything about her. Lida barely even remembers her from the one time she stopped at the library, looking for you. Cynthia Woolridge spoke to someone named Connie Victor on the phone, but of course never saw her because she was in COVID quarantine, and Cynthia says she was so out of it with her fever, she hardly remembers what they talked about. All Cynthia can remember is Ms. Victor's offer to run Feldpausch House this year—an out of the blue offer, by the way—and that Cynthia felt *compelled* to let her.

"Utica College has never heard of her. There *isn't* a theater or film club on campus. No students 'volunteered' their time working at Feldpausch House. Despite the renovations clearly done there, when I called around this morning, no one in town ever remembers *seeing* workers there. People said it was almost like the renovations were appearing overnight."

Chris leaned forward on his elbows, piercing Ed with his best "cop gaze," for all the good it did. Earl's expression remained placidly resigned. "Also, you claim she arranged the change in venue through Norman Fuller. Conveniently, after Bob Phillips disappeared, by the way. And we know what happened to Norman, don't we? Which, of course, makes me wonder about that 'out of town woman' Bob's secretary said visited him, right before he disappeared."

Chris sat back and folded his arms.

Earl said nothing. Face an impassive mask, eyes deep and hollowed out. Fighting back a surge of frustrated anger (knowing it was futile) Chris said, "Earl, who *was* that woman? She was, by your account, heavily involved in this. There's a few sketchy eye witness reports of what she did last night . . . but the only DNA we found on Danielle was *yours.*

"Who was she? Where did she go?"

Earl leaned back, arms in motion to fold across his chest, until they were checked by the handcuffs latched to the metal table. Looking almost *annoyed* that he couldn't strike a pose, Earl refolded his hands on the table, flicked a small smile at Chris, and said, "*Who* isn't the correct question, Sheriff. *What* is more fitting. As to where she came from, and where she went?"

Earl leaned closer, elbows on the table, a sudden fire lit in his eyes. "In the Paul Wenger and Henrick Galeen 1915 film *Golem*, a being created by the will of another being wrecks havoc, killing and causing mayhem. This created being had its own urges, desires, and needs, though it was created out of nothing, at the hands of another. In the movie's case, molded out of mystical clay by Rabbi Loew, to avenge his people."

Cold fingers trailed down Chris's neck. "What are you saying? You . . . *made* Connie Victor? Out of *clay*?"

Earl's wide, white-toothed grin turned Chris's stomach. "What a fascinating town we live in, that you can actually ask me such a question seriously."

His grin faded, expression empty once more, as he sat back. "No, not clay, Sheriff Baker. But I made her, sure as Rabbi Loew made his golem. I called her into existence through my unconscious will, my thoughts, desire, anger, and bitterness."

He shook his head sadly, expression somber and regretful, now. Unfortunately, not only did I realize that far too late, I also didn't understand the *price*, Sheriff Baker. The wages of bringing her to life. What she would ask of me, in return."

"What were the wages, Earl? What did she want from you?"

"My devotion," Earl replied, "my undying, sole devotion, to her alone. But instead, I committed the greatest sin. I rejected her and chose another, and everything which followed happened because of that."

39.

The memory—both emotional, and physical—of Earl's lovemaking with Danielle lingered with him for the next week and a half. Multiple times a day, he'd find his attention at the library drifting, his mind floating back to that moment when he'd cut Danielle off and kissed her, after she'd turned up unexpectedly on his doorstep. Alternatively, his mind also replayed shadowy, erotic images of their night of lovemaking in his bedroom, an experience which still hummed along his nerves, pulsed in his blood, and even buzzed on his skin.

Before meeting Danielle Lathrop, Earl had simply assumed he'd remain celibate for the rest of his life. The prospect hadn't bothered him all that much. He'd created a simple, orderly existence for himself, and the inclusion of another person—an *intimate* other person—would only disrupt that orderly existence. Better to remain alone in his simple existence, where everything happened the way it was supposed to.

Danielle's arrival in his life had erased such concerns and reservations. Of course, Earl knew he was basking in the glow of taking their new relationship to the next level, and that the tide could turn very easily. If some kind of unpleasantness rose between him and Danielle, (like at that Saturday lunch), that was when things could get messy or complicated. For now, however, he felt *whole* in a way he'd never thought possible, and decided it was impractical to dwell on matters out of his control. Even *that* resolution was groundbreaking for him, which only made him feel even more accomplished.

The only dim spot, of course, was the faint flicker of guilt (of all things) when he realized he'd spoken very little to Connie Victor since he and Danielle made love. A ridiculous notion, of course, because he and Danielle were together, and Connie Victor was nothing more than a stranger (even though, certainly, she was attractive, and had *kissed* him, also).

That, of course, was another point of guilt. He'd never told Danielle about Connie kissing him, and her clear intent to initiate something between the two of them. Earl tried to tell himself it didn't make sense to tell Danielle. That it would only upset her, but he was only partially able to convince himself of that. For several days after, his guilty conscience gnawed at the edges of his newfound joy.

As the days passed, that guilt faded. Especially after his only two conversations with Connie; brief phone calls (though he didn't remember giving her his number) which had remained brisk and business-like, focusing on logistical matters for FrightFest, nothing more. She hadn't expressed the slightest bit of personal interest in him, nor had she hinted he return before Halloween night.

The only other thing which poked Earl's conscience was the strange death of Norman Fuller, which Earl learned of in uncomfortable fashion: the next day during breakfast with Danielle (a breakfast she'd cooked after spending the night). They'd been halfway through ham and cheese omelets when a knock came on the front door.

Earl frowned at Danielle. "That's odd. Who'd be calling on a Sunday morning?"

Danielle grinned mischievously, as she raised a forkful of omelet. "Obviously your *other* girlfriend, Ms. Victor. She's found out about us, and now she's come to take her revenge."

Earl chuckled as he rose from the kitchen table, but something cold and unpleasant twisted in his belly, as he couldn't help but think of the dark, green-eyed form he'd imagined standing on Danielle's side of the bed last night. It was a foolish thought, but for some reason, Earl didn't like the idea of Connie knowing about last night.

When Earl opened his front door, instead of a vengeful Contessa Victoria Williams (why her, instead of Connie?), he was greeted with the sight of a somber-looking Sheriff Baker. He felt an unusual flush of relief (had he really expected the Arglwyddes y Cors?), followed by an odd premonition, a flicker of the odd nightmare he'd suffered last night.

Earl forced a smile he hoped looked convincing as he stepped outside and closed the front door quietly behind him. "Sheriff Baker. What can I do for you?"

In a slightly blunter fashion than a few weeks ago, Sheriff Baker responded, "Earl, when did you talk to Norman Fuller last?"

For a moment, Earl couldn't speak, his mind blank. Mercifully, however, his memory quickly kicked in. "Yesterday. Late afternoon, early evening, I think? He called to finalize the change in venue for FrightFest."

Sheriff Baker tipped his head. "Not having it at Raedeker Park this year?"

For some reason, Earl found the question intrusive. As if Sheriff Baker hadn't any right to question FrightFest's venue. Doing his best to restrain his irritation (irrational, he knew), Earl said in as bland a voice as he could muster, "Yes. We're holding it in the backyard of Feldpausch Horror House, at the invitation of the house's interim director this year, Connie Victor."

Sheriff Baker's face became an unreadable mask. "Interesting. I'd heard of someone taking over for Cynthia this year because she came down with COVID, but no one's filed a zoning permit for the FrightFest at Feldpausch, yet."

"Well, they wouldn't have," Earl pointed out (too hastily, he felt), "because I only just spoke with Norman yesterday. I believe Ms. Victor will most likely submit her permit soon." Earl paused, then added, speaking carefully, "Did . . . something happen to Norman?"

Sheriff Baker gave Earl an odd look. "Why would you ask that?"

The sheriff's voice remained even, tone neutral, but the accusation was there, nonetheless. Earl heard it, ringing like a Klaxon in his head. "Well, you asked when I last spoke with him," Earl replied slowly. "I just assumed something had . . . happened."

Sheriff Baker nodded, expression still impassive, giving away nothing. "He died in an accident last night, on Bassler Road, heading out of town. Plowed his truck into a tree, just past old Bassler House. Someone discovered it this morning. Whole cab stank of whiskey, so we expect his blood/alcohol level to be extremely high."

Flickers of last night's dream passed through Earl's thoughts. Of swooping down out of the sky, at a truck careening along the interstate. "Oh, my. That's awful."

"There's a few . . . irregularities about the crash we're looking into. Did Norman sound . . . strange on the phone? Anxious? We talked to his ex in Booneville this morning, and she said he called shortly after 6 PM, babbling something about 'making restitution' and how he was 'sorry for everything.'"

He looked at Earl, gaze probing. "He say anything like that to you?"

crave your pardon

"No," Earl lied, "absolutely not. He sounded perfectly normal."

Sheriff Baker looked at him for a heartbeat, then relaxed, face becoming less suspicious, and now just plain tired. "Okay, Earl. Thanks for your help. Norman drank like a fish, everyone knew that. Just a weird crash is all, I guess." He shook his head and offered Earl a weary smile. "This town, am I right? Never boring."

Earl smiled, hoping he looked genuinely commiserative. "Indeed not. Don't hesitate to reach out for any more questions."

"I won't, don't worry." Sheriff Baker nodded. "Have a good day, Earl."

"Same to you."

Earl re-entered his house, closed the door quietly, and returned to his breakfast with Danielle. When she asked him what the sheriff wanted, Earl told his second lie of the morning, saying Sheriff Baker was just checking on the details of FrightFest's new venue. Danielle seemed to accept this explanation, and they finished their pleasant breakfast, though something greasy turned over in Earl's gut for the rest of the morning.

As the days passed and Halloween approached, and as he and Danielle grew closer (making love several times, each time more wonderful than the last) Earl's troubled thoughts faded. The air grew crisper, and the trees along the streets and back roads and in backyards turned into riotous tapestries of red, orange, and yellow. Front lawns exploded into Halloween vistas full of ghosts, goblins, witches and zombies, with jack o'lanterns grinning merry fire from every doorstep and porch until, finally, it was Halloween, and Earl's night of glory had finally come.

November 1st

Chris glanced at the wall clock again. He was, essentially, out of time. Unless he could get Earl to give him at least *some* kind of accounting for what happened at Feldpausch Horror House, the former librarian clerk was most certainly going to be charged with the bloodiest and worst crime in Clifton Heights' recent history. The worst part?

Earl Flanagan was done. Finished. Life as he knew it was over, and there wasn't anything Chris could do about it. Even so, he felt compelled to try, as always.

"Earl, we're pretty much out of time. County boys will be here in ten minutes, maybe less. Honestly, I don't know if there's anything I can do for you at all. But if you don't tell me *something*, there's nothing I can do, for sure. What happened last night? How did it start? When did it go . . . "

"Wrong?"

Earl looked up at Chris, eyes now hollow and empty, devoid of life or spark. Even his strange mania had faded. Whatever remained of Earl Flanagan, Chris now understood it was nothing but a dried out, emptied husk of a human being.

"It would be most accurate to say everything went *wrong* from the moment I unconsciously willed the Arglwyddes y Cors into being. But seeing as I *lied* to myself every step of the way after that, and made myself completely oblivious to what was going wrong, let's begin, then, with last night. At first, everything seemed perfect. A dream come true . . . "

40.

Halloween
8:oo PM
Feldpausch Horror House

At first, everything seemed perfect. A dream come true. I arrived at Feldpausch Horror House early, at 7 PM, and went around back through the side driveway, as Ms. Victor had instructed me. Based on the line of children, teens, and adults down the sidewalk out front, and the gleeful yells and screams emanating from the depths of the house, I imagined Ms. Victor's renovations were proving to be a success.

In the backyard, nearly six dozen chairs had been set up, with an aisle running down the middle. To my delight, half the seats were already full. The movie screen the town provided had been erected at the lawn's farthest edge. The framing of trees towering behind and around the screen proved wonderfully atmospheric.

With Danielle accompanying me—busily snapping pictures for another web feature—I proceeded to the back porch, where I'd run the movie. When I mounted the steps up onto the back porch, I saw Ms. Victor—Connie—had fulfilled her promise. The film equipment had been set up . . . but, Sheriff Baker, this wasn't the equipment I used every year. I've always had to make do with a fairly cheap projector/DVD combination until I'd guilted the Town Board into purchasing a better option from the Best Buy in Utica.

This, Sheriff . . . this was a *vintage* reel-to-reel theater projector, of a kind I'd never seen before (and of course, isn't that what she'd promised? Something *vintage*). It didn't correspond to any of the vintage models I've studied over the years; also, *somehow* it had been wired into a much more modern speaker system in a way I didn't quite understand. The final shocker?

Somehow, somewhere, Ms. Victor had acquired reel-to-reel prints of all three Contessa Victoria movies. They sat, stacked neatly, on a folding table next to the projector.

This should've been my first indication something was amiss. It would be difficult for a seasoned cinemaphile to obtain prints for such obscure movies, almost impossible for an avid devotee like me, absolutely impossible for someone like Ms. Victor to have obtained those films. I was just too caught up in it all, Sheriff Baker. Too blinded by what I'd come to feel was my due, my . . . *restitution*. I should've known better.

Any questions I had about how she could've possibly obtained such rarities as those films vanished as soon as the backdoor opened, and Ms. Victor glided out to join us. And I don't use the term lightly, sheriff. For the event, Ms. Victor had chosen, of course, to dress as Contessa Victoria's most well-known role, the Arglwyddes y Cors. She wore a flowing, white, diaphanous gown of timeless cut which was somehow revealing and concealing all at once. Her hair shimmered darker than night, and her skin shone an alabaster white, her green eyes glimmering with a kind of ancient *knowing* which sent cold shivers racing down my spine.

Indeed, it wasn't Ms. Victor at all, sheriff. It never had been, I know that now. And it wasn't some psychic apparition of an obscure, long-dead black and white horror movie actress. It was the Arglwyddes y Cors. The Daughter of the Mists, and I'd summoned her with my heart, and my pain.

And of course . . . I'd also rejected her, too.

I think maybe I sensed it even then, but on a basic, instinctual level. I'm quite afraid that in that moment I ignored Danielle completely as I stared at the approaching ethereal figure, even going so far as to whisper, "Contessa."

She smiled, and in a voice somehow husky and smooth, said, "You approve?"

Again, much to my chagrin, I acted as if Danielle wasn't even there. "Very much so," I rasped. "Very . . . authentic."

She gestured at the reel-to-reel projector, and the movie tins lying on the table next to it. "As I said. Something special. Something vintage. Does it meet your satisfaction?"

"Looks great," Danielle piped up, sounding slightly annoyed (and with good reason, of course). "Where'd you get the old-school projector? That must've been hard to come by."

Connie—Contessa?—looked at Danielle, face hardening, as if offended Danielle dared speak to her. "Not for one such as me. What I desire, I obtain."

She swung her burning gaze back to me. "Or *else*."

A strange silence fell between us. Another heartbeat, and Contessa (that's who it was, and that's how I'll continue to reference her), spoke to me, dismissing Danielle entirely. "The last tour of the house is almost done," she said smoothly, "and your time has finally come. Are you ready?" She swept a grandiose hand at the mostly filled seats, "To show them the true face of the old monsters?"

Of course, I remembered the last time she'd said something similar. *Reject me, and I'll show you the true face of an old monster.*

All I could do was nod. Contessa laid a hand on the strange-looking vintage reel-to-reel projector. "I assume you know how to operate this?"

"I'm sure I'll manage."

"Very well. I'll leave you to it, while I conduct the final tour of the night to their seats."

She turned to retreat back inside, but paused before doing so. Once again completely ignoring Danielle, she looked at me, her face twisting into a slightly scornful expression of regret. Then, she whirled away, and was gone. Her absence felt like a sudden splash of cold water on my face. I blinked, strangely feeling lost, and rejected, also.

"Well. She's certainly got your number, hasn't she?"

It shames me to admit it, but the voice of someone I'd come to adore now sounded like nails on a chalkboard in my ears. I couldn't keep the annoyance out of my voice as I turned to examine the strange, vintage projector, and said, "I have no idea what you're talking about."

"It doesn't strike you as a bit convenient that she's cosplaying as your favorite old horror movie actress?" Danielle's tone sounded sharp and needling, not like anything I'd heard from her the entire time we'd been together. "She's trying too hard, y'know? Kinda pathetic, when you think about it."

"Maybe you should show a little more respect," I said, my tone short and quick, an unreasonable *anger* at Danielle swelling in my heart. "And if you don't mind, I need to concentrate on familiarizing myself with this projector."

Danielle didn't answer. Only snorted and walked away. A few minutes later, I heard her camera clicking, as she took more pictures. I guiltily considered apologizing to her, but her hectoring voice echoed in my mind, and I remained silent.

I'd never speak to her ever again.

41.

Twenty minutes later, the last tour was finished, and the chairs in the backyard were filled. The crowd hummed softly, most likely sharing their experiences in the spook house, but I also fancied them buzzing in anticipation of the night's events.

Finally, Contessa strode down the aisle and turned to stand before the screen. As if a switch had been thrown, the crowd hushed as one. Silence descended, as Contessa looked out over the crowd. For a moment, I believe she looked directly at me. I'm sure of that, sheriff. She was looking directly at me, and on her face was the same contemptuous look of regret from before.

When she began speaking, I believed—and still do—that she was speaking to me, also.

"Tonight promises to be transformative. It will be a night of change. A night of growth. *Evolution*. I assure you, whomever you are . . . *whatever* you are . . . after tonight, you will not be the same. You will expand beyond the limitations of your existence, you will become, and you will *know*. You will know the true face of the old monsters."

She spread her arms wide. "Open your minds and souls, and prepare to embrace the beauty . . . of the monstrous."

Silence.

All eyes, I truly believe, rested on her, and her alone. Though I wasn't looking at Danielle (she'd positioned herself near the screen and to the side, to get shots of the audience, I assumed), I'm convinced she was enthralled, also.

Contessa nodded at me. I returned her nod, and flipped the movie projector on.

42.

That was something else which should've alarmed me. I didn't give my usual speech about the old monsters of black and white cinema. She never gave me the chance. She made her strange speech, then nodded at me. I flipped the projector on without the slightest hesitation.

It whirred softly to life. The screen lit up, a brilliant white rectangle blazing against the semi-dark of the dimly lit backyard. After several seconds of this, the movie began.

But it wasn't *Daughter of the Mists*, or one of the others. It wasn't a *movie*, at all.

What was it?

I'm afraid words won't adequately describe it. After several minutes of that bright white rectangle and silence, a low, droning hum built, rising from seemingly everywhere. A gray kaleidoscope of moving and shifting patterns slowly faded into existence on the screen, and I saw . . .

I saw . . .

Teeth.

Gnawing on flesh. Limbs torn to shreds by jagged black claws. Looping and purplish entrails spilling to the ground and consumed by grunting mouths and clicking teeth. Creatures of indefinite shape, size and color clawed, ripped, tore, and disemboweled other creatures; and still other creatures were . . . they were *fucking*, sheriff. They were rutting and fucking even as their guts were being torn out, as they rolled and writhed in their own blood and filth . . .

Inhuman limbs with too many joints entwined, as too long fingers grasped, ripped, and tore. The creatures—too many to number—continued to rut and fuck, even as they gutted each other and ate each others entrails, their flesh turning translucent, as they melted together into one teeming, surging mass.

I can't . . .

We all watched, open-mouthed, with drinking eyes. The audience, myself, and, I'm certain, Danielle. Scenes of the most depraved and grotesque violence imaginable, abominable creatures visiting defilement upon each other in gleeful abandon. It was impossible to tell what the creatures were or what they looked like, and the longer we watched, the harder it was to determine whether they were eviscerating each other, sexually defiling each other, or both at the same time.

I don't know what we watched.

And I can't tell you how long it lasted. Eventually, after what seemed like an eternity, the screen snapped back to bright light, as the tape clicked against the reel as it spun, but even then . . . I could still *see* it all happening on the screen, as I stared and stared . . .

That's when the screaming began.

43.

The screaming started in the front row, near the screen. A high-pitched, frenzied, manic sound. At first it was the only sound, and the audience simply sat in numb shock, most likely still reeling—as I was—from the visual depravity we'd all just witnessed.

Minutes later, everything exploded in a flurry of thrashing bodies, screams . . . and blood.

A struggle broke out in the middle of the front-left row, and a person—a young woman of indefinite age wearing nondescript clothes—broke free from what looked like two other figures grappling with her. I recognized the screams as coming from her.

She stumbled into the aisle, screaming in that same, high-pitched wail. Hands clasped to her neck . . . to a ragged gash, which sprayed blood past her fingers, down her neck, staining her white shirt.

The two figures she'd struggled free from leaped after her, and tackled the woman in the middle of the aisle. They bore her down, and in a flash, opened their mouths wide—wider than human mouths should—and plunged down and latched onto both sides of her neck like gruesome lamprey eels. Blood spurted and geysered as she disappeared beneath the two hungry, feeding bodies.

The bloody scene served as a trigger, flipping a switch in the audience, a switch which flipped one of two ways. Many screamed and shouted, struggling up from their seats to flee. The others, however, instantly turned on their neighbors and attacked them. They grasped and tore at people with hands which looked like they were too long-fingered and tipped with claws, ripping clothes free and slashing flesh to ribbons, opening double-hinged jaws wide and feasting on torn and bloody flesh.

To my great horror, I saw several forms sexually defiling the people they were flaying alive, rutting in the midst of the bloodshed, regardless of gender. There were couples, there were threesomes, there were small orgies of violence and carnal lust, until the audience was nothing more than a surging sea of thrusting, twisting, eviscerating flesh as these things fucked and disemboweled each other with engorged and grotesque members. The air rang with mingling screams of torment, agony, and a wild, orgasmic ecstasy. Just like the hideous depravity we'd all seen on the movie screen only moments before.

And as I stood there, paralyzed, *she* drifted down the main aisle, somehow moving among the grappling, rippling, heaving and thrusting bodies without touching a single one, her flowing white gown somehow remaining pure white despite the blood spraying from those *things* feeding on and fucking their friends and neighbors.

When she reached the screen, she turned and looked out upon the depraved bloodshed . . . and looked at *me*. Not Connie Victor, not Contessa Victoria Williams, not even the Arglwyddes y Cors from those black and white films, but something *older*. Ancient. A thing my will had conjured into being. The thing which had restored my fortune, and dragged me from the watery depths of Clifton Lake. The thing <u>I</u> had rejected, by choosing another.

A figure broke from the mob and stumbled toward the aisle. It was Danielle. She'd lost her camera, but though disheveled and torn, her clothes were intact, and she didn't look badly injured. Her expression, however, was one of stark, mad terror. Eyes wide, like an unreasoning animal, an animal driven insane by fear. She raised her eyes, and her gaze found mine. I saw desperate recognition there, and she lurched forward, hands reaching for me, even though I was so far away.

In a flash of white, the thing I'd called forth with my pain and anger leaped after Danielle. It landed on her back with its hands and feet, like a feline beast of prey. It drove her face-first into the ground, and buried its mouth—open too wide, with far too many teeth—into the base of her neck. Blood flashed, black in the dim light.

Danielle's high and shrill scream, which seemed twice as loud as the mingled screams and groans of the ravaged crowd, cut off in a wet gurgle, as the thing on her back fed. It didn't content itself with her neck, however. It flipped Danielle over onto her back. With a swipe of its claws, it slashed Danielle's blouse open and jabbed its claws into her belly . . .

Paused.

And looked up at me. Its bestial green eyes glittering through a mask of blood and viscera, mouth spread inhumanly wide and ringed with needle-point teeth, and at that moment, I knew. Danielle's death was my fault. I'd chosen Danielle over it, and doomed her to death.

We stared at each other for a long moment, which seemed to stretch into a hellish eternity, as these *things* ravaged and thrashed in the bloody mess of what used to be human beings. Believe it or not . . . at that moment, I still wished to give myself to that thing, completely, and utterly. She could have me to do what she would, even if it meant my end.

It was too late, however.

My fate would not be so kind.

It grinned, a horrible thing to see on a face stretched and distorted by an inhuman skull structure, coated with blood, dripping with gore. Then, while looking at me, it *dug* its claws into Danielle's belly, and ripped her open from neck to groin, like she was a wet paper bag. Her innards—looping and slick intestines, kidneys, liver and lungs—spilled onto the ground, and the thing I'd called forth buried its face in that mess and began to feed.

I screamed, from the very depths of my being. Danielle's name, or just an inarticulate howl, I can't remember. I stumbled away from the projector (a hideous-looking thing now, alien and otherworldly, an infernal design not like anything on this earth), down the back porch steps and toward the teeming mass of creatures (none of them looked human anymore) clawing, biting, and slashing at each other. I glanced around wildly, trying to find my way through, and then I saw it.

Jammed blade first in that tree trunk on the edge of the

backyard. The ax. Still there, after all this time. How and why I don't know. It didn't matter, of course. It was there, and my mind seized on it. I crossed the yard to it—with the cries and screams of the damned in the background—in several strides. Grabbed the handle, tugged the blade free, turned, and waded into the sea of turgid flesh slashing and wildly copulating with each other.

I *hacked* my way through them. Swung and buried the ax in the back of the head of this *thing* (not a person) humping the prone form of what used to be someone from town; who, I didn't know, because their face had been torn off. The ax slammed into the back of the thing's head and cracked its skull open. I jerked it free from the twitching body, then swung it in a looping arc into the snarling face of another thing just looking up from its meal of someone's intestines. The ax's blade smashed into the thing's face, destroying its jaw and caving its face in.

As the thing fell away, I stepped over the disemboweled corpse it had been feeding on and swung the ax again, sideways, like I was chopping down a tree, at another thing which was frantically coupling with one of its own kind, while they both slashed and ripped at each other with their claws. The ax's blade struck the humping thing in the back of its head, and cleaved it off its hideous and misshapen shoulders with a *thump* I felt all the way up my arms. Grotesquely, its headless body continued its frenzied hip-thrusting, and I don't even think its deformed partner knew the difference.

This was how I made my way to what was left of Danielle and the thing feeding on her. I chopped my way through that teeming mass of bodies, caving in heads, burying the ax in chests, chopping off heads . . . but it didn't matter, you understand. They weren't human anymore. They'd been transformed. They'd become *monstrous*, Sheriff Baker, but not like the monsters in those silly black and white films of mine, you see. They'd become something *older*. Ancient, and inhuman.

I finally made my way to the thing feeding on Danielle. It looked up from her hollowed abdomen, viscera and blood dripping from its mouth, strings of shredded flesh clinging to a face which bore no resemblance to anything on this earth. An all-consuming rage pulsed through me, and I raised the ax above my head and brought it down as hard as I could. I slammed that ax down, over and over, screaming as the blood and innards splashed all over me.

It seemed to go on forever.

Until the strength left my arms, and the ax fell from my nerveless fingers.

All had gone quiet.

Gone was the moaning and screaming cries of the beasts violating each other. I closed my eyes, and stood, swaying blindly on my feet. That's when your men found me, of course. Standing over what remained of Danielle's body, covered in her blood, and the thing gone, because of course . . . restitution had been made.

November 1ˢᵗ

Sheriff Chris Baker sat in his office, feet propped up on the corner of his desk, hands clasped behind his head as he stared into nothing. He had reports to write—*God*, did he have reports to write—and, as always, he grappled with the very real truth that no matter how hard he tried, the reports he wrote would never match up with what actually happened, simply because there was no way anyone could ever know what *actually* happened.

Thank God Halloween wasn't for another 365 days.

The county police had taken Earl Flanagan away an hour ago. He'd fallen unresponsive by then, as if the last of his essence had slipped away into nothing with the story he'd told Chris. The county sheriff's deputies—Sullivan and Koloski—were old hands at picking up prisoners from Clifton Heights. They'd merely nodded at Chris as they collected the catatonic Earl, and took him away.

Chris closed his eyes, fighting against a familiar weariness. None of the stories about last night matched up, of course. Most specifically, Earl's phantasmagoric, hallucinatory movie which turned the audience into ravening beasts who turned on their neighbors. The eye witness reports they'd managed to collect said *something* had showed briefly on the movie screen, but no one could remember what, and that it had only lasted for a few minutes. Most assumed something had gone wrong with the projector or movie reel. A projector which—along with the movie reels Earl mentioned—were somehow gone.

Several of the stories agreed that someone had screamed shortly after the projector cut out, which panicked the crowd into a low-grade stampede, but no one seemed to know *why* someone screamed, or why the crowd panicked and started pushing and shoving their way to the exit, all at once.

Of course, no one had changed into strange, inhuman creatures. However, of the dead, seven of them died from ax-inflicted wounds. That was one of the few points all the stories agreed upon. As soon as the panic began, Earl Flanagan screamed, descended from Feldpausch House's back porch, picked up the ax (an ax forensics hadn't yet found) waded into the crowd and started attacking random people.

The biggest monkey-wrench was Danielle Lathrop's gruesome death. Several eye-witness accounts swore that a woman in a white gown had "killed a woman with her bare hands." The woman matched Danielle Lathrop's description, though all the testimonies were vague as to *how* the woman in white had killed her with "her bare hands."

Early forensic evidence showed Danielle Lathrop had indeed been disemboweled in a way inconsistent with an ax blow . . . though the body *did* show evidence of mutilation by ax *post-mortem*. Which also matched several eye-witness accounts of Earl's last victim: Danielle, as Earl struck her repeatedly in the belly with the ax no one could find.

And of course, as he'd already told Earl, Connie Victor didn't exist. No one knew who she was, or had spoken to her. The rest of the Town Board swore they knew nothing of the arrangements both Bob Phillips (still missing) and Norman Fuller (dead in a still suspicious drunk-driving accident) made with said woman. Cynthia Woolridge—who was still on COVID quarantine—said she indeed talked to someone on the phone named Connie, who offered to run Feldpausch Horror House this year, but also admitted to being so fatigued and sick at the time, she barely remembered any of their conversations.

Chris sighed. Unclasped his hands from the back of his head, closed his eyes, and rubbed his face. With a grunt, he kicked his feet off his desk and to the floor. Sat up, and pulled himself closer to the desk.

Last night, seven people died in a seemingly random burst of senseless violence, and an eighth died, possibly in a crime of passion, or love gone bad. Earl would most likely not stand trial. Chris didn't think he was faking his catatonia. He thought Earl's last burst of cognizance came with his story, and now there wasn't anything left. He'd most likely be institutionalized and rot in a padded room, drooling, for the rest of his life.

Cynthia Woolridge had announced she was stepping down as director of Feldpausch Horror House. Based on the call he'd received from acting Town Board Chairperson Joanna Kinner, both Feldpausch Horror House and FrightFest would be discontinued indefinitely.

It was November 1st. Friends and loved ones of the dead would grieve, and those around them would rally to their side. It was the Clifton Heights way, of course. Support your own. There would be a flurry of Town Board meetings as townspeople clamored for answers, but from past experience, Chris knew it was a reflex only. A show for appearance's sake. No one wanted answers, really. Not that there were ever answers to be had in this town, anyway.

Which, of course, left *him* to sort everything out. Write up reports, file them, pat agitated members of the Town Board on the back, assure them no one could've seen this coming, and reassure the town that everything eventually would be okay. Bad, unexplained things happened sometimes, and there wasn't anything anyone could do but move on. And move on the people of Clifton Heights would do. They'd had lots of practice, after all. It was practically a survival instinct, in this town.

This town.

It and the people who lived here were his responsibility. He'd stay and fight the good fight until he no longer could, and also, Clifton Heights wasn't *all* bad. Good people lived here; people he cared about, people who needed and deserved someone fighting for them. Even so? At times like this? He couldn't help but think . . .

Fuck this town.

ONCE UPON A HALLOWEEN NIGHT

JEREMY BATES

1.

THE HOUSE SMELLED of damp wood and wet mud. Rain had fallen for most of the day, an intermittent drizzle that occasionally rose to a full-throttled assault that beat down on the shingled roof. It had seemed to stop for good about a half hour ago. Our mom had told me that the forecast for the rest of the week was for sun and clouds, a huge relief. Halloween fell on Saturday in three days' time. The last thing anybody wanted was to be trick-or-treating in a soggy costume.

Standing at my bedroom door, I listened to make sure our parents weren't in the living room. Our mom wasn't usually in there at this hour. Our dad, however, would often crash out on the sofa, so he could be sleeping there or just lying on his back, awake, who knew? Nobody wanted to disturb him when he was working off a night of boozing. He wasn't very nice to be around when he was sober; when drunk, he was about the most frightening person in the world.

Let me say a word or two about our house. The first floor is divided between the bedroom I share with my brother, our parents' bedroom, the living room, and the kitchen. The second floor has a low and sloping ceiling, and nobody goes up there much. My brother and I don't because we avoid stairs whenever we can. Our parents don't . . . well, I don't know why. Probably for the same reason people with attics don't spend much time hanging out in them. They're cluttered with junk, and you have to stoop so you don't knock your head on the rafters.

I heard nothing in the living room now. That meant our mom would be in her bedroom, either sleeping or reading one of her books. That was all she ever did: read. She'd start a book after my brother and I left for school in the morning, and she'd be close to finishing it by the time we got home. She would work at putting dinner together before our dad rumbled up the driveway in his rusted Ford pickup truck. After everybody had eaten and the dishes were tidied up, she would spend the rest of the evening finishing the book or starting a new one. She was Mr. Jeffries' best customer, no question about it. Mr. Jeffries owned the used bookstore on Main Street. I went there with her whenever the opportunity arose. I loved the crowded, narrow aisles filled floor-to-ceiling with stories. I loved the foxed-paper smell that permeated the place. And I especially loved the dungeon-like basement because that was where all the kids' books were kept. I got my hardcover collection of Hardy Boys books there. And just last week our mom, with the credit from the stack of paperbacks she'd brought to trade, bought me *I Love You Broom Hilda*, an old paperback filled with black-and-white comics. I didn't understand a lot of the jokes, but so far I was enjoying it.

"Coast is clear," I said softly.

"Ready Freddy," Red said.

My name, by the way, is Fred. My brother's name is Red. I think my parents chose his name simply because it rhymed with mine. Can you think of any other reason why they'd christen their kid a color? I can't.

We started quietly into the living room. Red had our Eveready flashlight in his hand, but he didn't turn it on yet. For one, we didn't want to waste the two D-cell batteries that powered it. Batteries were expensive, as our dad was always telling us, and we wouldn't get any new ones unless we asked for them for Christmas in a couple of months time. And two, we didn't want to alert our mom. She rarely closed her bedroom door, and she might spot the sweep of the yellow beam if we turned the flashlight on prematurely.

I could hear Red's shallow breathing right next to me, and I suppose he could hear mine. I kept my hand outstretched, anticipating the big wooden dining table, which would be somewhere in front of us. One step, two . . . three, four. You've heard of the fable *The Tortoise and the Hare*, I'm sure. Well, Red and I are the tortoise. We don't get anywhere fast, ever. But that's all right as long as we get where we need to go in the end.

My fingers brushed the back of a chair.

"Stop," I whispered. We stopped. "Left or right?"

"Right," he said arbitrarily.

We moved around the table in a counter-clockwise direction. I trailed my hand from one chair to the next so we didn't get lost or turned around in the dark. When we reached the far end of the table I said, "Kitchen's straight ahead."

"Don't trip."

"*You* don't trip."

"*Quiet*. Mom will hear you."

I knew when we reached the kitchen because the hardwood floorboards disappeared beneath our bare feet, replaced with smoother and cooler linoleum tiles. The refrigerator would be to our right, the sink and oven and pantry to our left in a horseshoe-shaped space. I felt for the counter, found it, and moved alongside it.

"Okay," I said after a few steps. "You can turn on the flashlight, but keep it pointed at the floor."

"I know that," Red said. "I'm not stupid."

We lowered ourselves to our knees. Light bloomed. I found myself staring at the linoleum tiles, which featured an orange stone pattern. Our mom hated them and was always talking about getting new ceramic tiles instead. Our dad's reply to that was the same each time: "Money don't grow on trees, sweetheart."

Red raised the beam to the cupboard door directly before us. He shifted it left then right to make sure we were in front of the proper door.

We were and I said, "I'm gonna open it."

"Do it quietly."

I didn't know how you could open a cupboard noisily, but I didn't mention this. I opened the door by the round knob—and there it was, our prize. On the upper shelf waited a large glass bowl filled to the rim with candy bars, their wrappers glittering in the beam of the flashlight like so many colorful jewels. I eyed them hungrily, trying to decide which one I would take for myself.

We'd first discovered the stash this morning while making breakfast. The brown sugar had been all but gone except for some sticky lumps in the bottom of the jar, so we rooted through the cupboards looking for a new package. We ended up finding one in the pantry—but not before we'd discovered the Halloween candy. We'd been too chicken to snatch a candy bar for ourselves then. But over the course of the day our confidence (and hunger) grew until we hatched the plan which we were currently carrying out.

"Which one do you want?" I asked, licking my lips because my mouth had gone dry.

"A Snickers," Red told me immediately. "Hurry up before Mom catches us."

"You think she would tell Dad?"

"Hurry up!"

I had to sift my hand through the assortment of candy bars to reach a Snickers. I hated the brittle noises the disturbed wrappers made; they sounded as loud as firecrackers.

Finally I located a Snickers. I plucked it out and stuck it in the breast pocket of my pajamas. Then my hand was back in the bowl, searching for a Reese's Peanut Butter Cup.

'Hurry *up!*" Red said.

I settled on a Kit Kat and dropped it into the same pocket.

"Get one more," Red told me.

"No way! Dad will know."

"How will he know? Lookit how many there are!"

"He might have counted them."

"Then he'll know we already took two."

Red was right, and we would get in just as much trouble for stealing three candy bars instead of just two, so back in my hand went. A Twix would have been perfect because there were two evenly divided pieces we could share. But I didn't see one and chose a Crunchie. It joined the Snickers and Kit Kat.

Grinning triumphantly, I closed the cupboard door. Red, with a grin mirroring my own, flicked off the flashlight.

Mission accomplished.

2.

Back in our bedroom I snapped on the overhead light. The first thing I saw was my reflection in the full-length mirror that leaned against the wall directly across the room from the door. The mirror, with its gold filigreed frame, looked as though it belonged in a queen's castle, not some kid's bedroom. It was old because it had been my grandparents' (and anything they had owned had to be old). My grandfather had died three years ago when I was seven. My grandmother was never the same after that. She stopped smiling and no longer seemed interested in Red and me when we went to her house on weekends. She died recently at the end of July. Our mom said it was from a broken heart. I think all the wrinkles in her face and the gray in her hair also had something to do with it. Her funeral had been sad, especially when we had to look at her in her coffin. Why did our parents make us do that? She'd looked rubbery and not like the grandma I remembered, but that was the grandma I *now* remembered.

Her stuff was divided between our mom and her sister, our Aunt Jenny. One of the things our mom got was the mirror. She didn't think it fit with anything in the house, and it was destined to go up to the great wasteland of the second floor. But then Red asked if we could have it in our bedroom. I would have preferred it disappear upstairs because I didn't like looking at myself in the mirror, but Red persisted, and we got it.

And now there it was, capturing my reflection and beaming it back at me, a ten-year-old kid in blue pajamas with white pinstripes. I had a bright, shiny face with clear blue eyes and red lips. I parted my mop of brown hair on the right and brushed it over to the left side of my head. If you looked at me from the neck up, you would probably say I was handsome. The problem was, I had a second head growing out of me. That would be Red. He looked just like me except he parted his hair on the left and brushed it right. Also, his neck angled only five-degrees, while mine angled closer to fifteen, making him appear taller.

We were what doctors called conjoined twins, and what most regular folks called Siamese twins. I wished we were just twins and not conjoined or Siamese, but there wasn't anything I could do about that. Our mom had told us that when we were born the doctors had wanted to separate us, but she didn't let them because one of us would have died. That probably would have been me because I was weaker than Red, and on the animal shows that Red and I watched on YouTube, the weaker babies always died first. So I guess she made the right decision. But sometimes I think it might have been better had the doctors separated us and let me die. I thought a lot about death, probably more than most kids my age. And I didn't think it was so bad. Nobody could stare at you or hate you or make fun of you when you didn't exist anymore.

"Let's feast!" Red bugled suddenly. That was what he always said when we had something good to eat. He took his Snickers from the breast pocket of our pajamas and tore off the wrapper with his teeth.

We might have two heads, but we only had two arms and two legs between us. I controlled the arm and leg on my side, and Red controlled the ones on his side. This meant we had to do most thing in coordination with one another. Like walking or dressing or typing on a keyboard. But not opening candy . . . because you could use your teeth to help you out with that.

He bit into the Snickers. His face was right next to mine. I could smell the chocolate and peanuts and hear his sticky chewing. This made me all the hungrier. I tore the wrapper off my Kit Kat with my teeth and chomped down.

"*Mmmm*-mmmm," Red said around a full mouth.

"Mmmm-mmmm," I agreed.

The chocolate-covered wafers were the most delicious food I'd eaten in a long time, maybe all year. Our parents, you see, never took us out to Dairy Queen or Baskin Robbins or other fast-food places where the real tasty stuff was. Our dad would tell Red and me (just as he would tell our mom when she mentioned she wanted new ceramic tiles for the kitchen floor) that money doesn't grow on trees. And while money might have been a considering factor why we always ate at home, I think the *overriding* factor was that he didn't like being seen in public with us. Because it wasn't just fast food joints he didn't take us to; he didn't take us *anywhere*. It was like he got more embarrassed by the gawkers than Red and I did.

So we weren't used to eating junk food, and while the stuff our mom put in our brown paper lunch bags or whipped up for dinner at home was all right, it rarely included anything chocolate or sweet.

That was why Halloween was the best night of the year. I didn't care much for dressing up in a costume, or all the walking involved in hunting down the candy. But the effort was worth it. Last year Red and I had each filled a pillowcase with candy. We probably could have amassed even more loot, but some of the parents only doled out one piece of candy between us. Which was a gyp. We had two separate mouths, didn't we?

Nevertheless, this was something people always seemed to struggle with: Were we one person or two? It was a complicated matter, I can tell you that much. We had our own birth certificates, for example. And Mr. Green, the counsellor at school, told us that we'd need to get separate passports if we ever wanted to travel outside of the country, and that we'd have to take our driver's license test twice when we turned sixteen, once for Red, and once for me (which seemed pretty idiotic because if one of us passed and the other failed, how would anyone know which one of us was driving?). On the other hand, Mr. Green also told us we'd probably only get one salary whenever we got a job; we'd have to choose a single wife if we wanted to get married, as two would constitute something called bigamy; and if either of us ever committed a crime, we'd both likely end up in the slammer.

So, yeah, a complicated matter.

But if you're asking me what I believe, we're two separate people. There's no doubt in my mind about that.

When we finished our candy bars, Red said, "Open up the last one."

"I think we should save it," I told him. "That way, we'll have something to look forward to tomorrow."

"But I want it now." He reached for the pajama pocket.

I batted his hand away. "I wanna save it."

"I wanna *eat* it."

"Forget it." I took the Crunchie from the pocket and held it far to my left so it would be impossible for Red to reach.

He snorted. "You can't hold it there all night."

He was right. My arm would get tired soon. But I couldn't hide it anywhere either because he would be looking.

I decided I had only one option. I tossed the candy bar into the corner of the room. It bounced off the wall and landed next to a clothes basket filled with our stuffed animals.

"What the hell, man?" Red said, knowing it was now out of play for good; he needed my leg to get anywhere.

"We'll get it tomorrow."

"You're such a dweeb, you know that? I have to go pee."

"And then we better get to bed."

Along with having our own heads, we had our own hearts and lungs and stomachs. Because of this, when Red needed to go to the bathroom, I might not, and vice versa.

Red set the flashlight on the dresser next to our curio box, which contained all our favorite things, including bottle caps, desiccated insects, and keychains (the wackier the better). We went to the bathroom, urinated, brushed our teeth, and then climbed into bed. Although the latter took our full collaboration and coordination, we didn't communicate anything verbally to each other. When it came to things we did day in and day out, we could intuit what the other was going to do, how he was going to move. It was almost like telepathy. I'm not saying we could read each other's thoughts, but we could pick up, consciously and subconsciously, on the smallest tells.

Once we were lying on our backs with the patchwork cover pulled up to our chins, Red said, "Night, Fred."

"Night, Barney," I replied.

That was our joke.

I added, "And you better not . . . "

"Sheesh! Will you let up? That was just once."

Several weeks ago, just after school began in September, I woke in the middle of the night to find Red playing with our penis (which we did share, along with our lower spine and digestive tract). I freaked out and yelled at him loud enough that our mom came into our room to check on us. I told her I'd had another of my nightmares, and she left us with the dire warning: "Go to sleep— you don't want to wake your father . . . "

No, Mother, we most certainly did not.

When we were alone again (as much as conjoined twins could be "alone"), we whisper-argued for a few minutes before giving it up. By then our penis had returned to its normal shape and size, and I didn't want to think about it anymore. I knew how sex worked. I knew in a vague kind of way that some people did it to themselves . . . but having Red do it to our thing felt almost like he was doing it to *me* . . . and a part of me, a deep-down part not yet fully realized or recognized, understood that things were only going to get more complicated and difficult between us the older we got.

I closed my eyes and hoped to fall asleep quickly. I seemed to have a ten minute or so window to do this. If I was successful, I would sleep straight through until morning. However, if sleep proved elusive, then I could be in for one heck of a long, wakeful slog. I can't roll over onto my front if I so wanted, you understand. I can't toss and turn to find that "just right" position. I can't do anything but lie there on my back like our grandma in her coffin. And that can get uncomfortable—so much so that the elusiveness of sleep plays out as a kind of self-fulfilling prophecy. I know I'm uncomfortable; I know because of that I won't be able to get to sleep quickly; and lo-and-behold, I never do.

It really sucked. The boredom of being awake when you were supposed to be sleeping was as bad as the time Red got pneumonia and I had to sit beside him in bed doing nothing until he got better—only that ordeal had lasted two long weeks.

Thankfully, tonight I got lucky and fell asleep almost immediately.

I always looked forward to my dreams, as they were much more interesting than reality, or at least my reality. About two years ago I discovered I could manipulate them to my liking. I learned how to do this due to a recurring nightmare I used to have. I would be falling from the roof of a tall building. The wind would be in my hair, my heart would be in my stomach—and then I would wake up just before I pancaked the ground with a breathless scream trapped in my throat and sweat on my skin. It got to the point I was having this nightmare three or four times a week. I didn't know why. To my knowledge I wasn't afraid of heights, and I'd never been in a tall building before.

In any event, one night I was having the nightmare . . . and I thought, *Well, it would certainly be nice if I had a parachute right now*. And—voila! One was strapped to my back. I pulled the ripcord and floated safely to the ground and didn't wake until morning.

I began using this powerful sleep-magic not just in other nightmares but regular dreams as well, and it was the best thing that ever happened to me.

Most of my dreams, to give you some context, start out with Red and me fused together at the pelvises. But when I want to (which is more often than not) I use the sleep-magic to imagine us as distinct individuals. Sometimes I imagine myself strolling through a park on two strong legs of my own. Sometimes I imagine myself swimming in a cool, deep lake, something Red and I had never been allowed to do because we would sink to the bottom like a dumbbell. And sometimes I imagine myself at Clifton Heights Elementary School, showing off to everyone that I'm my own man.

Tonight the dream I would remember upon waking was of a time when Red and I had been sitting in the sandbox behind our house. We hadn't yet learned to walk—even crawling was a challenge—which was why we couldn't get away when a rabid porcupine trundled out of the woods and came toward us. Back then, our mom had heard us yelling and had scared it away with a broom. Now, with my sleep-magic, I stood up, unmerging from Red the way a soul might from a dying body. Imagining myself in a knight's shining suit of armor, I approached the porci-pisshead. I was planning on kicking it back into the woods . . . only it was no longer foaming and slobbering at the mouth. In fact, it had donned a small white tuxedo and was smoking a black pipe. Then it smiled, revealing yellowed buck teeth, and said, "Hello, good chap! May I have some of your tasty chocolate?"

I realized the Kit Kat I had eaten was now in my hand, back in its wrapper.

"If you don't share it," Mr. Porcupine went on, "I'm going to tell your father on you. You wouldn't want me to do that, would you? Tell him that you stole Halloween candy meant for the trick-or-treaters?"

"Please don't," I said. "He'll hit me."

"You should have thought about that before you stole the candy. Because he's home now, and he's going to find out—"

I snapped awake. The ink-black bedroom was silent as a tomb—

A crash sounded from the living room, what might have been a chair toppling over—or being kicked over. Red, I sensed, was awake too.

A moment later he whispered ominously, "Dad's home . . . "

I didn't say anything in reply. My throat had shrunken to the size of a straw, making it hard to breathe let alone speak.

Another crash, this time what sounded like a glass or dish shattering on the floor.

Our mom's voice came next—shrill, frightened, pleading. Her last word was decapitated by a roar. That was the only way to describe the sound our dad made. A roar. It was guttural, primal, void of language or anything human.

Something scraped loudly over the hardwood floor, maybe a chair, maybe the entire dining table. Other glasses or dishes shattered. Our mom began sobbing. Her bedroom door slammed shut with a resounding clap.

Our dad screamed after her, loosing profanities and threats. Yet worse than those were the personal attacks interspersed between, the adjectives demeaning her as "worthless" and "feeble" and "good-for-nothing" and the like.

Tears burned in my eyes, but I wasn't strong enough to stand-up for our mom. If I tried, our dad would be more than happy to use that as an excuse to lay into Red and me. And he knew all the spots that hurt but wouldn't show at school, like our kidneys or tailbone or bladder or groin. Or armpits. He especially liked beating up our armpits. He would dangle us in the air by one of our arms the way fishermen hold their prized catches by the gills and whack our exposed armpit with whatever he could get his free hand on (usually some type of cooking utensil such as a ladle or spatula or the hinged end of a pair of tongs). We could never do anything but shriek and squirm and wait for the assault to end.

A plate or bowl clattered as it was removed from its stack in the cupboard. The microwave issued consecutive beeps. Then silence—unknown, black, threatening.

I pictured our dad crouched before the cupboard that held the Halloween candy in the glass bowl, counting the chocolate bars on the floor, discovering that three were missing. He'd know it was Red and me who took them. He'd come for us to teach us another of "life's little lessons"—lessons that involved cooking utensils and pain . . . lots of pain.

A sound right outside our bedroom door, the scuff of a heavy boot on the hardwood floor.

He was there. He was right there.

The straw that was my throat closed up completely. I couldn't breathe. I didn't dare try. He would hear. He would know we were awake, and that would be enough to tip his indecision. He would bust into the room, drunk and gleeful with hate—

Liquid warmth spread down my inner thigh. I wasn't sure whether Red or I did that.

The doorknob turned quietly . . . and then stopped when the microwave beeped three times.

A creaking floorboard, then another, farther away than the first. A bang that would have been the microwave door closing. The clatter of the silverware drawer opening and shutting. Then nothing. A minute passed like this, then two, then five. Finally I was convinced our dad had finished eating and had passed out in his usual spot on the sofa.

Red whimpered as he did his best to cry quietly.

I closed my eyes, thanking God for letting us escape this encounter—and knowing all too well we might not be so lucky the next time our dad came after us in the middle of the night.

3.

I woke to the gray, gloomy light of the new morning sifting through our bedroom window. No birds chirped or chattered. They were likely still tucked away in their nests, wet and tired from the rain that had fallen throughout the night. Our mom had said it wasn't supposed to rain any more this week, but she'd been wrong. I had laid on my back for maybe two hours after our dad came home, listening to the on-and-off again pitter-patter falling outside.

I'd also spent some of that time thinking about killing our dad.

I would never do such a thing, of course. I'd been fantasizing. But the fantasies had been compelling and entertaining nonetheless. Of all the ways I'd considered doing it (and there had been many), the method I'd preferred the most was taking a chisel and hammer from the cellar, sneaking up behind him as he slept on the sofa, and driving the chisel through the shell of his skull into his brain. This won out over the other options because I didn't see how I could screw it up—and that was what I had feared most. Screwing up and having him come after me, knowing I had tried to murder him.

My face was turned towards Red's. Our mouths were close enough we were almost kissing. His hung open, and his breath stank like garbage. Wrinkling my nose, I looked away. I tapped him on the stomach with my hand.

"What . . . ?" he grumbled.

"Time to get up."

"Not yet."

I clenched my jaw. In moments like these, I felt as though I was being held hostage to Red's whims, and I suppose I was.

I began humming my morning wake-up song. Sometimes it was "Start Me Up" by the Rolling Stones. Other times it might be "Here Comes the Sun" by the Beatles or "Wake Me Up" by Avicii. Today I chose "Bittersweet Symphony" by the Verve.

We have a great playlist on YouTube, if you're wondering.

"Shut up," Red said.

I continued humming.

He reached over and whacked me on the head the way you blindly whack the snooze button on your alarm clock. I turned my face away from him and kept humming.

"Aaaargh!" he said. "Fine! I'm awake!"

We lumbered out of bed and went to the bathroom. I guess I had to pee more than he did because I grabbed our thingy first and aimed it at the toilet bowl. Afterward we pulled off our urine-stained pajamas (altered by our mother like all our clothes) and showered. There were no glass partitions, or even a porcelain tub with plastic curtains. Just a shower head poking out of the tiled wall, a drain in the floor, and a rubber mat to stand on so we didn't slip and fall over. Red washed our hair while I soaped our body. We rinsed off, toweled, and returned to the bedroom to change. This was always another sticking point in our morning routine. I liked to wear muted colors like blacks and grays and browns, while Red preferred bright splashes and patterns. I'd once proposed we wear what I wanted one day, and what he wanted the next. That never worked out. Instead, we would mix and match our favorite articles of clothing. Today we settled on a gray sweatshirt with some goofy-looking chickens in football helmets on the front of it (my pick), and firetruck-red sweatpants with BULLS written in black down one leg (Red's pick).

We crept through the living room so we didn't wake our dad, who was snoring loudly on the sofa, one arm folded behind his head, the other hanging down to the floor. The door to my parents' bedroom was open, and I figured our mom was already sitting in a chair on the front porch, reading one of her books.

"What do you wanna eat?" I whispered. We had our own favorite foods. But if we were preparing something for ourselves, we would often settle on the same thing; it was easier than whipping up two different meals. For breakfast we usually compromised on cereal.

"Special K," Red said.

We ate at the kitchen counter because it was farther away from our dad than the dining table. After rinsing our dishes in the sink, and collecting the lunches our mom had made for us from the fridge, we left for school.

On the front porch our mom looked up at us from the paperback novel she was reading. She had once been a pretty woman—in our photo albums I'd seen pictures of her when she was younger—and she still was. But there was a tiredness about her nowadays that made her seem more like our grandma's age before she'd died. Worry wrinkles creased her forehead and the corner of her hazel eyes, while the gray in her hair had almost completely overtaken all the brown.

She said, "Did you boys get your lunches?"

We both nodded.

"Then go on, before you're late for school."

"Mom?" I said.

"Yes, Fred?"

"Dad didn't hurt you last night . . . did he?"

"No, he didn't. And don't you worry about what he does when he's like that. He's just having a difficult time finding work right now."

Red said, "Is our Halloween costume ready yet?"

"I'm putting the finishing touches on it. Now giddy-up along. You're going to be late."

We didn't say much on the way to school. I think we were both reflecting on how frail and melancholy our mom had become over the last few years. This made me depressed because I knew Red and I were the cause. Sometimes I couldn't help but think it would be best if we killed ourselves so our mom and dad could be happy again without us, like they'd been in the photographs before we were born.

The cruel truth was, nobody liked kids with two heads, not even their parents. That was why in the past, before it became illegal, parents would sell their conjoined twins to the highest bidder, usually a showman, who would exhibit them throughout Europe and the US.

One exception to this practice that I'd read about was Chang and Eng Bunker, conjoined twins born in Thailand when it was still called Siam. The king had been so shocked at the news of their appearance he ordered them executed. But their mother, a good woman like our mom, never turned them over to his minions, so they got to live. They still ended up being paraded around as two-headed aberrations, eventually becoming famous enough that "Siamese Twins" came to describe all conjoined twins.

And I say their mother was a good woman like our mom because our mom *is* a good woman. She didn't let the doctors separate Red and me because she didn't want one of us to die, remember? And when we were younger, and she had more energy and life in her, she'd loved us with all her heart. I knew that because I had felt loved.

So what happened? I think she still loves us the same as before; but I think she's been worn down by our dad. He's been getting drunk almost every night for as long as I can remember, that hasn't changed. But he's been getting more and more violent. So can you blame our mom for being frail and sad when she's getting beat up all the time, or watching Red and me getting beat up all the time . . . by the man she had once loved enough to marry?

Behind the clouds I could see the brightly burning glow of the waking sun. Hopefully last night was the last of the bad weather for a while. If it rained on Halloween night, Red and I would have to carry an umbrella, which meant we could only bring one pillowcase with us instead of two . . . which meant less candy. And while you might think a pillowcase-full of candy is still a pretty good haul for two ten-year-old kids, you should know that our dad makes us dump our candy on the dining room table when we get home so he can take what he wants for himself, usually three-quarters of everything (of course he would claim he was only doing it for our own good; preventing tooth decay and bellyaches and all that, he would say).

The trees lining the street were deciduous and denuded, their once green leaves now shriveled and dead on the front lawns we passed. Also dotting several of these lawns were piles of dog crap, some old and hardened like fossilized bones, others fresh and soft and buzzing with flies. In the poorer parts of Clifton Heights, it seemed people didn't believe in the common courtesy of picking up after their dogs.

Red and I were not fast walkers, so it typically took us about twenty minutes to get to school. That was if we followed the direct route. When we detoured along Black Creek, we added an extra ten minutes to the trip. I thought it was worth it. Not only was it peaceful to see the ducks and birds that hung out by the water, it also meant we didn't have to pass Cujo. That was what we called the big brown Mastiff in the front yard of one of the houses we had to pass.

That dog hated our guts. It would always start barking before we could see it and continue barking long after we'd passed it. And although it was trapped behind a chain-link fence, it nevertheless scared the hell out of us. For starters, it must have weighed twice as much as we did, and if it *did* escape its yard and come after us, we would be screwed. We weren't coordinated enough to run. We certainly couldn't scamper up onto a parked car to get away from its snapping jaws. We'd just have to stand there and hope it killed us quickly. But here was something to think about. It *wouldn't* kill us quickly, not the both of us. If the Mastiff ripped out your throat, you'd be dead before it began eating you. Red and I, however, had two throats. If it ripped out one of them—say, Red's—I'd have to wait around watching it gobble him up until it turned its teeth on me.

Another reason we liked taking the detour: we didn't run into as many bullies along the river. Kids could be terribly mean, especially outside the jurisdiction of teachers. They would circle us on their bikes, taunting us with some of the worst possible names you could imagine. They would call our dad a tosspot and our mom a witch. They would urge us to commit suicide. They would say whatever they thought would cut through our skin to our souls. We tried our best to ignore them. That would only make them hate us more, and they would trade their insults for rocks and sticks and pinecones and whatever other projectiles they could get their hands on. These bullies weren't only boys, mind you. Girls would partake in our tormenting just as gleefully, and they seemed to know the things to say that cut the deepest.

Kids never used to be so mean. Up until Red and I were five or six, they had accepted us. When we met them for the first time in kindergarten or at the park or wherever, we might get a curious look, or a question like, "Why do you have two heads?" But after we told them we were born that way, that was the end of it. They played with us. They shared their toys with us. They traded stickers with us. It was around grade three when they changed. That was when the insults began, the blackballing, the us vs. you mentality. We were different from them, and so we were the enemy. And what do you do to the enemy? You hate them. You demean them. You defeat them.

If you want to experience true human nature, don't look to adults. Adults are masters of masking their honest feelings. They might smile at Red and me, but they're secretly repulsed and maybe a little frightened by us, the way a doll that looks a little too human can make you a little frightened. They would never call us a bad name to our faces because they had clothed themselves in manners and civility. They knew that to fit into a society of many they needed to follow the rules of decorum.

Kids are still naked, so to speak. They're savages. They speak what's on their minds without filters; they act out their impulses without restraint.

And so that's where you'll find true human nature, misters and misses. That's where I saw it every day.

Red had been talking excitedly about Halloween and now he said, "I hope Mom has our costume ready when we get home. If she does, you wanna try it on?"

"Not really," I said. "Why do you wanna try it on?"

"So we can play Batman and Robin in the backyard!"

"Why do you get to be Batman?"

"Because the costume was my idea. What's wrong with being Robin?"

"Nothing, I guess. I just don't like dressing up."

Red snorted. "You don't like doing anything fun."

"I like finding insects."

"Yeah, I guess. But that's not as fun as dressing up. Anyway, you can pick our costume next year."

"Maybe . . ."

"Maybe? If you don't wanna, I'm gonna pick again."

"No way. You said it's my turn."

"Then pick!"

"Stop rushing me! I have all year—"

"Hey look!"

Red had stopped walking, so I did too. Sitting on the grass to the right of the path, before the rocks that fed into the water, sat a huge green-brown bullfrog—and it had a pair of smaller frog legs sticking out of its mouth!

"Gross!" I said. "It ate another frog!"

"Or maybe it's having a baby?"

"Babies don't come out of mouths!"

"Why's it eating another frog then?"

"Guess it was hungry."

We crouched to see it better.

"Think we should help it?" Red asked.

"The one in its mouth?" I said. "Nuh-uh. It's probably already dead."

"But shouldn't we *try*?"

Red was a pacifist like me. If we found a spider or cockroach inside the house, we wouldn't smush it with a shoe or flush it down the toilet; we'd catch it and let it go outside.

So seeing the small frog getting cannibalized by the larger bullfrog tugged at our heartstrings. Life was already tough enough without getting eaten alive.

"You do it," I told him.

"How?"

"Just grab it by its feet and start pulling."

Red leaned close and pinched one of the frog's webbed feet between his finger and thumb. I thought the bullfrog might hop away. It simply sat there, its bulging black eyes looking everywhere at once, including up at us.

"Is it slimy?" I asked.

"Not really. But the froggie's really stuck in there."

"Pull harder."

He did because the smaller frog began to emerge from the larger one's mouth—

"The circus called, they want their freaks back!"

We'd been so focused on the frogs we hadn't seen Billy and Ted Myers speeding toward us on their bikes. Now they skidded to a halt on the path and smiled down at us with their superior, smug faces. They both had bright blue eyes and fine blond hair that reached to their shoulders. They weren't twins, but they looked a lot like each other. Billy was a year older than Ted and two years older than Red and me. Their house was two streets over from ours. Last year while trick-or-treating we knocked on their door. While their mom (dressed as a French maid) was giving us candy, Billy and Ted (dressed as Power Rangers) had appeared behind her, about to head out to trick-or-treat themselves. They didn't say anything mean to us in front of their mom, but they caught up with us later on and made us give them all our candy. Luckily it had been near the beginning of the night and not the end, so we didn't lose too much. But giving away your candy, *any* candy, was a hard pill to swallow.

"What're you losers doin to that frog?" Ted demanded.

"We didn't do nothing," I said. "The big one was eating the small one and we're trying to save it."

"The big one was eating the small one," Billy singsonged in a voice that sounded more like a baby's than my own, "and we're trying to save it."

"I know why they're tryin to save it," Ted said. "Cuz that's what happened to them!"

We had no idea what he was talking about. It must have shown on our faces because Billy said, "Our mom told us that's why you freaks are the way you are. Your mom had two em-bros instead of one in her stomach when she was pregnant, and one of 'em started eating the other but stopped halfway."

"Leavin' you two twerps stuck together," Ted finished happily. "Bet you losers don't even know what em-bros are, huh?"

I shook my head.

"Fuckin' losers!" he bugled. "Fuckin' em-bros!"

"And you know what happens to loser em-bros, right?" Billy said threateningly. "They get beat up! So which one of you two loser em-bros wanna get beat up? Or should we beat up both of ya's?"

"Leave us alone," I said. "We didn't do nothing to you."

"Weave us awone," Ted mimicked. "How about you go for a swim in the drink." He hopped off his bike and let it drop to the ground with a loud clatter of shiny new metal.

Frogs forgotten, Red and I stood up.

"If you let us go," Red said, "we won't tell."

"Tell?" Ted said, stepping toward us. "You gonna tell your rumpot dad on us? You gonna *rat* on us?" He kicked the bullfrog, sending it sailing into the river.

We turned our heads to watch it go, and I said, "Hey!"

"Better join your friend, freaks!"

He shoved us in the chest. We fell on the loose stones and somersaulted ass over teakettle into the river.

Cold blackness engulfed us. I swallowed brackish water. Out of instinct, I kicked my leg and clawed at the water with my hand. My eyes were squeezed shut in fear and I couldn't see Red, but I imagined he was flailing like me.

Where's the bottom? Why can't we touch it? How deep's the river—?

My head broke through the surface. I gasped for air and realized Red and I were on our knees. The water only came a little past our belly button. I coughed up the water I had swallowed and rubbed it from my eyes.

Ted and Billy were on their bikes again, speeding away from us.

I grabbed a handful of underwater stones. They shifted beneath my hand, and we slid deeper into the water. We let out a cry. But then we were working in coordination, grabbing and crawling until we'd dragged ourselves out of the river.

We flopped face-first onto the footpath, soaked to our bones and out of breath.

When we got ourselves into a sitting position, I realized my shoe was missing. The muddy bottom of the river must have sucked it off my foot.

"My shoe!" I said, my eyes scanning the water.

"Now you've done it," Red said glumly.

"I didn't mean to! I didn't even know it was gone! We gotta go get it!"

"We can't get it."

"What are we gonna do?" I answered my own question: "We gotta go home and get our other pair."

"No way," he said. "You know how mad Dad will be if he finds out we fell in the river?"

"We'll tell him those bullies pushed us."

"He'll still say it was our fault. And he'll go crazy if you tell him you lost your shoe."

"But we can't go to school with only one shoe and soaking wet."

"We're gonna hafta," he said.

4.

Our school had many different ways into it. There were the main doors obviously. But there were also a number of ancillary doors, one of which opened into the hallway where Mr. Green's office was located. Red and I entered through that door now and hurried to his office. We were still soaking wet but no longer trailing watery footprints behind us like we had on the river footpath. My foot felt uncomfortably exposed in nothing but its sock.

Mr. Green opened the door a moment after he'd called out "Coming!" His long black hair was tied back into a ponytail, and a week's worth of beard growth shadowed his jaw. He wore a white dress shirt, red tie, khaki pants, and brown loafers. He seemed surprised to see us but not disappointed. If there was anyone in the world completely at ease around someone like Red and me, it was the school's counsellor.

"Hiya, boys," he said. "What's on your mind?" He frowned. "Are you *wet*?"

"And I lost my shoe," I told him, sticking my foot forward and then planting it back on the ground quickly before we toppled over.

"Um, why don't you guys step inside?"

His office was a big space, almost half the size of a regular classroom. A large wooden desk was in one corner with three chairs on the other side of it. The blackboard running the length of one wall suggested the office might have been a classroom at one point in its life. The rest of the space was occupied by a few student desks and chairs, as well as an entire play area complete with bins of Lego, kids' books, board games, Play-Doh, toy cars, dolls, and other fun stuff.

Mr. Green closed the door and said, "All right, boys. What's going on?"

"We fell in the river," Red blurted.

"What were you doing by the river?"

"That's how we come to school sometimes," I explained. "Today we saw a bullfrog eating a smaller frog."

"Were you trying to catch it?"

"We tried to save the little one by pulling it out of the bigger one's mouth."

"Jeez, guys." He shook his head. "You should probably just leave Nature to its own devices. Your intentions were in the right place, but you might have hurt the bigger frog doing what you did. Anyway—how did you end up in the river?"

"We slipped," Red said and stared at his feet like he always did when he was lying.

I looked anywhere but at Mr. Green. I didn't want to tell on Billy and Ted either. If they got a detention, they would know we blabbed on them, and they would come for us.

"You slipped, huh?" Mr. Green said.

Red nodded. "On the rocks."

In the silence that followed I could feel Mr. Green studying us. I knew *he* knew Red wasn't telling the truth. "So there wasn't anybody else around . . . who saw you go in?"

"No," Red said.

More silence, and I couldn't stand the guilt any longer. Mr. Green wasn't the bad guy; he was on our side. "Billy and Ted Myers were there . . . " I said quietly.

"And did they have anything to do with you two ending up in the river, Fred?"

"No," Red said.

"Fred?"

"Well . . . " I said.

Red shot me an angry look. I shook my head.

"Guys," Mr. Green said, "it's all right if you tell me they pushed you—"

"You'll get them in trouble," Red said.

"I'll have a word with them, yes—"

"And then they'll know we told! They warned us once. They said if we ever told on them for teasing us, they'd sneak into our house when we're sleeping and tie us up and cut off our parents' heads . . . "

Mr. Green was quiet again. After a long ten seconds or so he sighed. "Let's not worry about them right now then, okay? We need to get you both into something dry—Fred, where's your shoe? Did you lose it in the river?"

I nodded.

"I guess I better call your parents. I can drive you home so you can—"

"No!" Red and I shouted at the same time.

Mr. Green frowned. "No?"

"We don't . . . " Red said, then faltered.

" . . . want our dad to know," I finished.

"To know what? That you fell in the river?"

We nodded.

"But it wasn't . . . " He sighed again. "What are we going to do about clothes? I suppose I could scrounge some up . . . but they wouldn't fit quite right, would they?"

"We're okay," I said. "We're already drying."

"Can't we just stay here?" Red asked. "The other kids will make fun of us if we go to class wet."

"Sure, you can stay here for the time being. I'll let Mr. Lasarow know where you are. But you can't remain in those wet clothes. You'll catch pneumonia again."

"I never had it," I said. "Only Red did."

"Well, you both might get it this time. Hold on a sec."

Mr. Green went to the phone on his desk and dialed a four-digit number. "Hi Ellen, it's Jeff. I have Fred and Red here, and they're a bit . . . wet . . . I'll explain later. Right now I was wondering if I could put their clothes in the dryer over there? Great . . . well, that's the thing. I was hoping you might have something . . . ? Okay, I'll be there in a sec." He hung up and said to us, "Mrs. Webber says she has some blankets in her room that you two can wrap yourselves in while we dry your clothes. I'll go grab them and be back shortly. Okay?"

"Okay," I said.

"Okay," Red said.

Mrs. Webber was the Special Ed teacher for the kids with disabilities inside their heads. We had been in her class for grades one and two, but by grade three it was decided we could learn just as well as any of the normal kids and should be put into mainstream classes. She had a washing machine and dryer combo in her room because some of her students would pee themselves or worse. We didn't see Mrs. Webber much anymore, but she would smile at us when our paths crossed.

When Mr. Green left, Red and I hurried to the back of the room and took the bin with the Play-Doh in it from the shelf. We came to see Mr. Green every Wednesday afternoon to talk about how we were doing and everything. We didn't mind because Wednesday afternoons were when we had religion study in Mr. Lasarow's class, and we hated religion. Besides, Mr. Green would always let us play with all his stuff while we talked. It was probably the best afternoon of the week.

I rolled some pink Play-Doh into a ball and used purple bits for eyes and lips and a nose. Red was using the plastic shape cutters to make different kinds of food.

When Mr. Green returned, he carried two folded blankets in his arms. "You guys are going to have to drape one of these blankets around you until your clothes are dry, if that's all right?"

"Like Batman's cape," Red said in approval.

"Sure," Mr. Green said. "And don't worry about anybody seeing you. I have the first two periods free, so nobody's going to be in here except us. And look." He set aside the blankets on a desk to reveal a pair of shoes that had been hidden beneath. "They look like they should fit, don't they? Mrs. Webber said you boys can have them, if you want."

"All right!" I said, and high-fived Red. "New shoes!"

"Well, they're not new, but they're better than nothing."

Red and I pulled off our sweatshirt over our heads (it was heavy with water and smelled swampy) and set it on the nearest desk. We took off our pants, one leg at a time like everybody else. They went on the desk with our sweatshirt.

We looked at Mr. Green expectantly, waiting for him to pass us one of the blankets. He was frowning, and I realized why. I looked down at our abdomen. Sure enough, the bruises that our dad had given us were still there. Earlier in the week they had been angry twirls of purple and red; now they were splotchy brown but still visible.

The awkward moment passed. Mr. Green handed us one of the blankets, which we wrapped around our shoulders.

"Can we keep playing with the Play-Doh?" Red asked.

He nodded. "I'm going to take your clothes to get dried. I'll be back shortly."

After we received our clothes, still warm from the dryer, we hung around Mr. Green's office until recess, so we could slip back into Mr. Lasarow's classroom when the bell rang without telegraphing that we had been absent. At lunchtime we went outside with all the other kids and climbed inside the orange crawl tunnel in the playground. It always smelled a bit funny in there, but that was where we liked to eat our lunches. Sometimes kids would poke their heads in one end or the other and complain that we were blocking the way, but we ignored them. Today nobody bugged us and we ate in peace. Our mom had made us identical lunches—a ham and cheese sandwich, a juice box, and a small bag of mixed nuts—with the exception that Red got an apple and I got a pear, which I preferred. When we finished eating, we watched everyone running around and playing games through the little round windows in the tube. We talked a bit about how much we hated Billy and Ted as well, and what we'd do to them if we were bigger and stronger. My idea was to bury them in our sandbox to their necks and pee on their heads. Red's was even better: fill their underwear with peanut butter and make them sit atop an ant colony (I didn't know if ants ate peanut butter, but I sure hoped so).

Like usual, the afternoon classes felt about twice as long as the morning ones. Finally the last bell rang and we were on our way home.

We followed the footpath along Black Creek again. Given what had happened to us there this morning, it probably would have been more prudent to take Main Street where we could flee into a store if we were harassed. But nine days out of ten we didn't run into any bullies along the footpath, so we figured it was a safe bet.

We were wrong.

When we were about halfway home, we heard hooting and hollering from behind us. We spun around, and the blood in my veins turned to ice. Riding toward us on their bikes were Billy and Ted Myers. Running beside them were Kelly Needham and Pipi Buchanan—two of the meanest girls in school. They always made disgusted faces when they looked at Red and me, and they would say rude stuff about us to their friends when they knew we were close enough to overhear.

Billy pedaled straight at us, like he was going to run us over. He swerved at the last minute and skidded to a halt behind us. Ted and the girls stopped in front of us. They were all smiling, though none of their smiles reached their eyes.

"I knew they would be dumb enough to come this way again!" Billy crowed. "We shoulda checked here first."

"Who cares?" Ted said. "We found 'em, didn't we?"

"They're so gross," Kelly said, as if we weren't standing right there. She had blonde hair and blue eyes like Billy and Ted, though while their faces were soft and round, hers was sharp and bony. She was so skinny she looked funny when she wore pants, which was likely why she mostly stuck to dresses like the yellow one she had on now beneath a denim jacket. The hem ended above her knees, two knobby, mangled softballs on otherwise twig-like legs. "Like, I can't believe their parents actually let them walk around in public."

"They probably can't stand looking at them all day," Ted said. "That's why they let them out. They need to give their eyes a rest. Can you blame 'em?"

I swallowed with difficulty, wondering what they had planned for us. I had been in this position enough times before to know it wasn't going to turn out well. It was times like these that I wished most that Red and I could run. At least then we'd have a *chance* of getting away. But now, as always, we were sitting ducks.

"We never told on you!" Red blurted, and he sounded as scared as I felt.

"You never told on us, huh?" Ted said. "Then how come Mr. Green called us to his office during lunchtime, huh? How did he know we pushed you in the river, huh?"

"And he called our mom!" Billy said from behind us. "He told her we were picking on the two-headed freaks!"

I gleaned a sliver of hope and said, "If you beat us up, we'll tell Mr. Green. He'll tell your mom again, then you'll *really* get in trouble."

"Then you'll *really* get in trouble," Pipi mimicked in her snobby voice. She was the odd one out of the four savages with her curly black hair and dusty skin. Her eyebrows were thick and fat and angled downward, giving the impression of a permanent frown. The way she always squished her lips together like she could smell something bad that nobody else could didn't help her angry look.

Pain shrieked in our butt. I didn't have to look over my shoulder to know Billy had kicked us there.

"Don't!" Red said, twisting us to look anyway.

"*Don't*," Pipi said, and she and Kelly snickered.

"Just let us go," Red said. "Please?"

"*Pweasssse?*" Ted said. "You guys are so fuckin' pathetic. Who has the bag?"

"I do!" Kelly took a plastic grocery bag from her backpack.

Ted hopped off his mountain bike, took the bag, and came toward us. "We're gonna do an experiment for science," he said, his blue eyes bright with malice. "Gonna see if one of you two freaks can breathe for the both of ya's."

Lunging forward, he tugged the bag down over my head. I tried to yank it off, but Billy grabbed my arm. In the next instant the bag tightened around my neck. I gasped. Plastic vacuumed against my nostrils and mouth, preventing me from drawing oxygen. I thrashed my head back and forth but couldn't free it from the bag, and I knew right then I was going to die.

I kicked my leg and felt my foot strike Ted in the nuts. For a moment the bag loosened around my neck. I sucked back some air . . . even as Red and I lost our balance and fell to the ground. We landed on our tailbone. Pain sliced up through me. I didn't care. My arm was free. I tore the plastic bag from my head and gulped back the brittle October air.

Through watery eyes I saw Ted and the two girls pointing at us and busting their guts laughing.

I hated those kids right then. If I could have killed them, I would have. Red and I didn't do anything to them. They simply hated us because we were different. Didn't they know we didn't *want* to be different? Didn't they know it wasn't our fault? Didn't they know if we could be normal like them, we would do so in a heartbeat?

Ted stepped forward and kicked Red in the stomach. He blurted "Ooof!" and sagged inside our clothes.

Even though I didn't feel anything, I could imagine how much it would have hurt and yelled, "Stop!"

Ignoring me, Ted grabbed our sweatpants and yanked them down to our ankles. His fingers curled around the elastic band of our underwear and tugged them down as well.

"Oh, lookit that!" he said, glancing back at the girls. "They only got one dick! I thought they would have two!"

"I thought they would have three!" Billy said.

"I'm gonna barf!" Kelly chimed.

Embarrassment burned inside me like a hot fire, but I didn't kick or struggle. The fight had left me. Tears washed down my cheeks.

"What are you waiting for?" Ted said. "Hurry up and take it!"

"Ready," Pipi said, and I realized she had her phone out. She aimed the camera lens at Red and me laying crumpled and exposed on the footpath. She snapped a picture. "Yuck! I feel gross for even having this on my phone!"

"That's insurance you don't go crying to Mr. Green again," Ted told us. "If you freaks do, that picture is going up all over Instagram for everybody to see. Understand?"

"Yes," Red mumbled.

I didn't trust my voice and simply nodded.

Ted slapped me across the cheek. "I said, *understand*?"

"Yes!" I cried.

"You pathetic pieces of shit," he said, standing. He picked up his bike and mounted it. "Come on, guys, let's split."

Red was trying to pull up our clothes, and I helped him.

Ted zipped past us. Kelly and Pipi paused next to us before following, their arms locked together like sisters, and Pipi said, "Why don't you two do the world a favor and just kill yourselves already?" She hawked a loogie that missed me but got Red right on the chin.

Giggling in fainting, witchy bursts, they ran away.

5.

We didn't speak to each other for the rest of the walk home. We were too depressed, I think. I know I was. Getting the plastic bag pulled down over my head was bad enough, but the photograph that Pipi had taken of us with our pants down was much worse. It was *personal.* And what if they decided they didn't care if we told Mr. Green on them? What if they decided the picture was too delicious to keep to themselves and posted it on Instagram anyway? Everybody at school would get an unforgettable eyeball of Red and me naked. They would laugh at us and call us more names than they already did. I didn't know if I could live with that. Maybe Pipi's suggestion we kill ourselves might prove true, after all. Maybe if Red felt as bad as I did about the humiliating photo going public, he would agree to kill himself with me.

Something changed in Red's gait. He'd slowed, and I instinctively slowed too.

"Uh oh," he said.

In the next instant I noticed what he meant. Our dad was sitting in a chair on the front porch of our house, next to our mom. He never sat out there with her. The fact he was doing so now didn't bode well for anything. I had the feeling he was waiting for us.

"What does he want?" I asked quietly out of the side of my mouth.

"Maybe he knows about us falling in the river? Maybe Mr. Green told him?"

"Uh oh," I said, repeating his sentiment. "What should we do?"

"We gotta go home. He's already seen us."

Indeed he had. He was staring in our direction.

Red and I continued walking at the same slow pace. We were in no rush to get whatever was coming to us. As we turned up the walk to the porch, my heart was hammering inside my chest, and my palm had gone sweaty. Was he going to notice our new shoes? Was he going to know I lost my old one?

My mom set down the book she was reading and smiled tightly at us. Our dad's stony expression didn't change. The bill of the trucker's cap that sat atop his nest of greasy black hair pooled his eyes in shadows. The baleful shine of his pupils reminded me of the eyes of a wild animal peering out from the depths of its cave. Stubble covered his gaunt cheeks and dimpled chin. His overgrown mustache masked his upper lip and most of the thin bottom one.

We stopped at the top of the porch steps. I looked from our dad to our mom and back to our dad.

"Hi, Dad," Red said meekly. "You're home . . . ?"

"Can we go inside?" I asked, and the question had a begging quality to it.

"Can you go inside?" our dad said, drawing each word out lazily, mockingly. "You hear that, sweetheart? This one wants t'go inside. All right, boy, go on ahead inside."

We took a step.

"Whoa, there!" he snarled, sticking out his hand to stop us. "What the fuck you doing?"

"Going inside?" I said quietly, knowing it was the wrong thing to say.

"I said *you* can go inside, boy. I didn't say nothing about *that* one going inside." He fingered Red.

Red and I exchanged uneasy glances. It was hard to tell whether our dad was drunk or not if he didn't have a bottle in his hand. By the way he was talking now—slowly and sludgy—I guessed he was.

"Well, go on, Fred!" he told me. "Go on inside!"

We just stood there.

"*Go on!*"

"James . . . " our mom said softly.

"Quiet," he said just as softly, though there was a whole lot of menace in that single word.

Without taking his shadowed, feral eyes off us, he slid a hand into the front pocket of his dirty blue jeans. When I saw what he produced in his hand, my leg almost buckled beneath me.

It was the Crunchie we had thrown into the corner of our room the night before. We'd forgotten to collect it this morning, and our dad must have found it—though why he'd been in our room, I had no idea. He never went in there unless he was looking for something to get mad at us about.

"I see this rings a bell," he said, scowling at us. "Or maybe *two* bells? *Well?* Does it?"

Red and I nodded at the same time.

"I wonder where you might've gotten it from? Cause I know you don't get no allowance from me. So you must have a part-time job then? Is that it? Cause it's either that, you have money I don't know about, or you stole it from somewhere. You tell me, boys. You tell me."

"We stole it," Red mumbled.

"Speak up, boy! I can't hear you when you whimper like a wet cur."

"We stole it," he said louder.

"And who'd you steal it from?"

"We took it from—"

"Quiet, Fred!" he snapped at me. "I'm talkin' to the other one! One at a goddamn time, for fuck's sake."

"We took it from the bowl in the counter under the sink," Red told him.

"Is that right?" our dad said, leaning back in his chair, a satisfied, relaxed air about him that was all show. "Is that fuckin' right? I s'pose you never stopped to wonder who put that candy in that bowl in the first place? So lemme tell you. *I* did. And that makes the candy mine, don't it? And you know what else that makes? That makes you two a couple of ratbag thieves. *Fuckin' thieves.*" He appeared so disgusted I thought he was going to spit on us like Pipi did. But he only shook his head. "Is that the kind of boys I raised? Fuckin' ratbag thieves?"

We didn't say anything. My chin was trembling, and any second I was going to burst into tears. The only bulwark preventing me from doing so was our dad's wrath. One thing he loathed more than anything was weakness, and to him, tears were weakness.

"Answer me!" he said. 'Is that what I raised? A pair of ratbag thieves?"

"No, sir," Red said, and I could tell by the sound of his voice he was already crying.

"No, sir," I said, biting my lower lip, which had begun to tremble along with my chin.

"And you know what's worse than having a pair of thieving ratbags for sons? Thieving ratbags that steal from their own daddy."

The tears came, hot and shameful, silently streaming down my cheeks.

"Lookit you two pissing wussies. Two. Pissing. Wussies." He

sighed, shaking his head again in disdain for us. "You know what this means, don't you? It means I'm gonna hafta teach you another one of life's little lessons."

Red moaned, and I felt a wave of heat rush through me that was pure, high-wire terror.

"Inside, now," our dad told us, reaching down beside his chair for a brown beer bottle I hadn't seen. "Don't make me tell you twice."

6.

We waited in dread in our room for the door to bust open and for our dad to appear. We didn't have to wait long. He arrived less than a minute later, a fresh beer bottle in one hand, a metal spatula in the other. He slammed the door shut behind him.

"Take off your shirt, you thieving little pricks," he said, tilting the bottle to his lips.

We both shook our heads, blubbering nonsense.

"Take it off!" he shouted, raising the spatula like a sword. It would have been an almost comical scenario—a drunk, out-of-work middle-aged man threatening a two-headed kid with a spatula—had the pain and suffering about to be delivered not been so real.

With great reluctance, Red and I began tugging our sweatshirt up our torso.

A knock sounded at the door, followed by our mom's cowed voice. "James . . . ?"

"Not now, Donna!" he barked. "Jesus Christ, I'm busy in here!"

"There are some men here to see you."

Our dad's entire demeanor changed in a heartbeat. His smug vitriol dropped from him like a discarded stage costume, revealing a man more pauper than king. He opened the door a crack and said in a hushed tone, "Some men?"

"The counsellor from school," our mom told him, "and a caseworker who says he's with social services."

Our dad didn't say anything for several long moments, then, "I'll be right there." He eased the door closed, turned around, and glared at us. "What the hell have you boys gone and done?"

"Nothing," I said, not understanding what was going on.

"We fell in Black Creek on the way to school this morning," Red said. "We had to take off our wet clothes so Mr. Green could dry them. I think . . . he saw our bruises."

Our dad cursed. "Did you tell him how you got those bruises? Hurry now! Did you?"

"No, sir," Red said.

"No, sir," I said.

"You better not have. And you better not tell 'em the truth now. When they ask—and they're gonna ask—you're gonna tell them you got them playing around and falling over, like you always do. You hear me?"

"Yes, sir."

"Yes, sir."

"I hope to God you do. Cause if you don't, if you tell 'em I laid one finger on you . . . well, they're gonna be gone later, and I'm still gonna be here, and I'll put you in so much pain you'll wish you were dead. You'll wish you were never born. You boys understand what I'm saying?"

We told him we did.

He stuffed the spatula down the back of his pants and left the bedroom.

Maybe five minutes later there was a light knock at the door, and then it pushed open.

"Hi, boys," Mr. Green said. "It's just me and a friend of mine. Can we have a word with you?"

We nodded.

Mr. Green's friend was short and stocky with curly brown hair and a broad, deeply tanned face that looked as though it might have belonged to a wrestler or mafia boss. But the eyes beneath his bony and bushy brow were friendly and almost made you want to smile. He wore a brown suit with elbow patches and a red tie. In his left hand he carried a manila file.

Mr. Green closed the door behind them, and the man said, "Hi, I'm George—you know, like George of the Jungle. Only I don't like bananas so much."

We looked at him cautiously.

"It's all right, boys," Mr. Green said. "Like I said, George is a friend. We just have a few questions for you, and we'll be on our way. Is it okay if we ask you a few questions?"

I looked at Red, who shook his head. I said, "I don't know . . . "

"They're not hard questions or anything like that. They're just . . . they're about the marks on your body. I saw them today when you gave me your clothes to get dried. Do you remember how you got them?"

"No," I said, hating lying to Mr. Green.

"We fall a lot," Red said, focusing on his hand that was tugging at the bottom of our shirt nervously.

"So does my son," the man named George said. "He's seven, so a bit younger than you guys. But it seems he can't get anywhere without falling over in the process. I have to put Band-Aids on his nicks. Those are usually on his knees and elbows. Sometimes he might scrape his hands or his chin. A real crazy kid, right? But I don't seem to recall him getting any bumps or bruises in the places Mr. Green told me you had your bumps and bruises."

A silence followed this remark. I think he wanted us to say something, but I didn't know what.

"Would it be okay," Mr. Green said, "if you showed George the marks I saw earlier? You don't have to take off your shirt. You can just lift it up a little."

"I guess," I said. Our dad had never told us we couldn't show them anything. I looked at Red. He shrugged.

We lifted up our shirt to about our nipples.

George knelt close and asked us to turn in a circle. When we finished, he said, "Would you boys mind if I took a couple of pictures of those marks?"

Red immediately began crying, and I think he was having a flashback to the picture that Pipi took of us.

"Hey, hey, hey," George said quickly. "Look, I'm sorry. I won't take any pictures, if you don't want me to." He stood back up.

"Red, you okay there, buddy?" Mr. Green said, cupping him on the shoulder with his hand.

I said, "He's just sad because some kids we're teasing us today . . . "

"Do you want to tell me who was teasing you?"

I shook my head.

"No, I didn't think so." Mr. Green smiled and cupped me on my shoulder too. "I want you two to know I think you're very brave.

You put up with a lot, more than most kids have to. And you know what? You're better than them. You really are. And you're better than anyone who may hurt you. I want you to remember that."

Red sniffled, getting his crying under control, and I nodded. Mr. Green always had a way of making us feel better about ourselves.

"That's about all the questions for now. You guys did great."

"It was really nice meeting you both," George said. "And, um . . . I want you to know. I'm going to be coming by once a week from now on to pop in and say hi. Is it okay if I do that? Pop in to say hi every now and then?"

"I think so," I said, not sure how happy our dad would be with this arrangement.

As if reading my mind, George said, "Don't worry about telling your dad that. I'll do it on our way out. I'll let him know I'll be coming by to say hi . . . and maybe have a quick look to make sure you're not getting any new bruises from falling over. If you are, we might have to do something about that. Okay?"

Red and I nodded.

"Okay, then," George said, smiling at us.

"Have a great Halloween tomorrow, boys," Mr. Green said. "I'll be taking my daughters out trick-or-treating. Maybe we'll see you out there?"

I woke in the middle of the night in a cold, sweaty panic. When my mind shook off the sleep, I found myself lying on my back as usual, staring up at the black ceiling. I remembered the nightmare perfectly. It had been one of the worst ones in a while. Red and I had been covered head to toe in virulent purple and red welts. We felt fine but looked as though every inch of our body had been pounded on with a rubber mallet. George had come by to check on us, but we weren't letting him into our room because we didn't want him to see the bruises. Somehow, though, he ended up next to us, as such things tend to happen in dreams. He didn't seem to notice the bruises and went about asking us ordinary questions about our day.

Before he left he said, "Who did that to you?"

"Did what?" I said, playing dumb.

"Did you think I didn't see those bruises? You boys look like a sunburned grape."

"We fell down," Red told him.

"No, you didn't," he said. "I know how you got them. Everybody knows. And we're going to do something about it. We're going to arrest your father."

"I heard you!" our dad shouted. He stood outside the house at our bedroom window, glaring in at us. "I told you not to say anything, you thieving ratbags! *I told you!*"

"We didn't say anything!" I shouted back.

"The hell you didn't!" He smashed the windowpane with a large wooden club and climbed into the bedroom. His greasy black hair was longer than normal and tangled in knots, and he was covered in mud. He wore animal skins like a caveman. "You're going to arrest me, huh?" he said to George. "That's your plan, huh?"

George took out his phone. "I'm going to call the police right now."

Our dad leapt at him, swinging his club. The fat end smashed George's face, caving half of it in like a broken egg. Blood and gray brains flowed out from between the shattered bone.

"Boys!" It was Mr. Green. He was pounding on the bedroom door. "What's going on in there? Let me in!"

Our dad yanked open the door with one hand and swung his club with the other. It struck Mr. Green in the face and knocked his head right off his neck. He turned his attention to Red and me, whooping and screeching like a monkey.

That was when I remembered my sleep-magic.

I instantly turned Red and me into a large rock . . . only the magic trick didn't work out as well as it usually did because the rock had a pair of eyeballs. Our dad's club was suddenly a spear, and he jabbed the pointed end into one of our eyes.

And that's when I woke up.

Talk about a strange nightmare. It seemed silly when I replayed it all in my head, almost like something you might see on the Saturday morning cartoons.

Closing my eyes, I fell back to sleep rather quickly, but it wasn't real sleep. It was surface sleep, from which I kept waking to make sure our dad wasn't sneaking into our bedroom with a bloody club.

7.

At lunchtime the next day, Red and I were once again hunkered down inside the orange crawl tube, eating our sandwiches.

After chewing thoughtfully on the rubbery meat and plasticky cheese, I mentioned what had been on my mind all morning. "Do you wanna help me kill Dad?"

Red stopped chewing and angled his head to look at me. "Kill Dad?" A bit of bread crust fell from his lips to our chest. "Are you kidding?"

I shook my head and flicked the crust away with my finger.

Red swallowed what was in his mouth. "We can't kill him."

"Why not?"

"Because he's our *dad*."

"He would kill *us* if he could get away with it," I pointed out. "And I think we have to do it first. Because he's not going to stop hitting us. I don't think he *can* stop doing that. And George is going to be coming by every week to check on us. When he finds new marks on us . . . I think Dad might try killing us and George to keep things secret. Maybe Mr. Green too."

"Or maybe he'll just stop hitting us?"

I shook my head again. "I had a dream about it last night. He killed all of us."

Red was silent for a long time. I thought he might've started thinking about something else when he said, "If we kill him, we'll go to jail."

"Not if nobody knows it was us."

"How are we going to kill him without anybody knowing?"

"With Mom's sleeping pills. People can die when they take too many of them. It puts them to sleep forever."

"How do we make Dad take too many?"

"We'll mush them up and put them in his whiskey bottle. He'll never know he's taking them."

Red frowned. "I don't know, Fred. What if he finds out? Then he'll definitely kill us."

"He won't find out," I said confidently.

"You don't know that."

"Don't you want to go home and not be afraid every day, Red?

Imagine we could just go home and eat dinner and play with our stuff and not worry about Dad coming back drunk and beating us up."

"I guess that would be pretty good . . . "

"You *know* that would be pretty good."

"So how do we get Mom's sleeping pills?"

"She'll be reading on the porch when we get home. We just go inside like usual, but instead of going to our room, we go to her bathroom and get them."

"Is that where she keeps them?"

"Behind the mirror over the sink. Don't you remember? Sometimes she would give me one when I was having nightmares about falling off the building?"

"I guess. I wasn't paying attention. I wasn't the one having the nightmares."

"They're in an orange bottle with a white top." Seeing his reluctance faltering, I added, "Dad deserves it, Red. You know he does. And once he's dead, he can't hurt anybody ever again."

8.

When we arrived home, we said hi to our mom, who was planted in her chair on the porch with a book, just as we'd known she would be. She told us she'd finished our Halloween costume. It was laid out on our bed in case we wanted to try it on before tomorrow. We told her we did and went inside.

We stopped before the open door to our parents' bedroom. We glanced at each other—it was a perfunctory, instinctive reaction; the choice had already been made—and crossed the threshold. Our dad might be a slob, leaving his dishes and beer bottles and clothes wherever he wanted, but our mom liked things to be clean and tidy. Not surprisingly their bedroom was spotless, the bed perfectly made, the cushions on the rocking chair in the corner neatly arranged, all the paperback novels on the bookshelf sorted according to size and color.

Red and I hurried to the bathroom. I opened the mirrored front of the medicine cabinet above the sink and snagged the orange bottle of sleeping pills from the middle shelf. I held it in front of us. Red twisted the cap.

"It's stuck," he said.

"It's kid proof. You have to squeeze the sides before turning it."

He still couldn't open it and moaned in frustration. I gave him the bottle to hold and tried removing the cap myself. It took a few tries, but I got it off in the end.

"Okay!" I said excitedly. "Pour some into my hand."

"How many?"

I hadn't contemplated this. How many would it take to kill someone? Our mom had only ever given me one when I couldn't sleep, so that was probably the regular dosage. Then again, I was just a kid. Maybe two was the regular dose for adults. So should we double that? Triple it?

"How *many*?" Red pressed, glancing back into the bedroom.

"I don't know! Five?"

He dumped six into my palm.

"Shoot, that's too many!"

"No, that's okay," I told him. "We want to make sure Dad doesn't wake up."

I screwed the cap back on the bottle. Red returned it to the medicine cabinet and closed the door. We exited the bathroom just as our mom entered the bedroom.

She jumped, pressing a hand to her bird-like chest. "Oh my! You boys nearly gave me a heart attack! What are you doing in here?"

"Getting toilet paper," I said, blurting the only excuse that came to mind. I squeezed my fist tightly around the pills.

"Toilet paper?" she said. "I thought I put a new roll in your bathroom yesterday?"

"But we're all out."

Our mom studied us silently. I think her eyes even went to my fisted hand for a moment.

"If you're finished in here then," she said, "I would like to use the toilet myself."

Relieved, we hurried past her into the living room. When it was clear she wasn't going to follow us, we went into our bedroom, where I hid the six sleeping pills under my pillow.

"I think Mom's a bit suspicious," I said. "So we better wait before putting the pills in Dad's whiskey."

Red nodded. "Wanna try on our costume?"

We took off our clothes and the shoes Mr. Green had given us.

The costume was folded on the bed. We pulled on the pair of gray tights (we would never wear something so girlish normally), then the shorts. Our mom had sewn two different pairs together. Red's half was blue because he was Batman; my half was red because I was Robin. The shirt was equally divided color-wise down the center, Red's sporting the Batman logo, mine a big yellow R. Topping everything off was a blue/yellow cape, as well as black velvet masks with eyeholes cut out in them.

When we finished dressing, we admired ourselves in our grandma's gilded mirror. I thought we looked pretty good. Boots and gloves might have been a nice touch, but people couldn't mistake us for anybody other than the dynamic duo.

We were turning around to see what we looked like from behind when our mom entered the bedroom.

"How does it fit?" she asked us.

"Great!" I said.

"You're the best, Mom!" Red said.

She held up a roll of toilet paper in her hand. "You boys forgot this earlier." She went to the bathroom. When she emerged a few moments later, she looked at us quizzically. "Seems you boys still have half a roll in there, after all . . . "

We managed to shrug in unison.

She went to the door—and paused there, like she'd forgotten something. She faced us. "By the way, I seem to be missing some of my sleeping pills. Would either of you know where they went . . . ?"

I think I might have fallen over had I not been attached to Red. I couldn't find my voice, and neither could Red. We both stared at her, looking about as guilty as anybody could.

"That's what I thought," she said, and held out her hand.

Our eyes downcast, we went to the bed. Red lifted the pillow, and I retrieved the forbidden pills. I placed them in our mom's hand without looking up at her.

"I hope you boys weren't thinking about taking these yourselves?" she said sternly.

"No," Red said.

"No," I repeated.

"So why did you take them?"

We shrugged in unison again.

"Perhaps you were thinking about making your father go to sleep?"

My mind tripped up at those words, while my heart clenched into a tiny, cowering ball. *Nice plan, Fred! Now you're dead meat! Mom's gonna tell Dad when he gets home, and he's gonna beat you and Red into a sunburned grape for real—*

"And if that's what you *were* thinking," our mom went on, "you're going to need more than six pills. Come with me to the kitchen."

9.

Dumbfounded, we followed closely behind her, stopping on the opposite side of the counter. She set the six sleeping pills on the wooden cutting board next to the sink. She took the orange bottle from her pocket and dumped another eight pills next to them. She withdrew a spoon from the drawer and used the round side to mill the white tablets into a fine powder.

She didn't say anything while she prepared the poison, nor did Red or I. We simply watched in a kind of religious, out-of-body trance.

Our mom was helping us kill our dad!

"That should probably do it," she said when all fourteen pills had been pulverized.

She glanced at us, and I couldn't read a thing in her expression. She may as well have been preparing scrambled eggs.

She opened one of the upper cupboards and produced a bottle of Wild Turkey. It was half full with amber liquid. She rummaged through a drawer for a plastic funnel. She upended the cutting board so the white powder slid through the funnel and down the neck of the bottle. She replaced the cap and shook the concoction like she was mixing a milkshake.

Finally she replaced the Wild Turkey in the cupboard and dumped everything else in the sink to be washed up later.

Her hazel eyes met Red's, then mine. She appeared older and more tired than ever.

"Your father has chosen to live in a way contrary to the will of God," she told us slowly and steadily, to emphasize the weight of her words, "and in doing so he has chosen death over life. I shouldn't have waited so long to do this. I'm sorry, my babies. You've deserved much better . . . so, so much better. I pray your torment ends tonight."

Red and I had been tucked into bed for several hours before our dad came home. Neither of us had slept a wink. I wouldn't say we were too excited; I'd say we were too alert. We talked quietly to each other for much of this time, mostly about Halloween tomorrow, and how much candy we were going to have now that we didn't have to give the lion's share of it to our dad. Well—that was what we hoped. We weren't positive the pills would work and our dad would die tonight. The best-case scenario was that he would come home and drink all the poisoned whiskey and die on the sofa. The worst-case one was that he would realize the whiskey tasted funny and come after us for trying to kill him. There were plenty of mid-case scenarios too, such as him not drinking anything and going straight to bed, or him only drinking a little bit so he still woke up in the morning.

I was in the middle of brokering a deal to swap all the boxes of raisins I got tomorrow evening for all of Red's Tootsie Rolls (he didn't necessarily like raisins, but for some reason he couldn't stand Tootsie Rolls) when the front door banged open. I went immediately silent. My hyper-vigilant ears heard everything. The clomp of his booted feet on the hardwood floors. The gasket popping as the fridge door opened. A glass jar clanking on the countertop, what might have been the sweet and spicy pickles he liked, or maybe the Great Value mayonnaise which he would eat straight from the jar with a spoon or his finger.

Then what I was waiting for: the bang of a cupboard door.

Our dad could have been retrieving a plate or a glass, but I heard nothing more until the groan of the springs in the sofa and voices on the TV. The image I conjured in my mind was crystal clear: our dad slumped on the sofa in the glow of the TV, his feet propped up on the ratty ottoman, the jar of pickles (or maybe the mayonnaise) in his left hand, the bottle of Wild Turkey in his right.

The voices on the TV changed as he surfed the channels. He stuck with a sports program for a long time, the commentators discussing the recent baseball World Series. I was wondering if our dad had fallen asleep when the channels began switching again. The show he settled on sounded like some kind of boring drama movie until a woman started making sex noises. This went on for even longer than the baseball talk. Red and I had heard our dad watch this type of stuff before, and we could imagine what was going on because we had seen pictures and videos of sex on the internet. And although seeing a pretty girl naked was a little exciting, I didn't know why anybody would want to keep watching her for a long period of time. It wasn't like she was doing anything special except having sex.

Nevertheless, I hoped the porno held our dad's interest now.

The longer he remained awake, the more poisoned whiskey he would consume.

The TV was still playing an hour later. There were no longer any sex sounds, just an enthusiastic man and woman selling kitchen knives. I turned my face toward Red's and said as quietly as I could, "I think Dad's fallen asleep."

"I think so too," he whispered, his breath warm and smelling faintly of toothpaste. "Is he going to wake up again?"

"I hope not."

"We better go to sleep now."

"Okay."

I closed my eyes and stretched my leg as I tried to get comfortable.

I was fast asleep in seconds.

10.

The next morning I woke to the wonderful smell of cooking bacon. This was so unusual—our mom only made us bacon and eggs on special occasions like Christmas morning—that I almost forgot everything that had happened the night before.

Was our dad dead?

I tapped Red on the head.

"Huh?" he said, waking up. His eyes sprang open. "Bacon!"

"Mom might be celebrating because Dad's dead," I told him.

We lumbered out of bed and went to the living room, still in our pajamas. Our dad was sitting on the sofa exactly how I'd imagined him the night before: slumped back in the cushions, his feet up on the ottoman, his eyes closed. Whether he was asleep or dead, I couldn't tell. I'd been right about the jar of sweet and spicy pickles. It was tipped on its side on the cushion next to him. The bottle of Wild Turkey lay on the floor, empty.

A cartoon was playing on the TV, the happy voices and music contradicting the grim scene.

"Uh . . . Mom?" I said.

"Yes, Fred?"

She stood in the kitchen wearing her pink bathrobe, her long brown/gray hair bound in a ponytail. Her back was to us as she cracked an egg open and dumped its gooey innards into a plastic bowl.

"Is Dad . . . okay?"

"Looks like he had another one of his big drinking nights, doesn't it? Why don't you go and wake him up? Ask him how he wants his eggs cooked."

I blinked in confusion, and for a moment I wondered whether I had dreamed everything that had happened yesterday. I didn't think I did. It had felt too real. It had felt just like *now* felt, and I was definitely not dreaming at the moment.

Red raised his eyebrows questioningly at me, and I shrugged. We went over to our dad. His mouth was slightly parted, though I couldn't tell whether he was breathing through it or not.

"Dad?" Red said quietly.

He didn't reply.

I noticed he hadn't drunk all the whiskey, after all. A fair bit of liquid pooled around the bottle on the hardwood floor.

"We're having bacon and eggs, Dad," I told him. "Mom wants to know how you want your eggs?"

He didn't reply.

Red and I shuffled closer.

His chest didn't appear to be moving up and down, and his skin looked paler than usual . . . or was I imagining that?

We were going to have to get close enough to shake him before we knew whether he was really dead or not. This terrified me because I was pretty sure he was faking everything. When Red and I were in range, his hate-filled eyes would snap open. His hand would seize my arm. He would drag me close to him, telling me it was time for another one of life's little lessons—

"Dad?" Red tapped him on the shoulder.

His eyes didn't open. He remained perfectly still.

Growing more confident, I waved my hand in front of his face. He didn't flinch.

"Check if he's alive," Red told me quietly.

"How?"

"Put your ear to his heart."

"No way! You!"

"You!"

I placed my hand over his mouth. "I don't feel his breath . . . "

"I think he might be dead."

I looked back at our mom. She was watching us while holding the plastic bowl against her chest, absent-mindedly beating the eggs with a whisk.

"Is everything all right, Fred?" she asked.

"I, um, don't think Dad is breathing . . . "

"Whatever do you mean?" She set aside the bowl and came over. "Oh my," she said quietly, stopping next to us. She crouched before our dad and felt the side of his neck for a pulse. "Oh my," she said again.

"Is he dead?" Red asked keenly.

"We need to call an ambulance."

Our mom dialed 9-1-1 on the rotary phone attached to the wall (our dad was the only one in the house who had been allowed to have a mobile phone) and when she'd hung up the receiver, she said to us, "An ambulance is coming right now, but there isn't anything the paramedics can do for your father, boys. He's dead."

The heavy steel ball in my gut suddenly vanished. I might have smiled weakly in relief, though I still didn't know why our mom was acting so strange. It was as though she didn't remember what we'd all done yesterday afternoon.

"The sheriff will want to speak to me," she went on. "He might also want to talk to the both of you. If he does, he might ask if anything unusual happened yesterday . . . "

"You mean the pills?" Red said.

"What pills?"

I think she was giving us permission to lie, so I said, "We came home from school and went to our room and tried on our Halloween costume. That's all that happened."

"And then . . . ?"

"And then you made us dinner," Red said, "and we watched TV for a little, and we went to bed."

"And this morning?"

"We came out here and you were making bacon and eggs," I said quickly, liking the lying game, "and you told us to wake up Dad."

"And?"

"We tried. But he wouldn't wake up. Then you came over and checked his pulse and called the ambulance."

"That's exactly right, boys," she said, nodding in approval. "That's exactly how everything happened."

11.

The paramedics attempted CPR on our dad, but not for long. They brought in a metal stretcher, loaded him onto it, covered him up with a sheet, and wheeled him away. Our mom followed the ambulance to the hospital in Dad's pickup truck, leaving Red and me home alone. We toasted some bread, slathered the slices with butter, and had a bacon and egg feast in front of the TV. Afterward we went up to the second floor to explore, just because we could. It felt strange to have free rein around the house, but great too. If this was what living without fear felt like, then we had been missing out big time.

When our mom returned around noon, we were back in front of the TV, watching a *Star Wars* cartoon.

"Is Dad still dead?" I asked her immediately.

"I'm afraid so," she said. "We won't know anything for certain until the town's coroner examines his body, but it seems he wanted to kill himself. A lot of my sleeping pills are missing, and when you mix too many of those with whiskey . . ."

"Why would he want to kill himself?" I asked, slipping back easily into the lying game.

"As you boys know, he was having a very difficult time finding work these last few months. He wasn't very happy. And he became even more unhappy when the school counsellor and the man from social services came by the other day. Sometimes these types of things can lead to depression. They can make a person not want to live anymore." She smiled sadly at us. "Now, I've spoken to the sheriff already. I've told him all this, and he seems to believe it, so I don't think he's going to want to speak to either of you, after all."

Red and I high-fived each other. I'd really been dreading lying to the sheriff.

"So what do we do now?" Red asked.

"It's Halloween tonight, darling. The best thing you boys can do to forget about this horrible tragedy is to go out and try to have some fun."

Even though it was hours before we would head out trick-or-treating, which was usually just before dusk, Red and I put on our Batman and Robin costume and went to the backyard to play. The sky was gray and gloomy. A light wind blew, shivering the skeletal branches of the giant oak that towered above our garage. The grass was patchy with mud and dead in places. My mom's rose garden along one wooden fence was dead too, the colorful blooms hiding away until the return of better weather in the spring.

For a while we ran around with invisible guns and handcuffs and arrested all the bad guys of Gotham City, including the Joker, Penguin, and Poison Ivy, whom we decided to let go because she was pretty. When we grew bored of this, we went to the swing that hung from one of the oak's lower branches. The yellow rope was frayed in places, and the wooden plank that constituted the seat was old and rotting . . . which was why we only ever sat on the swing and didn't actually *swing*.

"Do you feel bad about killing Dad?" I asked, toeing the ground to rock us gently.

"Not really," Red said. "It's a lot more fun without him around."

"Do you think he's in Heaven?"

"I hope not. That's where we're going to go, and I wouldn't want to run into him up there. He probably knows we're the ones who killed him."

"So he's in Hell?"

Red nodded. "I guess so. What do you do in Hell?"

"You just stand there and get burned in fire."

"And scream."

"Yeah."

"For eternity."

"Yeah."

"I guess he deserves that," Red said. "He shouldn't have hit us all the time."

"It was pretty easy killing him," I said.

"It was scary. Like, the scariest thing we've ever done."

"But it was easy too. And nobody even suspected us."

"Because Mom helped us."

"But we could have done it on our own, don't you think?"

Red hesitated. "I guess."

We sat on the swing in silence for nearly a minute. I continued rocking us with my foot. The rope squeaked occasionally. The wind messed my hair and chilled me through the thin material of our top.

"What are you thinking about?" Red asked me eventually.

"Nothing," I said.

"You are. I can tell."

I shoved my foot harder against the ground and kind of diagonally. The swing spun in a circle, the two lines of rope snaking around each other above us. When they disentangled, we twirled like a helicopter rotor. Holding tightly to the ropes, we yelled and giggled until we had slowed and faced forward again.

"Maybe we should kill Billy and Ted too?" I said.

Red's smile faded. "We can't kill them!" he said.

"Why not? Then they can't ever bully us again."

"I don't think Mom will give us any more of her sleeping pills—"

I shook my head. "Not sleeping pills. Real poison."

Red frowned. "What's real poison?"

"The stuff Dad keeps in the cellar to kill all the rats."

"Rat poison?"

I nodded.

"How are we going to make them drink *rat poison*?"

"Not drink it," I told him "Eat it. We can put it in their Halloween candy with the plastic needle Dad used to put it in the peanut butter."

Red considered this and said, "How are we going to get their Halloween candy?"

I explained my plan.

"What do you think?" I asked him when I'd finished. "Should we kill them?"

"You really want to?"

I nodded. "They made Pipi take that picture of us with our pants pulled down. They'll probably tell her to post it online whether or not we tell Mr. Green on them, just so everybody will laugh at us. And even if they don't, they're going to keep bullying us. Do you want them to keep bullying us for the rest of school?"

"No . . ."

"Remember what Mom told us. If you make God angry, you deserve to die. Dad deserved to die, and Billy and Ted do too. It's what God wants."

12.

After making sure our mom was on the porch reading her latest book, we filled our pockets with fourteen pieces of candy from the bowl under the kitchen sink (because that was the magic number of sleeping pills that our mom had put in our dad's whiskey). The bowl didn't look quite as full as it had before, but there must have been over a hundred candy bars in it to begin with, so the difference wasn't really noticeable.

We made our way down to the cellar carefully, as the unfinished steps were steep and narrow. On the shelf against one cinderblock wall stood our dad's plastic containers of rat poison. I counted seven in total, all different sizes and brand names. We had so many rats living in our house that killing them had become an obsession of his. For a long time he used traps. When the rats learned to avoid them, he switched to poisoned bait pellets. Yet the same thing happened: the rats stopped eating them when they realized their friends were dying, or at least getting sick. Eventually he settled on liquid bait, which he injected directly into gobs of peanut butter or slices of cheese, food the rats couldn't resist.

We emptied the candy bars from our pockets, dumping them on the ground next to the container of Tomcat Liquid Concentrate that I had selected.

"Get the needle," I told Red as I unscrewed the container's lid, "and fill it up like Dad used to do."

Red took a plastic syringe from the shelf and depressed the plunger so it cleared the tube of air. He stuck the needle down the neck of the container of poison and pulled back the plunger, sucking up liquid.

"Do you want to do it, or do you want me to do it?" I asked him, sensing his reluctance.

"You can do it," he said, handing me the syringe.

"Then you have to hold the candy bar."

Red selected a Crispy Crunch and held it toward me in the palm of his hand.

I poked the needle through the package and depressed the plunger, emptying a third of the tube.

"Is that enough?" Red asked skeptically.

"I guess so. We're going to fill all fourteen, remember. And we don't want Billy and Ted to taste the poison."

"What if they *do* taste it?"

"The rats never did. That's why Dad liked this stuff so much."

"But those were *rats*."

I shrugged, getting annoyed by all his questions. "Dad's whiskey covered the taste of the sleeping pills. The chocolate will cover the taste of the poison. Now hurry up and pick another candy bar."

13.

Mom made spaghetti Bolognese for dinner. After we finished eating, she gave us each a white pillowcase (embroidered with our names in orange thread) to collect our candy in because plastic grocery bags could rip open if they got too full.

I told her I needed to go to the bathroom. In our bedroom Red and I stuck the fourteen poisoned candy bars hidden beneath our pillows into our pillowcases, seven in his, seven in mine.

"Think Mom will notice it isn't empty?" Red asked quietly, raising his pillowcase.

"No way. You can hardly tell anything's inside it."

Our mom was waiting for us at the front door. She'd taken the bowl of candy from beneath the sink and had placed it on the small hall table. She'd stopped escorting us on Halloween two years ago. Since then she sat by the door with a book to greet the trick-or-treaters.

"You boys have a good time," she told us. "Don't stay out too late. Don't stray too far. And remember to look both ways before you cross any streets."

We assured her that we would be fine and stepped outside into the cool October evening.

14.

Numerous kids, decked out in homemade or store-bought costumes, were already on the hunt. Most traveled in pairs or small groups while they dashed from door to door, singing, "Trick or treat!" Their moms and dads hung back on the sidewalks, taking photos with their phones or chatting with the other parents.

For Red and me, the candy would have to wait.

We had business to attend to first.

We reached Billy's and Ted's street ten minutes later. The houses there were much bigger than those on our street and festooned with better Halloween decorations. One family had transformed their front yard into a full-fledged haunted graveyard, complete with tombstones, monsters, spooky music, flashing lights, and a life-sized skeleton strapped into an electric chair.

"I don't see them anywhere," Red said, sounding worried.

"That's their house right there," I said, pointing across the street to a house that was about twice the size of ours. It had hedges in the front yard and green window shutters and trim. Three jack-o-lanterns sat on the porch next to a bale of hay. One had triangular eyes and a goofy, gap-toothed smile. The other two looked a lot meaner, and I bet they had been Billy's and Ted's creations.

"So where are they?" Red asked nervously.

"They haven't come out yet."

"We can't stand here waiting for them. People are going to wonder what we're doing."

"Then let's start trick-or-treating. Just keep an eye on their place."

We knocked on five doors before we spotted Billy and Ted exiting their house. Billy was dressed in purple clothes and had white pancake makeup on his face with black rings around his eyes. Ted carried a plastic butcher knife in one hand and wore a red-splattered white apron. I couldn't see his face because he also wore a smiling hog mask, but who else could it be?

"There they are," I told Red, pausing behind a parked car so they couldn't see us. "We just have to stay a few houses behind them."

"Are you sure you want to do this?"

"No chickening out!" I told him. "We're not even going to do anything. *They're* going to steal the candy from *us*."

That was the plan anyway. We were going to follow them until there weren't so many people around. Then we would get their attention, and they would steal our candy just like they did the year before—including the fourteen poisoned ones.

"Now come on," I said, "before they get too far away."

We crossed the street and began trick-or-treating while doing our best to keep up with Billy and Ted. The problem was, they were a lot quicker than us, and we began to fall several houses behind. When they were approaching the end of the block, I told Red we had to beeline down the sidewalk to catch them.

Lucky for us, Billy and Ted had stopped on the corner and were arguing about which way to go. Even luckier for us, no other kids or parents were this far down the street.

Ted saw us approaching. "Hey, look, it's the two em-bros! And shit, they're dressed just like you, Bill. Maybe you should be hanging out with *them*?"

"Batman and Robin?" Billy said, scowling. "You guys are so lame."

"You're the Joker," I pointed out.

"The Joker's cool. Batman and Robin and fuckin' lame."

"You em-bros should have been Two-Face—get it?" Ted laughed behind his hog mask.

"Come on," Billy said. "We're wasting time. If you wanna go by Kelly's house, fine. We'll just do a big loop back to the good streets."

They started to cross the road.

I panicked. *They didn't even try to steal our candy!*

"Hey—Piggy!" I blurted. "Oink! Oink!"

They turned around. Billy cracked up laughing like he really was the Joker. Ted yanked his mask off and glowered at us in anger. "What did you call me, em-bro?"

"Couldn't you find a costume to wear?"

"This is my—" He caught himself. "*You stupid dick.*"

He stepped toward us. Billy grabbed his arm. "Screw 'em," he said. "We'll get 'em later."

Ted yanked his arm free. "He just called me a pig!"

"We don't got time for this now."

"Oh, you *are* wearing a costume," I went on, exhilarated by my newfound audacity. This was the first time in my life I was the taunter, not the taunted—and it felt wonderful. "You dressed up as your mom!"

Ted came for us, his face twisted in rage. Red tried to run; I held our ground. The result: we lost our footing and fell backward, landing on our ass.

Then Ted was looming above us. He kicked me in my side three times. Even though each kick was harder than the last, and the pain was acute, I began laughing.

"You think this is funny, shithead?" Ted said.

"What's wrong with him?" Billy said.

"He's retarded, that's what. Get their candy."

After Ted took all my candy, and Billy took all Red's, Ted kicked me a final time for good measure. "Don't think this is the end of it," he said threateningly. "Monday morning, you're both dead meat."

"We're gonna cut off your heads and piss down your necks," Billy added smartly.

They crossed the road and vanished into the night.

When we returned home two hours later, both our pillowcases were heavy with candy. I wanted to empty them and head out again, but our mom told us it was getting late. Instead Red and I flopped down in front of the TV and began sorting through our loot.

Sitting on the sofa behind us, sipping a peppermint tea, our mom said, "Looks like you two had a successful night."

"And we get to keep everything, right?" Red asked excitedly.

"Everything that's wrapped. You can set those two apples aside, for starters."

"What's wrong with apples?" Red asked.

"You don't know how many people have touched them."

"And someone might have stuffed razor blades inside them," I added helpfully.

I felt Red stiffen, and I realized I might have said too much, given our scheming that night. I picked out another Coffee Crisp and put it in the pile with the others.

"Do you boys know why I named you what I did?" our mom asked us.

We turned to look at her. This was a subject she had never broached before.

"Because 'Red' rhymes with 'Fred'?" I said.

"Not exactly, sweetie. When I held you boys in my arms for the first time, you both had bright red cheeks. They were like little candy apples. I thought Red would be a perfect name. But there were two of you, weren't there? So I needed another name. Fred sounded about right."

"I like Red," Red said.

"And I like Fred," I said.

"And I love you two so very much," she told us, tears touching her eyes.

We might have been used to seeing her sad all the time, but we'd never seen her cry before.

"Are you okay, Mom?" I asked her.

"Yes, Fred, I am." She smiled through the tears. "Everything is okay now."

EPILOGUE

In the end, my plan didn't work out quite how I'd wanted it to.

Neither Billy nor Ted died.

They did, however, get sick. They weren't at school on the Monday or Tuesday following Halloween. On Wednesday Mr. Lasarow announced that they were in the ICU at Clifton Heights Hospital. This had been a big deal over the next two days, with many of our classmates speculating about what was wrong with them. Chicken pox, diarrhea, pinworms, pinkeye, strep throat, you name it, we heard it.

Unfortunately, Billy and Ted were back in class on Monday morning, looking none the worse for wear. If the doctors had suspected that they had been poisoned, they never made the connection to Halloween candy; that would have been something we would have heard about. I guess they simply figured that Billy and Ted were the type of kids who would do something stupid like ingest poison.

In any event, Billy didn't die. Ted didn't die. Nobody died.

Bummer.

Still, I wouldn't say the attempted murders were a waste of time. They gave me the confidence that I could do this kind of stuff and get away with it. In fact, I probably would never have drummed up the nerve to kill Red had I not tried killing Billy and Ted first.

It was a brisk Friday morning in April. Six months had passed since Halloween, and Red and I were walking to school along the footpath next to Black Creek. When we reached the spot where we had seen the bullfrog eating the little frog all those months ago, I said, "Hey! Look! He's back!" I pointed at some reeds poking out of the water.

"Who?" Red asked excitedly. "Who's back?"

"The bullfrog! See him?"

"Where is he? I don't see him anywhere. *Is he eating another frog?*"

"He's just sitting there. Don't you see him? Let's go pet him."

We went to the riverbank. The loose stones shifted beneath our feet.

"I don't see him, Fred."

"He must've gone under the water. Let's wait for him to pop his head back up."

"We don't want to be late for school—"

I plunged forward into the river, taking Red with me. As the icy water enveloped us, I could feel Red thrashing madly. When my feet touched the mucky bottom, and I determined up from down, I scrambled forward until my head broke through the surface. Red's did too. He was coughing and crying at the same time. I took a deep breath, pinched my nose with my index finger and thumb, and sank beneath the water again. Red went bonkers, twisting this way and that. His hand kept whacking me in the face. Trying to ignore this, I focused on calmly holding my breath and counting to sixty, like I'd practiced in our mom's bathtub at home when she let us use it.

Red, I knew, wouldn't be calmly holding his breath. He would be screaming underwater, filling his lungs with water.

When I reached thirty, his wild movements had slowed considerably. Ten seconds later he went completely still.

I finished counting the last twenty seconds to be on the safe side before dragging myself—and Red's lifeless half of our body— up onto the shore.

When I opened my eyes, I found myself in a mechanical bed in a dimly lit hospital room. I was covered in tubes and hooked up to a beeping machine. It took me a few moments to remember what I'd done.

Before killing Red, I had figured that after he'd died, I would still be okay. I could wait on the footpath until somebody came by and helped me get to the hospital. This wasn't the case. Within minutes of crawling out of Black Creek, I began to lose all the strength in my body and ended up collapsing facedown on the pavement. I couldn't recall anything after that and must have passed out.

But I'm here now, in the hospital, and alive.

I turned my head to look at Red.

He was gone.

His arm—gone. His leg—gone. Where his head used to be—nothing.

Well, not nothing. There were bandages covering everywhere he used to be attached to me.

But who cared about that?

They cut him off me! My plan worked! I'm free!

These thoughts and a thousand others were zipping through my head when the door to the room opened and my mom entered, holding a magazine in one hand and a coffee in the other. When she saw that I was awake, she rushed over to the bed.

"Oh, Fred!" She set the coffee and magazine aside, delicately cupped my cheeks in her hands, and kissed me on the forehead. "I would hug you but . . . How do you feel?"

I didn't know exactly. Elated? Yeah. Guilty? A little. Dreamy? Definitely that. Just like in the dreams during which I used my sleep-magic to separate myself from Red—

Was this a dream?

My mom must have seen the horror cross my face because she took my hand in hers and squeezed it tightly. "I'm sorry, Fred. You must be so frightened by everything that has happened."

"Is this . . . a dream . . . ?" I asked, my voice barely a whisper.

"No, honey, it isn't. I wish it were . . . " She swallowed tightly. "Red drowned, Fred," she said. "You boys fell in the Black Creek and Red drowned. Someone found you on the footpath and called an ambulance. They couldn't save Red. You were dying. The only thing they could do . . . There wasn't any other choice. They had to separate you two." Tears spilled down her cheeks. "The doctors told me the operation went better than expected . . . "

"I'm okay?"

"You're going to be fine."

"Where's . . . Red?"

"Don't you worry about that right now. There will be a funeral for him, just like the one we had for your father. I know you're going to miss Red. Oh God, you're going to miss him. But we'll get through this. Together. You have to believe that, Fred."

I nodded, my eyes easing closed, my lips forming the faintest of smiles.

Yeah, Mom. We'll get through this together. It's just you and me now.

BROTHERS

JASON PARENT

Warning: This story contains scenes of rape and suicide.

RAND TRIED TO hold still as another man rubbed the hair-removing cream over his back. He shrank from the touch of fingers sliding across his bare skin. The sensation was not in itself unpleasant, but years of small-town conditioning where everything was *fag this* and *fag that* had rooted a phobia deep within his subconscious that he couldn't just expel. It didn't help that the man rubbing said lotion, his Greek god of a roommate, Henry, was not only gay but far more atypically masculine than Rand could ever be. The fact that he loved Henry, albeit in a platonic sense, amplified his discomfort. Rand was straighter than a ruler's edge. But he'd come from a Booneville graduating class of no more than sixty kids, none of whom were outwardly homosexual. His home was worse, a bastion for intolerance where he would have been called a sissy and much worse for even hugging a male friend. No matter how irrational he knew it to be, Rand couldn't shake the sensation of wrongness. Not entirely.

College life had been a culture shock from day one, but he'd welcomed it. Where his hometown life had been all white and all Christian all the time, Mount Marshall University, despite being nestled in the middle of Adirondack wilderness, was as diverse as New York City, which Rand had only visited once. Physically escaping Booneville had been the easy part, but being paired with Henry had shown him how much of Booneville he'd yet to escape. In just the first week, his charismatic roommate had opened Rand's eyes to countless walks of life and new experiences, and the two became instant friends. After only a few weeks, Rand didn't think he'd ever had a friend he felt as close to, or could be as open with, as he did Henry. And yet he couldn't help himself from shrinking away from his friend's touch.

"Oh, stop squirming," Henry said as he slid his hands down Rand's back. "It's not that bad."

Rand dipped to keep the roaming hands from going too low. "It's not that good, either."

"It'll all be over before you know it. Besides, unless you're double-jointed, like, *everywhere*, there's no way you could get it all yourself."

Rand's lower back tightened as Henry's hands brushed the top of his buttocks. He let out a breath and let his shoulders drop. "Sounds like you've done this before."

"Are you kidding?" Henry snorted. "I'm Portuguese. We come out of the womb looking like werewolves."

"Well, if it grows back fast enough, you'll have your costume for the Halloween bash . . . assuming we get in."

"Werewolves." Henry snorted. "How original."

"You got a better idea?"

"Yeah . . . kinda."

Rand stood silent and waited for his roommate to continue.

"Fine." Henry sighed. "I was thinking something along the lines of my heritage."

"Oh yeah? Are you gonna dress up like a big piece of chouriço?"

"No, man. My Native American heritage."

"Didn't you just say you were Portuguese?"

"I am . . . mostly. You wouldn't know it from looking at me, but I've got enough Mohawk in me to qualify me for a tuition discount but not enough to own a casino."

"That sounds racist."

"Is the hillbilly from Booneville giving the gay indigenous person a lesson in PC?"

"That *definitely* sounds racist," Rand said. "Anyway, what did you have in mind?"

"I don't know. Maybe . . . You know that Monster Bear thing all the students here claim lives out by the cliff? I doubt most of them know it, but that actually comes from Iroquois folklore. When I found out one of my great-great-grandparents was Mohawk, I got really into it for a while." His hands stopped moving. "Or was it my great-great-great grandparent?"

"You're thinking about going as a giant bear monster? That could be cool."

"Monster Bear, but no, probably not." Henry spread more of the thick cream over Rand's shoulders. "We could go as a pair. One of the Iroquois legends is about these two brothers, twin spirits who were like gods to their people. Of course, one embodied all that was good—that's me. And the other was a total shit—that's you."

"Thanks." Rand glanced sideways at his roommate. "You want to go as twins? I saw those conjoined boys in Clifton Heights once. I know I shouldn't feel this way, but . . . I'd be lying if I said they didn't give me the creeps. Poor kids probably get that a lot. Still, there's a lot of potential for a horror costume in the idea. Ever see *Basket Case*?" He shuddered. "But regular twins? Won't that just look . . . er . . . "

"Gay?" Henry chuckled. "You know it. And the loincloths around our junk probably won't do anything to dissuade that notion either."

Rand groaned.

"Relax," Henry said. "We can do the stupid werewolf thing if we have to." He slapped Rand's arms. "Done."

When Rand turned around, Henry was frowning as he scrubbed his hands with a dry cloth.

"Tell me again why you want to join the Alphas so badly," Henry said. "As far as I can tell, they're nothing but a bunch of privileged, pussy-chasing white boys out to destroy more brain cells than they'd likely ever need in life."

"My father was an Alpha. He reminisces about those glory days all the time, like they were the only time in his life that mattered. You know, before the wife and kid dragged him down. We've never been close. I guess I . . . I don't know. I guess I feel like I need to get in to prove something to him, you know?"

Henry clapped him on the shoulder, spattering Nair onto Rand's neck. "Fathers can really suck, man. You don't have to prove a thing to anyone but yourself." He gave that slightly crooked, somewhat mischievous but always infectious grin only Henry could pull off. "Besides, from where I'm standing, you're doing all right."

"I just want to feel part of—"

"Shit!" Henry stared at his hand. "Now I gotta wipe this crap off again."

"They could open doors for me."

"Yeah? Did they do anything for your dad?"

"My dad's a drunk."

Henry scoffed. "I bet I can guess where that started."

Rand sighed and studied his feet, noticing more hair that would need removal.

"I'm sorry. That was out of line." Henry offered his patented smile again. "Look, I said I'd do it with you, and I'm doing it. And I'm doing my best to keep an open mind. I know we haven't known each other for that long, but my gut says you'd do the same for me."

It was Rand's turn to smile. "What? You mean join a gay fraternity? I'm not so sure about that."

Henry laughed. "No, you asshole. I'm just saying . . . I know if I ever needed help with something, you'd have my back. Can't say that about a lot of people." He cleared his throat. "Anyway, you only got like two more minutes before that shit starts to burn." He picked up the bottle of Nair, handed it to Rand, and pointed at his boxers. "Plus, they said *all* of it, right? You need to clear the field, my friend. Front and back. And I'm sure those pervs will be checking. They'll probably have some pube detector or some shit." His crooked smile returned. "I can help you with it, if you'd like."

Heat rose in Rand's cheeks. "I-I-I got it. Thanks."

Henry snorted. "Aw, you're so cute when you're gawkward."

"Gawkward? Is that like gay awkward?"

"Yep, and I'm coining it. Put a little *C* in a circle next to it. But you can relax already, bud. I've already told you, you're not my type."

"Oh yeah? And what type am I?"

"Straight."

Rand adjusted his bra as he hobbled up the frat house's front steps. "This is so stupid."

"It's not too late to turn back," Henry said, batting his eyelash extensions. "I heard there's another party at the cliff tonight. There's going to be a séance or a sacrifice and everything."

"An offering to old Bear Monster . . . or is it Monster Bear? I always forget."

For more than a moment, Rand considered it. *Play bitch to a bunch of drunken fraternity pricks all night while dressed in drag, or relax and be myself while listening to goofy stories of the cliff monster hungry for the souls of unsuspecting college kids?*

His hand lingered on the rattling doorknob. A subwoofer boomed from seemingly everywhere inside Alpha territory. The nearby cliff was an amazing place to drink and maybe smoke a little weed, regardless of all the crazy stories too absurd to actually scare kids away from the place, if that was what they were intended to do.

One of Rand's first acts as an MMU student had been to look up articles concerning deaths at the cliff. True enough, people had died there, mostly intoxicated students stumbling over the precipice, plummeting over a thousand feet, and smashing into the rocky ravine. After a few suicides, several accidents, and as many lawsuits, the school had finally put up a railing six feet in front of the drop, even though the cliff wasn't technically on university property. Despite the railing, at least one kid fell over the cliff every year.

One of Rand's second acts as an MMU student was to sit atop that railing with his new roommate and smoke a joint. High and drunk, he'd made the mistake of looking over the drop at the dry creek bed. A sensation, vertigo he supposed, had sent his head spinning. He could have sworn, if just for a second, that he saw himself lying broken on the rocks below, draped over a boulder like a clock in a Dali painting. He'd begun to pitch forward, a part of him wanting to lean forward. *If Henry hadn't been there . . .*

He shuddered, but that was half in part due to him freezing his fake tits off in his skimpy cheerleader's uniform. He thanked God for his Spandex, which offered his freshly hairless privates some modicum of protection from the cold, early October night. With his athletic frame and blond wig, Henry looked like an androgynous superhero and yet somehow was still confident and attractive. Rand, on the other hand, felt wholly inadequate in his frail, slender but soft body. His teeth chattering, he groaned. "Let's just get this over with."

He pulled open the door, only to be accosted by the loudest music he'd ever heard. "Great. How are we even supposed to hear what people want?"

"What?" Henry shouted.

"I said . . . " Rand shouted back. "Never mind."

They stepped into a large living room. Its walls were lined with sparse furniture, clearing as much space on the stained carpet as possible. A large, unmanned sound system blared from the far corner. A keg stood beside it. A tingle ran though Rand, and he smiled. His first real college party was about to begin at the frat house of frat houses, a place affectionately called "the Wolves' Den" by those who lived there.

More like Animal House. Rand took in the room, which was already crowded and peppered with discarded cups trampled on the floor. People in various states of dress and undress sweated and pulsated to the near-techno dance beats, while others with bloodshot eyes and drooping lids swayed languidly on the outskirts. Not a single person was bereft of a red SOLO cup. And it was Rand, Henry, and the other pledges' jobs to keep those cups filled.

"You're late, pledge!"

A hand clamped down on Rand's shoulder. Hot, alcohol-infused breath whistled by his ear and dampened his cheek. Rand turned to face Turk, a dark-haired, pimply-faced stocky beast of a boy built like a Port-o-John. He was one of the senior brothers of Alpha Kappa Pi.

Turk crossed his thick forearms over his barrel chest. "Not a good start." He leaned in so close their noses nearly Eskimo kissed. "You know what that means?"

Neither Rand nor Henry responded, though Rand doubted his roommate could make out what Turk was saying over the din. But the ask seemed clear as Turk raised a bottle of gold-colored liquid over Rand's head. "You boys have some catching up to do." He tilted the bottle. "Open wide!"

Almost instinctively, Rand did as he was told, managing to catch the small waterfall in his mouth before it could rain down on his face. Cheap liquor—tequila, he thought, maybe mixed with rubbing alcohol—poured down his gullet like fiery oil, each swallow burning fiercer than the last. Tears formed in the corners of his eyes as he tried not to gag. What seemed like an eternity elapsed before Turk finally decided Rand had choked down enough and turned the bottle on poor Henry. Rand wiped his mouth even as he coughed and sputtered. A cherry-red lipstick stain marred the back of his hand. His stomach roiled, and he turned away from Henry, fearing his friend's punishment would only make his stomach worse, causing him to puke all over the place and annihilate his chances for passing initiation.

But Turk's sloppy grin suggested he was pleased with the results. He spun the two faux cheerleaders around, draped his meaty arms over their shoulders, and pulled them in close. "Not bad, kiddos. Now—" he slapped their asses and pushed them forward, "—get to work."

As Turk bounded through the crowd, Henry spit. "What was that? Gasoline?"

"Tequila . . . I think. Maybe we should avoid that brother as much as possible." Rand took in the room again. "Keg's over there. Seems to be a help-yourself kind of thing. Where do you suppose the hard liquor's at?"

Henry shrugged. "Maybe we should try the kitchen."

The idea sounded as good as any, except neither Rand nor Henry had any idea where the kitchen was. Guessing, they wound their way through the crowd toward a better-lit room at the opposite side and entered a slightly emptier kitchen and dining area. An island in the center of the kitchen housed dozens of bottles, cups, and a cooler filled with ice. Boxes of beer and hard liquor were stacked atop a massive oak dining room table, which was as oversized as everything else in the Victorian-style house. Both conversation and music were a notch quieter inside, and although they still had to shout, they were able to hear each other.

"Who was that idiot?" Henry asked, his expression souring. "I'll be tasting that shit for weeks."

"Yeah, Turk must have modeled himself after, like, every frat movie there's ever been. The guy's a walking stereotype."

"Turk?" Henry squinted. "How the hell did you remember that? We only met him once, and there were at least twenty other guys there that day."

"He's the biggest and doesn't seem all that bright, so I kinda just think of him as a big, fat Thanksgiving turkey. A little name association and—*voila*! Turk."

Henry laughed. "Maybe that's how he got the nickname." His face paled. "But do me a favor: let's not talk about food right now." He burped and blew it out. "Any guess what his real name is?"

"Don't know. Don't care. And don't expect me to remember too many more of them. There's D-Rod—he's like the president or whatever. I only remember him because he did most of the talking when we rushed. Then there was the guy with the mustache . . . and the other guy . . . I want to say there was a Mike."

"Yeah, what was with Mustache Guy? I'm not sure why people are trying so hard to bring it back, but if you're going to rock one, you should probably make sure you can grow one first. That shit on his upper lip was reddish and mangy."

"And yet he probably gets laid more in a week than you or I will see all year."

"Goats don't count, man." Henry keeled over, laughing at his own joke, then froze. "Oh wait, sorry. Did that hit a little too close to home?"

"Ha. Ha." Rand huffed. "That small-town-farm-boy crap never gets old, does it?"

Henry scratched his head. "Uh, not yet."

"And everyone knows us Booneville folk are into pigs." Rand shook his head and studied the various bottles on the island counter, set beside an industrial-sized box of plastic cups. He'd only tried a minute fraction of the wide assortment of liquor, liqueurs, and mixers before and had never used a shaker or any of the other tools of the bartending trade. He'd drunk before, of course. In Booneville, there wasn't much to do except drink and perhaps have sex with farm animals, if that was your thing. But he and his high school classmates had mostly drunk beer or whatever one of them could pilfer from their parents' stashes, which they'd almost always mixed with Coke, Jack and Coke mostly. Dear ol' Dad was a whiskey man and always spent his last cent to keep it in stock, even when Rand needed new clothes for school or money for lunches. Once, Rand had mixed the whiskey with Dr Pepper, but the combination lacked the same magic.

"So are we supposed to mix drinks for people or go out there with bottles and fill up cups? I didn't exactly go to bartender school or anything."

"Let's just mix whatever with whatever. People will drink anything we hand them. And if someone actually cares enough to ask, just make something up." Henry filled a SOLO cup halfway with vodka then to the top with cranberry juice. He half-filled a second cup with vodka and added a green syrupy liqueur to it. "That's cranberry surprise," he said, pointing at the first cup. "And that's green apple surprise."

Rand snorted. "Genius."

He began making his own mixes, throwing less alcohol into his creations than Henry and testing each before sending it out into the world. Partygoers picked up cups nearly as fast as Rand and Henry could fill them. No one seemed to care what was in the cups. When there was a lull in the alcoholic binge, Henry and Rand took turns waiting on the partiers in the other first-floor rooms, though a few other pledges were working a second bar at the other end of the house. Now and then a red-faced pledge, his belly protruding from under his halter top, stopped by the kitchen and absconded with a bottle. Handprints marred his exposed skin as if he'd been slapped repeatedly, but he continued serving the lords of the house seemingly without complaint.

The night went on, and Rand fell into a rhythm. He was meeting new people and actually enjoying himself despite the awkwardness of his dress. Henry, too, seemed to have gotten into the spirit of things. Each time the two met in the kitchen or cleared out the empties, they would do a shot together, raising their cups in a mock toast to Mount Marshall, the Alphas, and even the old Monster Bear, often mistakenly calling it the Bear Monster. By his fourth shot, combined with all the sips he'd snuck, Rand was feeling pretty good. Three Alphas burst into the kitchen just as he was knocking back another.

"Well, well . . . " The wolf pack's leader, a lean, wiry-muscled young man with a natural handsomeness blunted by the fierce intensity that seemed perpetually behind his eyes, pushed his way toward them. He looked at each of his flunkies, his two betas in tow, making a show of his apparent disapproval. "Who said the help could help themselves?"

Rand didn't recognize the back-up boys of the frat pack. The taller of the two was a trust-fund brat straight out of Bel Air, wearing a cardigan and khakis. The other was a diminutive, baby-faced boy with a slanted grin that resembled a sneer. The speaker, however, needed no introduction: D-Rod, the Alpha who would ultimately decide whether he and Henry should join their ranks.

"I-I'm sorry . . . sir. We thought it might be okay if we had just one."

"One, huh?" D-Rod scowled and peered down his nose at them, holding the glare for only a couple of seconds before bursting into laughter. "Relax, pledges. I'm just playing. You can and absolutely should be drinking. It's a motherfucking party."

Rand started to relax, but D-Rod held up a finger. "But not just one." He pointed at the counter and twirled that same finger as if he were stirring an imaginary drink with it. "Pour."

Rand glanced at the array of bottles in front of him. "Uh, yes, sir. What'll it be?"

"Oh, fuck. I don't care." His gaze landed on a dark bottle with an elk logo on it. "That one."

Rand lined up three cups and was about to pour when D-Rod held up his hand again. "Five cups."

"R-Right." Rand snuck a glance at Henry, who gave a short nod. "Sorry, sir." He poured roughly an inch of alcohol into each cup. He'd heard something about it being measured in fingers, but even the length of his pinky finger seemed far too much.

Just as Rand finished pouring the last one, D-Rod shook his head. "More."

Rand dumped another inch into the last cup.

Again, D-Rod said, "More."

Rand tipped the bottle and let a slow but steady stream of liquor flow into the cup, watching D-Rod the entire time for a signal to stop that never came. The bottle emptied when the cup was three-quarters full.

"Phew!" D-Rod pulled the cup in front of himself and stared into it as if admiring his reflection in the liquid's surface. Rand watched in silence, simultaneously impressed and repulsed by the thought of D-Rod pounding that drink.

D-Rod released a breath. "Nah." He looked up at Rand, a leering grin worming its way over his lips. "You do it." He pushed the drink in front of Rand and took one of the others. "Cheers." He raised his cup.

The other Alphas each took one of the remaining cups and tapped it against his. Henry followed suit, grimacing at Rand as he and the others waited for him to pick up the final cup.

Fuck me. His stomach aflutter, Rand sucked in a breath and grabbed the drink. As he raised it to cheers the others, he did his best to mentally prepare himself for what he knew was coming.

"Down the hatch," D-Rod said, the zeal in his smile more than just a little sinister. The smaller Alpha behind him actually tittered.

All three Alphas had downed their shots before the plastic of Rand's cup touched his lips. They watched him even as Henry pounded his shot. Closing his eyes, Rand kicked back the thick, syrupy liquor and chugged. Maybe that was what it would take to make his father proud. He sputtered, and alcohol spilled over the corners of his mouth. It burned his nostrils and ran down his chin, but he refused to stop—not for D-Rod, or to get into the fraternity, or even to exceed or rebuke his father's expectations of him. He finished that drink out of sheer stubborn refusal to be bested by anyone, the fear of the ridicule that came with failure, and the reminder of who his father was and what he felt destined to become.

As he thought of all that, the cup emptied. Tears blurring his eyes, he slammed it down on the counter.

"Good." D-Rod pursed his lips and nodded. "Good." He turned to Henry. "Now, your turn."

Henry crossed his arms. "I'm good."

D-Rod's eyebrows shot up, and his forehead furrowed, as if the concept of being refused were foreign to him. His lackeys looked equally puzzled, but their expressions were tinged by something that took Rand a moment to recognize: fear.

"Are you telling me no?" D-Rod turned to the smaller of his support staff. "Runt, did he just tell me no?"

"I think he did, D," the rodent-faced boy answered.

"Patrick?"

The cardigan-wearing Alpha shrugged. "Why not tell him again? Maybe he misunderstood."

D-Rod crossed his arms in a pose that matched Henry's. A muscle in his jaw flexed.

Henry leaned forward, meeting D-Rod's gaze with stolid determination. "I'm telling you I'll do it, but only if you do it with me."

D-Rod huffed. "I'm not sure you understand how this works, pledge." He jabbed a finger into Henry's chest. "If you don't do it—"

"I'll do his for him." The words jettisoned from Rand's mouth before his mind, already spinning, could comprehend their meaning.

"What?" Henry and D-Rod asked in unison, which Rand might have found funny had he not already regretted opening his mouth.

Henry nudged him and said into his ear, "You don't have to do this. I never really wanted to be an Alpha anyway."

Rand smiled at his friend, who stared back at him with pleading eyes. Henry was worried about him. For some reason, he found strength in that.

D-Rod chuckled, and the tag-alongs were quick to join in. "I like this kid. Alpha material all the way." His lecherous smile broadened. "I'll even let you pick."

Rand grabbed the bottle of Jack, the booze he knew best, and froze. He thought of his bastard father back home, who was probably drinking the same thing that very moment as he degraded Rand's mother.

The apple doesn't fall far from the tree.

Anger rushed through him. He denied any resemblance beyond blood type to that poor excuse for a man. *I will not end up like him.* With snappy motions, he topped off a cup and drank it without prompting.

Jack was not the right choice for swilling. About halfway through, Rand coughed and spit up on his halter top. He gasped then took deep breaths, trying to calm both his nerves and his stomach and keep the liquid down.

"Drink, drink, drink!" two of the three Alphas chanted. Cardigan Alpha looked away as if he'd lost all interest in the display.

Henry put a hand on his back. "Are you okay?" He reached for the cup. "That's enough, man. I'm stopping this."

Rand jerked the cup away, the alcohol sloshing over the rim and dousing his hand and the counter.

"Party foul," Runt chided him.

Rand swung an arm out between himself and Henry and gulped down the rest of the drink. His stomach twisting and cramping, he ran to the sink and hitched over it. Instead of vomiting, he let out a long burp. Pulling his halter top up to wipe his mouth and exposing his stuffed bra, he staggered back to the counter. He must have almost fallen. One second he was walking, and the next Henry had an arm around him, propping him up.

Rand raised the empty cup in front of D-rod and his boys, crushed it in his hand, and let it fall from his grasp. "Th-That's how it's done." He put a hand on the counter to steady himself.

"Not bad, pledge." D-Rod fist-bumped him. "I'm not even sure Turk could have done that."

Rand's head lolled on his shoulders, suddenly feeling heavier than it had a right to. His eyelids felt a little heavier too. "Than . . . thanks." His own voice sounded strange to him, as if spoken underwater.

Henry poured the Alphas fresh drinks, and Rand tried to keep the world from spinning. He saluted them as they left.

"That was really stupid," Henry said, his arm back around his waist. "We should get as much of that out of you as possible. Ever hear of alcohol poisoning?"

He tried to focus on his roommate, but with a flash of light and clarity, the roiling and cramping came anew. "Sink!"

They hurried over like competitors in a potato sack race, just in time for Rand to eject the first wave of vomit. Several more followed, the final throes releasing nothing but air. Rand turned and leaned against the counter, fighting to keep his chin off his chest. Henry ran the cold water and dabbed Rand's face with a wet paper towel.

"Thanks, Henry." He threw his arms around his roommate, falling like dead weight into his arms. "You . . . You-You're a good dude. Good dude. I'm sorry for being so . . . gawkward." He cocked his head back and hawed like an ass.

"And you're drunk." Henry ran water in the sink, trying to clean up the mess without touching any of it. "God, that stinks. Wait . . . " He straightened and examined his top. "You didn't just get that on me?"

Rand giggled. "And you're not drunk?" Through half-shut eyes, he stared at his friend, who seemed to be swaying in place. Or maybe the whole kitchen was on a boat.

But their eyes met for a moment, Rand holding what he thought must have been the best poker face anyone had ever seen before the grin refused to be suppressed any longer, and the laughing rose anew. Yet Henry laughed first.

"Okay, okay. Maybe a little. But you, good sir, are fucked up. I'm not the one who's going to be regretting this in the morning."

Rand snorted and curtsied. "Good sir." When he tried to stand straight again, he stumbled left then back against the sink.

In an instant, Henry propped him up again. "Whoa, there, buddy. I think it's time we got you out of here."

"But we gotta . . . " Rand rasped. "Fuck that! We got work to do." He reached for the nearest bottle.

"I think our work here is done." Henry helped him toward the living room, Rand's feet cooperating as best they could. "Think you could make it back?"

Rand leaned into his friend. He tried to clear his mind and take stock of himself. Yep, he was drunk and utterly exhausted, and his head was starting to hurt. And the taste in his mouth was god-awful. He slowly shook his head.

Around them, the party pulsed onward. A shrinking part of Rand wanted to join them, but a growing part wanted to find a quiet place away from all the noise and people. "I should . . . I should probably lie down." He staggered toward the couch, ready to face-plant into the couple making out at one end.

Henry redirected his course. "Not there. You'll wake up with dicks drawn all over your face or a jockstrap in your mouth." He tilted his head toward the stairwell. "Maybe we can find an unoccupied bedroom upstairs. You're going to have to help me on the steps, though."

Rand nodded. "Shheriously, Henry. Best friend I ever had." He kissed Henry's cheek. "I fucking love you, man."

Henry winced. "Your breath smells like a litter box."

"Dude, bro, I'm serious. I love you." He tried to stand on his own but couldn't. "Not like that, though. You know what I mean."

Henry shook his head and smiled. "Yeah, I know what you mean. I love you, too, but you are so gonna owe me for this in the morning."

With great effort, Rand climbed the stairs, using his roommate as a crutch. After what seemed like eons, they reached the top. Henry propped him against the wall as he began opening doors. He said something about the first room being loaded with jackets, which struck Rand as funny, though he couldn't say why.

After opening a second door, Henry hauled Rand over to it. Inside was an empty bed in all its glory. He let go of Henry and fell like an axed tree into it. The awful rotation of the earth on its axis finally slowed, but that might have been because all Rand could see was blanket.

"Can I get you anything?" Henry asked. "Water?"

Rand grunted. "Best friend . . . I ever . . . " He sucked in a breath, and with excruciating effort lifted his head to thank Henry for everything he'd done for him since the start of school.

But Henry was heading for the door. "I'll lock it. You can have the bed. I'll take the—"

The door swung wide open, and four men wearing plastic werewolf masks filed in.

"Well, well," the one leading the charge said. Aside from the mask, he wore only a wife beater and shorts. "Would you look at these two pledges, getting it on in here all by themselves. And on your bed at that, Turk. Can you believe it?"

The big man in the mask guffawed. "Can't let that slide. Not from pledges."

"Come on, D-Rod," Henry said. "You saw what he drank. Can't you cut him some slack? I'll take whatever punishment he's got coming."

"Okay, fag." D-Rod dropped his shorts. "Suck it."

Rand raised his head and squinted. It hurt to focus, but he could have sworn he was staring at a flaccid penis. "Is that a dick?"

Henry snickered. "You must be joking."

The room fell silent. No one moved. Just six guys in a room, one with his shorts around his ankles. The small-framed figure in the doorway let out a tinny laugh. Turk crossed his arms and stuck out his chest as if he were standing guard.

The fourth Alpha tipped up his mask—the preppy kid from earlier. "D, you *are* joking, right? I mean, hazing is one thing, and that's already illegal. What you're thinking . . . That's just beyond messed up."

"If I want your opinion, Patrick, I'll give it to you."

"Yeah, Patrick." Rand gurgled, proud he'd remembered the Alpha's name.

Patrick opened his mouth as if to protest, then looked away, shaking his head. "Screw this." He pushed his way past the omega Alpha.

"Runt," D-Rod ordered. "Lock the door."

Rand could sense his roommate's tension and had a vague notion of trouble, though he couldn't pinpoint its source. *Wait. What? Aren't we drinking and having fun? Why does he look like he wants to throw down?* "Hen . . . Henry. Be cool, man." He tapped his roommate's arm.

Henry shook off his touch. Rand propped himself up on his elbow but fell back to his side. A hollow pang ran through his stomach, and he groaned. The room blurred again, and he pulled a pillow underneath his head then curled into a ball.

"If you think for a second that you're coming anywhere near me or Rand with that dirty little thing of yours, you'd better think again. I'll rip it off and feed it to your fat-fuck friend."

"There's no need for body-shaming," Turk said matter-of-factly.

D-Rod pulled up his shorts. "Yeah, like you don't want it. You queers are all the same." He sighed and bit into his lower lip. "Have it your way. Turk."

His jaw set, Turk stepped forward. As soon as he did, Henry knocked him back again with a right hook that sent Turk's mask off-kilter. The mask beneath was one of pure rage, deep red with clenched teeth.

"Rand?" Henry called, a shake in his voice. "I could use a little help here, buddy."

Rand struggled to sit up, then kicked his legs over the side of the bed. "Leave him alone," he mumbled, eyes half open. The figures in the room vacillated between recognizable people and shadow monsters, not fully formed but menacing and evil. He tried to will his eyes to focus, which seemed momentarily to be working. Then he tried to stand and help his friend. He collapsed onto the floor, his back against the side of the bed, one leg bent awkwardly under him.

Turk fixed his mask and glowered through its eyeholes at Henry. D-Rod clenched his fist and shifted his feet. Even in his inebriated state, Rand could see what was coming. He tugged on Henry's pant leg, trying to warn him of the second threat. "He . . . he's . . ."

As Turk charged, Henry apparently didn't see D-Rod slide to his right and throw a jab into his stomach. He bent over and spun so that his back took the brunt of Turk's blow. Turk flattened him into the bed, putting all his weight on top of him.

"Get off me!" Henry shouted.

His friend's cry, combined with the festering anger rising within him, sobered Rand enough for him to stand. But as he turned to help his friend, a hard object collided with the back of his head. He pitched forward, catching a glimpse of D-Rod pulling down Henry's Spandex as reality flashed in and out. Turning to see what had blindsided him, he found Runt a couple of feet away, holding a textbook in one hand and a phone in the other. He snarled, but his eyes rolled back, and he fell onto the bed, his head inches from Henry's.

"Now you'll see why they call me D-Rod," the Alpha said as he straddled Henry's thighs.

"Rand! Help me!"

"Don't worry," Turk said. "He's next."

Though Henry was so close, his shouts seemed miles away. Rand passed out to the sounds of his best friend's pleas.

Rand woke with the taste of something sour on his tongue. His body ached all over, though he had trouble focusing on any specific injury beyond the massive throbbing in his head. Light stabbed his eyes each time he tried to open them, amplifying the heavy machinery operating inside his skull and the cramping in his stomach.

Squinting, he leaned over the side of the bed and heaved out stringy bile that clung to his lower lip. "Henry?"

No answer. His mind noted the blue comforter under him, not his. *Where am I?*

He struggled to lift his head, to shake off the remnants of sleep and intoxication, and took in the room. A small dresser had been arranged kitty-corner near the foot of the bed, and a desk stood against the far wall. A *Sports Illustrated* swimsuit calendar was pinned to the wall next to the poster of a band Rand didn't recognize. A nightstand with a lamp and a framed photograph sat next to the bed.

He reached for the picture. As he moved, his muscles ached. A stinging, more centralized pain came from other areas his head was yet too groggy to narrow down. Determining where he was took priority, and the photo helped him do that. In it, Turk held a trophy. A man stood at his left and a woman at his right, each with an unmistakable resemblance to him.

The party. Rand began piecing together the night. He remembered the syrupy liquid and how much of it he'd drunk. And that hadn't been all he'd had. He groaned. *That would explain my head and my stomach. Why'd you have to mix, Rand?* He frowned, and even that hurt. *Did I have a second full cup?*

He laughed, then groaned again. He was stinging in the strangest of places. Inside him. He slowly rose and planted his bare feet on the hardwood floor. "Henry?" he called again, even though he was fairly certain the room was empty. *I can't believe he just left me here.*

Fighting the spinning and the impulse to heave again, he rested his forehead against the wall. The pain in his head dulled and gave way to more stinging, like lemon juice poured on a fresh cut, in and around his thighs and buttocks. Panic skyrocketed within him, quickening his heartbeat and throwing his already-befuddled mind into further disarray. But the pain and anxiety battled away sleep and grogginess, clearing a path for less segmented thoughts. Still, he couldn't put a finger on what troubled him. Something in his gut told him he needed to find Henry.

When he took a step, he fell onto the floor, bumping his chin. The metallic taste of blood filled his mouth, but that was the least of his concerns. He'd tripped over his Spandex, which were down around his ankles. *Why?*

With shallow breaths, his brain scrabbling for comprehension, he rolled onto his back and yanked them up, as if doing so could somehow reverse the harm he sensed had already been done. Then he noticed the dried blood flaking off the skin of his inner thighs. He clawed at his hair. "What the actual fuck?"

He couldn't remember how last night had ended or how'd come to be sleeping in that bed. Every nerve in his body blared a warning beacon, screaming to him he did not want to remember. Bile threatened to rise again.

Find Henry. He'll know what happened. He'll know what to do.

His stomach twisted like a pretzel, and he held his breath until the pain passed. A whimper escaped his lips that had little to do with the physical injury but plenty to do with what his imagination filled in for his lost memories. Grasped by a sudden need to escape that place—to be back in his own room and his own bed, Henry there to help him through . . . whatever this was—he scurried to the door, not bothering to look for his missing heels.

Before exiting, he froze. His ear against the door, he listened for sound outside. Hearing none, he entered the hallway and headed down the stairwell. In the living room, he met the gazes of several stragglers strewn about the afterbirth of a frat party. Some snickered as they saw him. Others looked away, faces marred with disgust, pity, or fear, as if he were an instant pariah, worthy of exile when he'd been their party facilitator only hours earlier. A few were glued to their phones despite the early hour, while those beside them pointed at Rand with mouths agape.

He had to get out of there. His face flushing, he hurried out of the frat house, feeling like a child young enough to wet his pants but old enough to feel the humiliation of it.

As he crossed campus to his dorm, the pain worsened and his gait slowed. He experienced more of what he had in that living room: people pointing, some snickering, others turning away with just-swallowed-a-bug expressions. One student, a young woman he'd never seen before, asked if he was okay. He nodded curtly and hurried away, keeping his gaze glued to the ground the remainder of the walk back, his own tears a cause for further shame. Despite having been victimized. Despite knowing what had happened to him, even though he couldn't remember it. His body remembered it, as if it had been written on his skin. But *they*—those with their judgmental stares and those who couldn't bear the sight of him—could only see a weak young student in a skimpy cheerleader's uniform, doing what likely resembled a walk of shame. For all intents and purposes, it was, though the humiliation should have been felt by all who judged him.

They couldn't know his true shame and all the horror, anxiety, and desolation that came with it. He felt hideous, not only in his soiled clothes but also in his own skin. As he threw himself into his room, closing the door and the world outside with it, he wanted nothing more than to hide under his sheets until time forgot him. But his skin, he had to get it clean. He needed to feel clean.

Grabbing a towel, he headed for the showers. There, he scrubbed himself under the scalding water until his skin was raw and red. Then he curled up on the floor of the stall and sobbed quietly, his face buried in his hands.

He stayed under that deluge for a long time. Finally, he rose, dried himself, and headed back to his room. He drew the shades and climbed into bed, tucking the sheets so that they swaddled him. There, he lay through day and night, half awake and half in nightmare, shadows dancing like memories through his mind. In something of a fugue state, he stared at a pale blue wall for hours, oblivious to anyone or anything around him.

The sound of a door closing startled Rand from his daze. "Henry?"

He listened but heard nothing. He let his head fall back into the pillow, no part of him ready to rise and face whatever awaited him outside his door. The horrific events of the other night seemed too unreal even as his body screamed the truth to him. They couldn't have happened, not to him. Not to Henry.

"Henry?"

No answer. He squeezed his eyes shut and felt a trickle run

down his cheek. His pillow was damp. As much as he wanted to stay in bed forever, Rand couldn't shake the concern for his roommate. It wormed its way through the disarray of his mind and castled itself there.

And forced him to take a shaky, painful step out of bed.

A sheet of paper fell off his comforter onto the floor. He picked it up and read: *They taped the whole thing. It's all over campus.*

Even in its hastily scrawled penmanship, Rand recognized Henry's writing. But Henry himself was nowhere to be seen.

Rand dressed quickly, his worry for his friend trumping his disquiet over the note's contents. It gave him something other than himself to focus on, some good he could still do, some purpose he may yet serve. And he knew just where to find Henry.

When he reached the cliff, Rand found his roommate sitting alone on the railing, staring out over the drop. A bustling party place at night, the cliff on a late-Sunday morning was as dead as he felt inside. All the happier people were still sleeping off their minor indiscretions. The chill was better suited for folks like Rand and Henry, who sought to be numb.

Wordlessly, Rand sat beside his friend. Henry's gaze remained unbroken, endlessly downward. He hadn't changed out of his cheerleader's uniform. Black eyeliner streaks ran down his cheeks as if he'd cried ink. His lip was swollen and cracked, and his lower back sported a bruise the size of a softball. But he seemed otherwise unbroken, in a physical sense.

The smell emitting from Henry reminded Rand of hot dog water. Dirt smeared his friend's skin. Dead leaves caught in his clothes. *Did he spend yesterday . . . last night in the woods?* Rand lacked the courage to ask and took a modicum of solace in the fact Henry had, at the least, come back at one point to leave the note.

He draped the extra jacket he'd brought with him over Henry's shoulders. His roommate didn't seem to notice. Rand opened his mouth to speak, but when no words would come, he closed it again. After a few moments of uncomfortable silence, the dull pangs of helplessness tightening his chest, he forced himself to say something, anything. "I . . . I don't remember . . . what happened."

As if breaking from a trance, Henry wheeled on him, a fire burning behind the fresh tears in his eyes. "Didn't you watch the freaking video? I sent it to you."

Rand stuttered then fumbled his phone out of his pocket. Sure enough, he'd received a text from Henry with a link to a post entitled "Alphas Showing Their Bitches a Good Time." His thumb hovered over it, trembling. But his need to know won over blissful ignorance as he pressed play.

He saw D-Rod thrusting into his roommate as Turk held him down. Henry screamed for help, begging Rand to get up. Rand lay right next to the pig pile, unconscious and useless. With each grunt and every plea, Rand could feel Henry tensing beside him, forced to relive the moment in his head, then and probably forever.

Rand turned off the volume. Though the assailants wore masks, he knew who they were. Having seen both D-Rod and Turk earlier in the evening when his head remained marginally clear, he could guess who they were from their voices and builds. Their wolf masks and corresponding howling-wolf tattoos on their upper arms, the latter a trademark of the fraternity, made identification a certainty.

Again, his thumb hovered over the phone as he deliberated whether to fast forward. What was seen could not be unseen. Maybe it was better not knowing. Henry certainly didn't seem better off for it. And it was his concern for Henry's emotional state that kept his own from shattering again into a thousand smaller pieces. He couldn't help his friend if he couldn't maintain his own shaky composure.

Just like you were no help to him the other night.

An emptiness filled him, cold and suffocating. He swallowed hard and slid his finger to the right, advancing the story. His eyes blurred, and he wiped them with the back of his hand but continued scrolling. He saw himself and Henry used in all sorts of ways, Rand always unconscious, Henry not so much. Rage welled up within him, impotent and without an outlet, and secondary to feelings of humiliation and degradation. Most of what he felt—the hate, the rage, the guilt, and the shame—he directed at himself for allowing what had happened.

But not all of it. "I'll kill them," he said so low his voice was almost a growl. "I swear it, Henry. I'll get them back for what they—"

"What good will that do?" Henry ripped the jacket off his back and threw at their feet. "Huh? They'll be dead, but we'll still be raped." His breath hitched. "I can't even . . . Goddamn them! Goddamn you!"

"Me?" Rand studied his friend's wild-eyed and red-faced expression. "I-I'm in the same boat as you here. At least you're ga—"

"And you think that somehow makes a lick of difference? That me being gay means I must have secretly wanted that to happen? Fuck you, Rand. Go back to Booneville or whatever ass-backwards hole you crawled out of."

Rand bent over to pick up the jacket and drape it over the rail, not wanting to look his friend in the eyes. "I'm sorry. Poor choice of words."

"You're an asshole, Rand. If not for you, I wouldn't have even been in that room. Hell, I wouldn't have even been at that fucking party." Spittle shot from his mouth as he leaped to his feet and began to pace the few feet between the railing and the cliff's edge. "And you wanna know the worst thing about it?" He laughed something hoarse like a bark. "You probably still want to be one of them."

Rand sniffled and rubbed his nose, looking everywhere but up at Henry. *I don't still want to be an Alpha.* He considered it for longer than he felt he should have. *No.* Of that much, he was certain. Well, maybe that small part of him did, that inner child who always sought inclusion, affirmation, understanding, and acceptance . . . things only Henry had ever really shown him. *And look where that got Henry.*

His friend was right: it was all Rand's fault. He thought of apologizing. He'd apologize as many times as Henry wanted, but he knew nothing he said could heal Henry's hurt or his own. The two cried quietly, together but worlds apart, each lost in thoughts forced upon them, memories that could never be scrubbed clean.

"We can't just let them get away with it," Rand muttered, breaking the silence.

Henry inhaled deeply and went still, his resignation somehow scarier than his anger as he stared down Rand with blank indifference. "What can we do, Rand? Those people, the Alphas . . . Don't you get it? They were never gonna let us in. To them, we were always queers, playthings . . . their *bitches*."

"We can go to the cops. Believe me, if there were a way to sweep this under the rug, drink enough to permanently forget—"

"Oh yeah, 'cause that's been working out for you so far."

"—I would have been all for it. But we're never going to forget, so we shouldn't be the only ones paying for it. There's a freaking video. It's out there, and there's no sticking the cork back in after this, no matter how much we want to. But it's also evidence. We have proof of what they did, and they should go down for it."

"Man, what world do you actually live in? Back in Booneville, who does the law crack down on harder: the rich or the poor?" Henry threw up his hands then let them fall and slap against his sides, shaking his head with disbelief. "Rand, they're fucking Alphas! Their parents buy and sell people like you and me every day. Do you really think they're not going to spend more money than the government making it look like we're the bad guys here? Or that we consented?" He hovered over Rand, seething, the fire and fight returning if but for a moment. "You're right. I'm gay. And like you, they'll make me out to be just some queer who must have wanted it. In the end, we'll go through a whole humiliating investigation, everything we do and have ever done under a public microscope, only to be raped again, this time by a bunch of rich mommies and daddies and their puppets in the courts and precincts." He stepped toward the cliff. His whole body seemed to shrink. "I can't do this."

Rand was up and spinning Henry around before he truly understood what his roommate, the stronger of the two of them both physically and mentally, meant to do. Henry had been awake for it all, every indignity. In his friend's eyes, Rand saw the billowing dark clouds above reflected, spreading out from his pupils to cover all within, filling him with endless storms. The brilliance of life had died somewhere in that black mass. The darkness reached out to Rand as it continued to spread. Only his love for his friend kept him from staring over the edge himself.

And Henry broke. "I needed you, Rand." His body began to shake. "I was there for you. Why weren't you there for me?"

Those words hit Rand harder than all the other hurts he'd experienced the last several hours. He'd failed the only real friend he had. Searching for the means to make things right despite knowing they could never be right again, he pulled Henry into his arms.

Henry leaned limply against him. "I needed you, man." He buried his eyes against Rand's shoulder. "I needed you." He pushed hard against Rand's chest, staggered back a few steps, and dropped silently out of sight.

"No . . . " Shaking off a stupor, Rand dropped to hands and knees and peered over the edge. Henry's body lay far below, bent and mangled, striking an odd pose.

"Henry?" His lower lip quivered. "God, no. Henry?" He

searched for a path down, some way to help his friend in case he was somehow still alive.

Reason told him it could not be so. "What do I do? Henry . . ." He looked around for someone to help him, but there was no one. Just like there had been no one that night or the day after. He and Henry had only had each other.

And now?

A fury like nothing he'd ever felt before rose swiftly with him. He punched the ground, clawed at the dirt, and roared at the sky. "I'll kill them! I'll fucking kill them all!"

The power that came with his rage poured out of him as quickly as it had come. He was weak again. He could do nothing. He collapsed to the ground. "God . . . anyone . . . please," he mumbled between sobs. "Give me the strength to make them pay."

Rand could only recall bits and pieces of his walk down the mountain. He had some vague idea that he might find help or justice in Clifton Heights or one of the other nearby towns and had just started putting one foot in front of the other. Somehow, he'd had enough sense to avoid the campus police. They had never broken up an Alpha party, no matter how many underage drinkers were present. At some point, he'd been shuffled into a car and driven an indeterminable amount of time as he sat trapped in his mind, reliving the events of the last two days. He must have walked for hours, yet Henry's suicide seemed only moments ago, that particular memory replaying repeatedly like looped tape. His friend's final words chided him with every step. *I needed you.*

"He needed me."

"What?" asked a heavyset man with a campaign hat tilted forward over dark hair, dark eyes, and pockmarked cheeks.

Rand had been vaguely aware of his presence, asking questions for at least the last twenty minutes. He had introduced himself as Deputy Sheriff Tewksbury or something similar. Rand was having a difficult time concentrating on anything the officer said. The cop looked vaguely familiar, but Rand's scattered mind left no room to puzzle out where he might have seen the man before. Compared to losing Henry, all else seemed unimportant.

"Nothing," Rand muttered.

"You said they made a video? Can I see it?"

With mechanical motions, Rand opened his phone and clicked on the post. An error message replaced what had previously been an active link. "I don't understand. It was right here."

Deputy Tewksbury ripped the phone from his hand. "Well, it's not there now."

"You don't believe me?"

Tewksbury stiffened. "It's not that." He sighed. "Look, I'll level with you, kid. I haven't seen the video, but if you were unconscious like you say you were, then it may not play out like you think. Add to that the amount of alcohol you told me you had to drink, the fact that you washed away any physical evidence we might have been able to take, and that your only witness is a homosexual who you say jumped to his death—"

"He's down there now. Go look if you don't believe me."

"I'm just saying there're some obstacles to proving a crime took place. And without that video, it's your word against theirs, and your story is that you were unconscious and don't remember a thing."

"You can get the video . . . a-a-and witnesses! It already had like a hundred views."

Tewksbury leaned forward and lowered his voice. "It's more than just that. Between you and me, you have no idea who you'd be going up against here. If you want my honest advice—and I know this isn't what you want to hear, but it's true—you're probably best off going home and forgetting any of this ever happened."

"Forget . . . " Rand's lower lip trembled. For a few seconds, he couldn't wrap his mind around what he was hearing. Confusion gave way to anger, and he slammed his palm against the deputy's desk. "Forget this ever happened? I will never forget what they did to me and Henry or what Henry did because of it."

The officer raised his hands as if Rand had pointed a gun at him, then he looked around the precinct to see if the outburst had attracted any unwanted attention. "Just . . . keep your voice down. Please. I'm just saying . . . these are not the type of people guys like you and me cross. They will do whatever it takes to protect their children. They might say you pushed your friend off that cliff, and they have the money and power to make something like that stick.

After all, there were only two people at the cliff this morning, and only one came back alive. If you think things are bad now, you haven't thought about just how bad things could be."

He reached over the desk to touch Rand's wrist. Rand yanked his arm away.

The deputy softened. "Look, they could be your friends, too."

"My . . . my *friends*!"

"Again, between you and me, I heard they're preparing you an offer. You know, for your troubles."

Rand gasped. He stared with disbelief at Tewksbury. Then it all made sense. He narrowed his gaze on the deputy. "This 'they' you keep talking about . . . you're one of them, aren't you?" He groaned as he ran his fingers through his hair then leapt to his feet. "Who else is here? Who else can I speak to?" He looked around but only saw one other officer in the tiny precinct. The man's nameplate read 'Potter', and he seemed more concerned with cleaning out his ear with the eraser end of his pencil than anything Rand had to say. Rand would find no friend there.

Tewksbury scowled. "Listen to reason, kid. Don't make things worse for yourself."

Rand laughed. Though he found none of what was happening funny, he couldn't stop himself from snickering even as his chest panged. He glanced about for an escape route then headed for the nearest exit.

As Rand hurried out of the station, Tewksbury called after him. "Take the offer, kid."

The offer awaited Rand as he returned to his room. Upon seeing the Alpha seated on Henry's bed, he snapped. He charged the clean-cut poster child for *GQ*, knocked him flat on the bed, and wrapped his fingers around the young man's neck. Rand squeezed until the frat boy's face went purple.

Still, the young man did not retaliate. Rand recognized him as one of D-Rod's lackeys, but as far as Rand could remember or piece together from the video, this Alpha had not participated in the rape. *Unless* . . . He lessened his grip just enough to allow the young man to speak. "Were you the one who recorded it?"

The Alpha gently tugged Rand's wrists. His voice hoarse, he managed, "No. I had no—" He coughed. "No part in that."

Despite the fact that the young man had twice the muscle Rand had and could probably turn the tables on him at any moment, he showed no hostility or hint of violence. "Please. Can we just talk for a second?"

Rand backpedaled until his shoulders hit the wall. He slid down onto his buttocks, still seething with anger. "Why are you here?"

"I'm sorry we're meeting like this. I'm Patrick. As you know, I'm an Alpha—"

"What the fuck do you want?"

Patrick folded his hands. "To make you an offer."

"Get out."

"Rand, I get that you're angry, but—"

"Angry doesn't quite cut it, asshole. If you don't get the hell out of here in three—"

"Hear me out. That's all I ask."

Rand had no desire to hear anything Patrick had to say, but Patrick barreled forward as Rand considered attacking him again.

"What happened to you was . . . fucked up, to say the least. Fucked beyond anything I could possibly imagine. I had no part in it, and had I known they would take things that far, I would have tried to stop it." Patrick averted his eyes. His cheeks reddened.

Though his words rang with sincerity, Rand still wanted him dead. He wanted much worse for the other Alphas.

"I can't undo what they did, and I can't bring back your friend."

"Henry. His name was Henry."

"Henry. Right. I wish we could go back in time and fix this, but we can't. What I can do, though, is offer you a way out of this mess that will make your life a whole lot easier going forward. We know you're paying your own way here. We can take care of your tuition. Your grades can be bought, as well, paid for by us, of course. Job placements, your pick of the litter after you graduate. We can also give you a weekly allowance that will make your living arrangements as comfortable as you'd like them to be at any on-campus or off-campus location you prefer."

Rand scoffed. "And I bet you'll even make me an Alpha too, huh?"

Apparently, Patrick missed his sarcasm. "No . . . unfortunately.

Alphas must maintain a certain reputation—aggressive leadership, dominance, et cetera. Macho bullshit, for sure, but steeped in tradition. After what happened to you and its rather public disclosure . . . you wouldn't fit with our brand. It's all image and optics and shit I don't want to bore you with . . . "

The disgust must have shown on Rand's face because Patrick trailed off. As he began to stutter out an apology, Rand decided he'd heard enough. "And I suppose the price for all that is my silence? I just ignore what you did to me and Henry? I just forget that my best friend killed himself because of what you did to him?"

Patrick stood, his expression souring. "I did none of those things." He expelled a breath. "But yes, silence is the cost. I know it's a bitter pill to swallow, but think about it." He headed out but paused at the threshold. "Seriously, think about it. What we're offering could be life-changing for you. Otherwise—and this isn't a threat but reality—the school, the fraternity, and the families of the Alphas who . . . violated you . . . have a vested interest in keeping this quiet. They will do whatever is in their considerable power to make sure it stays that way. They own the administration, the board, the local law enforcement, and politicians. The video has been removed, and those who repost are being dealt with swiftly." His arms fell, palms out at his sides. "Let some good for you come out of this horrible situation." He opened the door. "Think about it."

Then he was gone, leaving Rand with only one thing to think about: how to get revenge on the Alphas.

That night, sleep did not come easily. Rand had spent the remainder of the day locked in his room, doing nothing except replaying the events of the last twenty-four hours and dreaming up ways to hurt the Alphas. He hadn't eaten or spoken to anyone, with the exception of a rare call from his father. He'd listened as his father berated him. Apparently, good ol' Dad had seen the video and had also been made an offer, because he was ordering Rand to take it.

"And anyway, what kind of faggot just lies there and takes it up the ass without a fight?"

According to his father, Rand was no Alpha, just a bitch like it had said in the post's title. He must be queer if he lived with a queer. The call had ended with his father telling him not to bother coming home if he didn't take the offer.

Rand hadn't said a word. He could hear his mother crying and pleading for her husband to give her the phone, an act that would likely grant her a few new bruises come morning. If not for her, he would never go back there anyway. If that was what it meant to be an Alpha, to bully and take advantage of the weak, then Rand wondered why he'd ever wanted to be one in the first place.

Because he was weak, and he didn't want to be weak anymore. Henry hadn't been weak, though. Henry had been strong, and he didn't need to be an Alpha to be so. They had taken that from him. They should learn what it was like to feel small.

God, he missed his friend. And when he saw him again that night, Rand hoped at first that the party and suicide had all been some vivid and awful dream. But as he lay in bed, it was Henry who was the dream. He hovered over Rand, his face a ghastly white except for strange markings that resembled war paint. And as he floated, ethereal, his peaceful expression contorted into a mask of rage. Foreign words spewed from his blue-tinged lips. Rand tried to make sense of them, but the language was unlike anything he'd ever heard. All the while, a malice almost alive itself grew behind Henry's black-orb eyes, amplifying with his temper. Rand couldn't shake the chill it sent through him.

Henry's brow furrowed. His gaze intensified, and he fell silent. Pain bored through Rand's forehead as if his friend's stare were actually drilling a hole through it.

Your tongue, Henry said, his lips not moving. His voice echoed as if out of a well or perhaps directly through the unused portions of Rand's brain—inside his head. It sounded low and guttural, nothing at all like Henry's. The tone was devoid of kindness, life, or anything else human. *So strange. Certainly not Mohawk or Mohican. To be sure, I would have tormented you in so many gratifying ways had you even the remotest of connections to those who confined me. How long has it been now?* Henry's eyes glazed over. He worked his jaw, seemingly lost in thought. *Too long . . . The world is not as I left it. No matter.* His gaze again found Rand. *I have seen your mind, boy. Assimilated your ways through your thoughts. I know what is in your heart. We are not so different, you and I.*

As sweat began to pool under his armpits, Rand studied the apparition floating over him. It was not Henry. He didn't know how or why it looked like Henry, only that something else, something sinister, was wearing his friend's skin.

The fear that came with that realization crippled him. Had Henry haunted his dreams, that, he would have been able to comprehend. That, he deserved. Whatever this thing was, wearing his friend like a Halloween costume, was not within his rational mind's realm of understanding. Nor were its motives, which made it all the more terrifying.

"Who . . . W-What are you?"

The Henry-thing laughed. *I am the timeless yet time itself, the devourer of men, the harbinger of oblivion, the conquering wyrm. I am that before which your squabbling kind should kneel and tremble, pray for charity, beg for mercy. I am the great and powerful Oz, the coyote, and the Monster Bear.* He smiled widely, revealing a grin full of pointed teeth. *I would say I am the Alpha and the Omega, but I fear that might strike too close to home for you right now.* It laughed harder at that. When it finished, it fixed Rand with Henry's borrowed crooked smile. *In truth, I have many names. Those before you called me Tawiskaron, one half of the whole, but I existed long before that name was given me. To you, I am simply a friend, here to honor the pact you made when you offered me the life of the one whose body now adorns me.*

"Pact?" Rand propped himself up on his elbows and scooted back against the headboard. "I didn't make any pact with you. I don't want anything to do with you."

You truly have no idea what you have done, do you? You sacrificed this one before my altar. His ancestral blood, though diluted, has given me the strength to come before you as I do now, has unbound my mind so that I might explore beyond the darkness in which I am kept. You have allowed my spirit to act for my body's betterment, without the confines of flesh or stone. I could tear your heart from your chest and keep you alive long enough to watch me eat it, but . . . Its smile grew. *I sense you have more to offer me than this mere sacrifice. So much to delight in! I will honor the pact so crudely made, as it amuses me to do so, and we shall see what other nourishment your heart has to offer.*

"I . . . I don't understand. You want to help me? Do what

exactly?" Rand forced himself to meet the Henry-thing's stare. "Get revenge on the Alphas?"

It chortled. *If that is the limit of your feeble imagination, so be it.*

"It's all I want . . . to avenge you, er, Henry before I join him. If only you were real—"

"I *am* real, boy!" the Henry-thing snapped, using a mouth and vocal cords not meant for its kind. It gnashed its teeth as it leered at Rand and edged closer.

Rand could smell its breath, fetid with rot, like bodies left to decay in a dank dirt cellar. In a wisp, it glided from over Rand to stand at the bedside, a trail of gray smoke following it like a comet's tail.

"Pathetic." The apparition *tsk*ed. "You are ruled by fear, worthy of only my loathing and contempt. Certainly, you are not fit for either adversary or prey, and I doubt you have the strength to even face your enemies, never mind enact your revenge. You are no warrior."

It turned its back to Rand and started for the door slowly, as if giving Rand time to build a retort.

"Wait," Rand said, his voice barely above a whisper.

"Yes?" the Henry-thing asked, its smile all teeth.

"They need to pay for what they did."

The Henry-thing sat beside him on the bed.

Rand scurried farther back, imagining disease and poison in its touch.

The apparition waved a hand in front of Rand's face. "They shall, my boy. They shall."

Rand's eyelids grew heavy. He slid down to his pillow and sank into bed. The Henry-thing lay beside him, its mouth an inch from Rand's ear, whispering endlessly as Rand slipped into darkness.

When he woke in the morning, Rand felt as if he hadn't slept at all. As he threw on some clothes and walked off campus, he could hear the Henry-thing whispering still.

Halloween.

Rand stood around the corner of the frat house, listening. His hood hung over his eyes, casting his face in shadow as he leaned against the cool vinyl siding.

On the porch, Turk was talking with that same officer who'd spoken to Rand after he and Henry were violated. Seeing their profiles side-by-side, Rand could not understand how he hadn't noticed the family resemblance before. The man in the picture on Turk's nightstand and Deputy Tewksbury were one and the same. 'Tewk' was close to Turk; perhaps that was how the Alpha had earned his nickname. Rand couldn't help but smile at his luck.

"It's how you pale faces say: the more the merrier," the Henry imposter said into his ear. It was always beside him, in spirit if not in body, unseen and unheard by anyone except Rand. He understood that the voice he heard might be his own, that he could be losing or might already have lost his mind. But he didn't care. The Henry-thing was granting him the strength, be it real or imagined, to do what needed to be done, what Rand would not have had the strength to do on his own.

"No one's even seen him since he left campus," Deputy Tewksbury said. "The Booneville PD wants him for questioning in his parents' deaths, though right now they're calling it some kind of freak bear attack."

"And you think that queer did it?" Turk snorted. "Come on, Dad."

"How many bears do you know that can close the door behind them?"

"Damn, ain't you a cop?" Turk chuckled. "A gust of wind could have shut the door. Maybe it had one of those automatic closer things."

"It didn't have one of those automatic closer things."

"Well, I know one thing: if that puss shows up here, he'll wish he hadn't."

Deputy Tewksbury placed his hands on his hips and shook his head. "I still don't think the party is such a good idea. My worries may be for nothing, but you should probably keep a low profile until we know if that boy's gonna cause any trouble for us."

"The Halloween party's one of the biggest and best we throw. Ain't no way D-Rod would cancel it, not unless the whole damn house burned down."

"Yeah, I know. I was an Alpha once, too, remember?"

"Once an Alpha, always an Alpha."

The deputy sighed. "Well, I'll be keeping an eye out, and I suggest you boys do, too."

"We will."

"And, son . . . Try not to get caught with any drugs. And definitely don't be mixing anything with alcohol. Some guy back home offed himself that way just this morning. Left a wife and two boys, or one boy . . . It's not important. Point is: I got enough of that shit to clean up in my work life. I don't need it in my personal life, too."

Turk laughed. "Just alcohol for me, Dad."

Deputy Tewksbury shook his head, slapped his thighs, and muttered something Rand couldn't make out. "Be smart for once, will ya?"

"I will, Dad. I will." Turks shuffled his feet. "So . . . what are you doing tonight? Handing out candy?"

"Nah. Baker's got me over at Kaminsky's, making sure no one causes trouble in the corn maze. But I'll be relieved early. Your mom and I were thinking of heading over to FrightFest. Supposed to be a good one this year."

"Not if that same douche is doing it. That guy won't play anything post 1970. And that's when they really started showing tits in horror movies. I bet he's queer."

"Is it really that big of a deal if he is?" Tewksbury huffed. "Anyway, be safe. Call me if you even think that boy might show up. Give Derek and the other boys my number, too." The officer walked back to his patrol car, and the frat boy returned to his roost.

Once he heard the door close, Rand peeked through the cellar window near his feet and found a dark basement. Its near side hosted a washer, a dryer, and discarded gym equipment spread out before him. He couldn't see the opposite side, only that it appeared to be as unoccupied as the rest.

He pressed his foot into the cheap pane, and it cracked as easily as thin ice. He cleared away the bigger shards with his sneaker. Tiny bits of glass embedded in his hands as he wiped away the rest and slid through the small opening onto the washing machine. Before climbing down to the floor, he reached back for his large garbage bag of supplies, which he had to shimmy to get through the window. It hit the washer with a *thunk*, but if anyone upstairs had heard, they made no attempt to investigate.

He searched the basement for a place to hide until the party began. Two storage bins were tucked under the cellar stairs, a space walled off on the opposite side of the stairwell and in back. He dragged them about a foot from the wall and squeezed into the cobweb-infested cubbyhole he'd made, setting his garbage bag in front of him to shield his feet from view.

Barely fifteen minutes had passed when he heard a door open above. A pair of voices, followed by footsteps, trailed down the stairs. As quietly as he could, he leaned forward and reached into his bag while he listened.

"How many more of these we got?" a male asked. Rand did not recognize the voice.

"Just a few more," another said. "Shit, you're lucky I'm helping you at all, pledge."

Pledge? Rand scowled. *Rush isn't even over yet. Hazing and tormenting people is a seasonal sport for these assholes.*

Footsteps drew closer. All that stood between Rand and the two speakers was the low barrier of storage bins, one stacked upon the other. The darkness under the stairs and his garbage bag at his feet provided additional cover but not much.

"Phew!" The pledge whined. "Why does it stink like gasoline down here?"

"Who knows? The sooner we get this done, the sooner we'll be out of here."

The top crate rose. "These two, right?" The pledge grunted as he lifted the storage bin up to his chest, hiding his face from Rand's view. He turned and started back toward the stairs.

The Alpha called Runt bent over to pick up the remaining bin. His gaze met Rand's, and for a second, neither of them moved.

Rand lunged, tripping over the crate and falling into the Alpha. The momentum accelerated his knife toward Runt's neck. The frat brother squeaked as the blade pressed into his skin.

"Get rid of him," Rand hissed. "Or you die."

"Do you need help?" the pledge called from near the top of the stairs.

"N-No," Runt stuttered. "I just . . . jammed my finger. Go and finish setting up. I got this last one."

Rand smiled. He couldn't believe his luck. Runt could have easily gotten away. Until Rand regained his footing, the Alpha was supporting most of Rand's weight. All Runt had to do was back up and run, but fear seemed to have rooted him in place.

Compounding Rand's luck, Runt was just the little bastard he'd been hoping to isolate first. "You recorded it, didn't you?" He pressed the knife harder against Runt's Adam's apple, matching Runt's every step backward with a step forward of his own.

"What are you talking about? I didn't do anything. Who are you? What do you want?"

Rand tore off his hood. "Perhaps you don't recognize me without my makeup on."

Runt's face paled. "Y-You . . . I-I-I didn't want to. D-Rod made me do it! I didn't touch you."

A hazy picture flashed across Rand's mind, an image of a boy about Runt's size holding a rectangular object. A textbook. He massaged his forehead, and the resolution became a little clearer. "You hit me with a book?"

Runt drove the heel of his palm into Rand's elbow and twisted away from the knife. He cried out as the blade dug a shallow gash across his neck. "Help!"

He tried to get by Rand, and had almost made it when Rand grabbed him by the shirt and yanked him back with one hand, simultaneously driving the knife to the hilt into Runt's back with the other. He assumed he hit a lung, because Runt immediately began wheezing and coughing up blood. The Alpha spun and fell.

Rand fell on him. "This is for Henry." He drove the blade past Runt's raised hands and into the frat boy's chest. More blood sputtered from Runt's mouth. After a moment, he went still, his eyes gazing blankly up at the crossbeams.

"You were right," Rand said as the Henry-thing appeared beside him. "It's so much easier the second time."

The Henry-thing ran its blackened tongue over a sharp incisor. "And so much more filling, er, *ful*filling." It placed a hand on Rand's shoulder. "Admit it. You rather enjoyed that, didn't you?"

Rand scowled. "He deserved much worse." He glanced at the milky, almost-translucent hand on his shoulder. He could feel the apparition's touch, which was unnaturally cold but weighted and present all the same. That meant the thing posing as Henry had to be real. *Doesn't it? Or can an insane person* feel *hallucinations, too?* He shook his head. "Whatever. Let's just get this done."

Rand opened his garbage bag of surprises and withdrew a relic from one of his father's many failed start-ups: a pesticide sprayer. The tank was the double-strapped kind meant to be worn like a backpack. He slung it over his shoulders then walked around the bascment, spraying its contents into the rafters and along the support columns.

"Would it not be better to spray that substance upstairs?" the Henry-thing asked. "While I see the logic in bringing down this structure from the bottom up, much of your . . . fuel . . . " it said the word as if trying it out, "is wasted down here. How will it ignite down here if we are up there and you have none left to spray?"

"That's what the costume is for."

The Henry-thing snarled. "You're not listening. You are wasting all your precious fuel where it is not likely to hurt the most people."

"You mean the most Alphas."

"Yes, them. Of course."

Rand pursed his lips. "You've obviously never been to a college party. There will be plenty of fuel upstairs."

"As you say, Rand." It bowed its head. "I have much to learn of this new world, it seems."

Rand paused, a question lingering on his tongue. But he let it die there in the silence. He didn't really want to know what wore Henry's skin or whether it was real or imagined. He knew what his father had called it—a demon, the devil even—when it had given Rand the strength to tear out dear ol' Daddy's throat. His father had seen it, even if he had been looking directly at Rand at the time. In any event, Rand could not possibly have done what he had with bare hands alone. This beast had claws. So, a demon was Rand's best guess. For once, he and his father could agree on something. It was too late for his father to agree to anything, though. Too bad— they would have also agreed that all stories concerning human and demon interaction had one thing in common: dealings with them always came with a cost.

So what? If it meant avenging Henry and either getting back what he'd lost of himself or taking from the Alphas equal payment with interest, he would gladly pay the price. And anyway, he was fairly certain he was already damned.

As if reading his thoughts, the Henry-thing said, "I will do all that you have asked of me. All that I have promised and more."

The creature or manifestation or whatever it was had repeated this mantra many times as Rand had tried to find sleep on cold ground, beneath stars, beside the cliff, as he imagined Henry had the night before his death. Except for a short time after granting

Rand the strength to destroy his father, when the might-be demon had faded nearly out of existence, it had kept its promises and remained by his side. Fear had marred its expression then, and for a moment it had truly looked like Henry right before he fell. It had flickered in and out of reality. But it had re-solidified soon after and had never left him. It remained always at Rand's side, always whispering in his ear.

Rand only wished he could remember what had happened to his mother, or if she'd even been there. She must have felt so relieved when she realized that abusive bastard was no longer in her life. He smiled at the thought of her having a better future now without her husband in it.

As for his own future, he gave it no thought beyond the night. It would be a Halloween like no other. The music came on upstairs and quickly grew in volume. Whistling, Rand stuffed the body and his knife into the dryer then changed into his Halloween costume.

His costume was a hit. A couple of sequels to the original movie had been released within the last decade, both offering a precedent for a female Ghostbuster, and Rand owned it. Thanks to the ecto-goggles over his eyes, a ghost trap strapped to his hip, a blond wig made from real human hair tied in pigtails, and the most obnoxious shade of red lipstick he could find, guys and gals flocked to him as soon as he hit the scene. Encased within a hollowed-out, authentic-looking proton pack, his pesticide sprayer sloshed with all sorts of alcohol and mixers pilfered from the house's stock. This trivial feat of engineering made him a life of the party as he squirted its contents into the mouths of many a college student eager to get shitfaced. He kept to the kitchen, where he could hide in plain sight and reload as necessary.

For the second time in his life, Rand had worn drag. For the second time, he had fully Naired. His tan jumpsuit, cinched at the waist to create an illusion of hips he didn't have, was open at his neck to reveal as much skin as possible, along with a bit of his stuffed, lipstick-matching bra. A lace choker partly hid his Adam's apple, and his slight hands were glossed and manicured. He was hot enough to fool the desperate, evidenced by the handsy vampire who kept trying to lay claim to him until Rand finally told him to fuck off. In his normal voice, it seemed to do the trick.

Rand had no interest in vampires. He was hunting another monster altogether—werewolves. And the Alphas would surely don fangs and fur. An hour into the party, not a single brother had made an appearance.

Maybe they're waiting on Runt. Rand didn't mind. He was patient.

The Henry-thing at his side was not. "The least you could have done was kept the poison in your tank. We could have killed a few of these imbeciles while we waited."

"We're not here for them," Rand replied, one hand covering his mouth as if he were yawning while the other arm stretched behind a giant M&M to squirt alcohol into the corner.

"But if they burn—"

"They burn."

"What?" a candy-costumed partygoer asked.

Rand raised the sprayer. "I said your turn."

The M&M opened her mouth, accepted the alcohol, and choked it down. "Whoa," she said, her eyes shimmering. "Thanks."

As she fled into the living room, leaving Rand to himself, he glanced at the Henry-thing. It leaned against the counter beside him, its black orb eyes twinkling with starlight. Wormy lips revealed a shark-like grin. As if to itself, it said, "I've waited this long. I can wait a little longer."

Rand heard the words but dismissed them. He winced as a twinge of fear shook his resolve. The vagueness around the question of the cost and consequences for the help he'd accepted lingered like an unpleasant odor. But the time to worry about that had long passed. Dwelling on it served no purpose. *What's done is done.*

Enthusiastic applause came from the living room. Their gracious hosts must finally have arrived. The Henry-thing trembled with anticipation, energy vibrating off it in infectious waves. They fed Rand's own jitters, but he kept his station in the kitchen. As eager as he was, he had little room for error. He was outnumbered and would be outmatched by any one of them in a fair fight. And although Rand had no intention of playing fair, dividing and conquering seemed the wisest play. He took deep breaths as he told himself to remain calm and stick to the plan.

Nevertheless, he did allow himself a peek. Raising his goggles onto his forehead, he watched as twelve Alphas dressed as werewolves of a variety of shapes, sizes, and fur colors cleared the floor. The music stopped and was replaced by mind-numbing techno music. The Alphas broke out into a ridiculous dance routine that included the Running Man, the Sprinkler, and some Flossing, which most of them couldn't do. Rand, having tried it himself before, had to admit it was a lot harder than it looked. Apparently easily impressed, the crowd cheered them on.

As the performance devolved into a jumbled mess of stumbling, gyration, and parodied sex acts, Rand tried to determine which of the costumed beasts were his primary targets. One Alpha wore a yellow basketball jersey with Beavers, the apparent team name or perhaps another sexual reference, and 42 written on its face. Another looked like the classic Lon Chaney version of the creature from the old Universal film. A third wore a cop uniform. Rand didn't even try to figure out the probably obscure reference. Had he seen one made up like the werewolf from *Ginger Snaps*, his favorite werewolf movie, he might have given that Alpha a pass, unless it turned out to be Turk or D-Rod.

The biggest of the lot, though, looked like he could be from *Underworld* or maybe *The Howling*. That had to be Turk. He was the only one Rand could identify, but that was as good a start as any. He studied the various bottles laid out on the counter, thinking he could use a drink and despising himself for wanting it.

The Henry-thing's clammy hands massaged his shoulders. "No need, friend. I will give you courage and strength."

Rand huffed. While all eyes were still on the Alphas, he sprayed down the rest of the kitchen, soaking cotton-ball cobwebs, dangling bats and spiders, and wind-chime-like skeletons with his party mix. He even managed to spray alcohol into the living room as the basketball werewolf opted to do a keg stand, drawing more raucous applause. The scorn Rand felt for all of them at that moment, not only the Alphas, contorted his face into a sneer, even though he knew if he could go back and undo what had happened, he would be cheering right alongside the mindless masses. *Well on my way to becoming like my father. Well, Dad, I hope you can see me now.*

The stream from his sprayer ran down to a trickle, and he reloaded the tank, barely making a dent in the fraternity's stock. Students came and went as he worked, and not a single one questioned him. Instead, they complimented him on his costume and left with drinks Rand poured, leaving him plenty of time to ponder how to isolate Turk. He would worry about how to pick D-Rod out of the crowd if he succeeded with the big man.

"*When* you succeed, Rand," the Henry-thing said. "This night is ours."

Rand ignored it. *Whoever barks out commands, that'll be him.*

The apparition snickered. "Barks."

"If you can read my thoughts, why do I bother speaking to you?"

"I am pleased to converse in any manner by which you feel the most comfortable."

"How incredibly civil of you."

"I do not understand."

"Never mind. Can you use your—I don't know, your powers to detect which one is D-Rod?"

"And which of my powers might I use to accomplish that?"

"I don't freaking know." Rand exhaled. "Can you . . . smell him or something?"

"Smell him?" The Henry-thing cackled. "In this form, I do not even have a sense of smell . . . yet." It stroked its chin. "I think your plan to isolate Turk is a good one. Why not start there and see how the night unfolds?"

Rand rolled his eyes. "Yeah, but how?"

"You know how, Rand. It has been your plan from the start."

Rand huffed. "Some help you are. Are you sure you can at least prevent them from leaving? Keep the doors locked?"

"I promised you that much, did I not? I always keep my word."

The Alpha antics apparently at an end, the party resumed its normal course. Partygoers squeezed into the house like field mice through dime-sized holes, nesting everywhere, bumping into each other, and spilling drinks. With his goggles over his eyes, limiting his peripheral vision, Rand intermingled with those who entered the kitchen. When the wolves came by for drinks, they were always in packs, and Rand could not decipher any details that would help him discern who was who.

Another hour passed with Rand wondering if he would ever get an opportunity. He considered lighting the place up and hoping for the best. Maybe he would get lucky and take out a few frat boys unable to escape. The cops would have a hard time discovering the cause of the fire, and his costumed ass would be long gone before they even suspected arson. *Live to play another day.*

With every passing moment, the Alphas were doing themselves in with drink. A better opportunity might never come. The cover of Halloween offered him anonymity he wouldn't have any other night of the year. Wearing a costume in November would just make him stand out more, not less.

No. They die tonight. Simmering, he raised his ecto-goggles and readied himself for a more aggressive approach. He moved toward the entrance to the living room and batted his long eyelash extensions at Turk, who was standing in the middle of the room. He appeared to be looking Rand's way, but it was impossible to tell for certain through his rubber snout. As the Alpha stepped in his direction, every nerve ending in Rand's body flashed out a signal. *This is it! This is it!*

A scantily clad female with fairy wings slid her hand into Turk's massive claw. She drew him across the floor to the stairs.

"No."

"This could be your opportunity. It appears this winged creature is isolating him for you."

"She's not a target."

"Oh, enough already!" The Henry-thing hissed. "Do you honestly care?"

Rand peered deep inside himself for an answer to that question. He found he was lacking, ready to admit to himself that he would kill everyone in that house so long as he took the Alphas down with them.

But it didn't change the fact that a small part of him thought he *should* care. Henry would have cared. *And if I'm truly doing this for Henry—*

"You are missing your chance," the Henry-thing spat.

Rand pushed his way through skeletons and zombies, slutty nurses and horror nurses and slutty horror nurses. He raced up the stairs and grabbed the fairy girl by the arm a bit more roughly than he had intended as Turk opened the door to his bedroom.

His wolf head turned toward Rand. "Who's this?" he asked, his words slurring. "Does your friend want to join? There's plenty of Turk to go around."

"Back off, ho," Fairy Girl said, ripping her arm free. "What the fuck?"

"Just a sec'," Rand said, his falsetto voice pleading. "We'll be right in."

Turk staggered into the room and sat on the bed. He began removing his costume. "You two better hurry up, or I'll take it out on your asses." He giggled so hard he snorted.

Rand met Fairy Girl's eyes and blurted out the first thing that popped into his head. "He raped me at the last party." The truth of the words hit him like a punch to the gut. He had to look away to hide the wetness that sprang to his eyes.

The girl placed one hand on her hip and pushed out her lower lip with her tongue. "Girl, it's not rape if I'm willing." Her tone was sobering.

"And gave me HPV."

"God, who doesn't have that?"

"And . . . and . . . " He lowered his head. "HIV."

At that moment, Rand realized he hadn't gotten checked for STDs after that night. He hadn't considered that the lies he was telling might actually be true. The past few weeks had been focused solely on taking from the Alphas what they'd taken from him, spurred on by the Henry-thing's incessant whispers. The thought that he might be permanently tainted, not just emotionally but physically, by those sons of bitches gripped him with such immediate hate and despair that his mouth opened in a silent scream.

His pain must have shown on his face. For the first time, the Fairy Girl showed some semblance of real human emotion. "Shit . . . Fuck . . . " She squeezed Rand's hand. "Thank you . . . and . . . " She pulled him into a hug. "I'm sorry."

"Still waiting!" Turk called.

Fairy Girl scurried away. Rand summoned the strength to compose himself and stepped into the room. He pulled the door closed behind him and watched as the Henry-thing, giving a mischievous grin, locked it, and nodded.

Careful not to dislodge his wig, Rand tugged off his goggles. He looked around the room, not really remembering what had happened there except for waking up disoriented, with that feeling that something was wrong and not yet knowing what. But having seen the video, he had seen it all. His hate made playing the role so much easier, but his feelings would be hard to disguise.

With his back turned to Turk as he took cleansing breaths, he slid off his backpack and unzipped his jumpsuit, letting the top fall around his waist. He slid his arms through the cheerleader top he'd been wearing like a sash underneath his stuffed bra, adjusted his stuffing, and turned, keeping his eyes downcast.

"Where's, uh, Tifa or . . . whatever the fuck her name is?" Turk asked.

Keeping his voice low, Rand stepped out of his jumpsuit and threw it and the ghost trap onto the bed beside Turk. Smoothing out his skirt, he said, "She wasn't woman enough to handle you. But I am."

He jumped on top of Turk, knocking him flat and straddling him while pressing his lips against the drunk Alpha's. He resisted the temptation to bite off Turk's probing tongue and break the fingers gripping his ass. Everything about the contact sent revulsion through Rand, so fierce it made his skin crawl. But he forced himself to endure it a little longer as he worked his advantage, planting kisses up the side of Turk's neck until he was close enough to whisper, "Lie back, and I promise I'll show you an animal like you wouldn't believe."

Rapists like Turk craved power and control. Rand wasn't sure if the frat boy would willingly give them up. He lacked the strength to force Turk to do anything, so deception had seemed his only option. If things went badly, he would have to take Turk out as quickly and quietly as possible, a better death than the prick deserved.

But the alcohol must have been hitting Turk hard, because he was all too happy to be compliant, a big, sloppy grin plastered over his dumbass face. He pulled down his boxers and flopped back onto the pillow. "I want your mouth first."

"Oh, you're gonna get it all. Believe me." Rand smiled, not at the erection that stood so near to him—he wanted to twist it off with his bare hands and feed it to Turk—but at the Alpha's compliance. He ran his fingers gently up Turk's chest and over one arm as he lifted it and placed it near the headboard. Pinning Turk's wrist in place with one hand, Rand opened and dug into his ghost trap with the other. He pulled out a pair of handcuffs. Slowly, so as to not raise any alarms in the drunken behemoth's alcohol-addled brain, he clasped one cuff around Turk's wrist and the other around the bedpost. After tearing the rubber cord from the trap itself, he tied Turk's other wrist to the opposite post.

"Ow." Turk drooled. His eyes rolled back in his head. "Kinky but, uh, kinda tight."

"You'll forget all about that in a second." Rand laughed, surprised by just how genuine it sounded. "Oh, the things I am going to do to you."

Still straddling Turk, he fumbled for the contents of his ghost trap. His fingers found a bottle, pressed open the top, and squirted its contents liberally onto Turk's stomach. He then massaged the cream-colored lotion all over Turk's chest. "How does that feel?"

Turk groaned with pleasure, spit bubbles popping between his lips. "You came prepared, didn't you, you dirty little slut?"

Rand snickered. "I certainly did." He squirted more lotion onto Turk's stomach and began working it lower and lower. He smeared it over Turk's pelvic area and thighs, all the while smiling as he focused on what was to come and not on what he still had to do to get there. He made sure the lotion fully covered Turk's genitals, pushed as much as he could into the Alpha's urethra, then slowly wiped the excess off on Turk's legs, biding his time. He sat back and waited.

"Well?" Turk raised his head off the pillow. The handcuffs rattled against the wood. "Massages are good and all, but didn't I tell you to use your mouth? Don't make me tell you twice now."

"Easy, big boy. I'm not through with you yet. I just want you crazed with anticipation." Rand lowered his gaze to Turk's chest. The skin looked red and inflamed, his nipples a dark purple. *Any moment now.* He squirted another glob into his hands.

"Hey." Turk pressed his chin against his chest, his eyes looking down his nose at his body. "What is that shit? It kinda itches. I'd better not be allergic . . . and my nipples . . . God, that stings."

"It should," Rand said, no longer whispering or disguising his voice. "It's Nair."

"Nair? What the fuck?" Turk raised his head. "Untie me now, bitch, or I swear to God, the Alphas will be running a train on you every night for the rest of your college career. I'll—"

"You'll what?" Rand straddled Turk's chest and gnashed his teeth. He tore off his wig and leaned over the frat boy. "Look at me." He grabbed Turk's chin and directed his eyes toward his. "Look at me! What could you possibly do to me that you haven't already?"

Turk's gaze narrowed. Slowly, comprehension came, and his eyes widened.

"Yes!" Rand was mad with hate and glee. He reveled in the moment. "You see me now, don't you?"

Turk turned his head toward the door. "Help!"

"Now you see me—"

"Help!"

"Now you don't." Rand shoved globs of Nair into Turk's eyes.

Turk screamed. As he opened his mouth, Rand jammed the bottle down his throat. Lubed up on its sides, it slid in easily as Rand hammered it down with the heel of his palm. Turk thrashed and bucked. The headboard groaned.

Still, Rand hammered, losing himself in the violence. Rage like nothing he'd ever felt before empowered his every strike as the Henry-thing cheered him on. The corners of Turk's lips split grotesquely. Blood trickled from fresh wounds, creating a sad-clown frown.

Thick strands of snot exploded from Turk's nose as he tried to breathe through the pain. But Rand wasn't done. He reached into his ghost trap for a twelve-inch souvenir bat from a minor league baseball game he'd attended back when life was simpler. He'd doubled its one-inch width by smearing it with glue and rolling it in broken glass. After coating it with as much Nair as he could, nicking his hand in multiple places, Rand hopped off the bed.

As Turk tried to work the bottle out of his mouth with his jaw, he kicked blindly at Rand, who couldn't get in close enough to insert his tool. After a few jabs at Turk's buttocks with no success, he called the Henry-thing for help. The creature began to fade as Rand filled with raw, unnatural power. With the flow of energy, something more came, feelings that were not his own, abhorrence for a world of men and a brother's love for them. With all the force of will fueled by that extreme animosity, Rand struck again and either found his entry point or created a new one.

Turk's eyes, red and tearing, bulged open. Even muffled by the bottle, his cry of agony was likely loud enough to be heard over the music downstairs. He thrashed with renewed vigor. The headboard post cracked, and the cuffs cut into his wrist, shredding flesh and vein.

For the briefest moment, and to his utter surprise, Rand pitied Turk. But it vanished in a flash as wood splintered, and a meaty fist swung wildly in his direction. One hand free, Turk wrenched the bottle from his mouth. His gritted teeth were stained with blood. With strength that would have previously terrified Rand, he tore the cord from his other wrist. Through eyes like bloodied milk, he searched for Rand but couldn't seem to find him.

"I'm gonna kill you," he managed through gasps and sniffles, his chest heaving. "You are so fucking dead."

The threat sounded weak to Rand, as if torment had crippled the Alpha's spirit. "Maybe." Rand scoffed. "But I won't be dying alone, asshole."

Turk charged at the sound of his voice. Rand dodged easily despite the limited space. Quietly, he slid the backpack over his shoulders and sprayed Turk's back with alcohol. "Just in case Nair isn't flammable."

Turk didn't even seem to notice. His blind attack had sent him sprawling onto his desk. "I can't see. I can't see." He no longer seemed concerned with Rand or revenge and appeared to have forgotten Rand was even in the room. Arms out like Frankenstein's monster, as naked as the day he was born and with a small bat jutting from his backside, he stumbled along the wall toward the door, found the knob, and shambled into the hall.

Rand shook off the shock of what he'd just done, swallowing the bile in his throat. The night was not yet over. He grabbed the final item he'd stored in his ghost trap, a utility lighter with a superglued snap-on grip so that he could fix the lighter to his sprayer. He'd been afraid the flame would ignite the alcohol inside the tank, but everything seemed to work in practice. Either that, or he'd been lucky. *If I go up, let's just hope I can give D-Rod a big hug when I do.*

"Help me. Help me." Apparently, Turk's cries had drawn the attention of a few students. Some giggled while others covered their mouths as they gasped and pointed. It triggered memories of Rand's walk back to the dorm. Turk's was much shorter. When he reached the end of the landing. he plummeted down the stairs.

Someone cut the music, and the room erupted in laughter. The crowd no doubt thought a drunk naked guy had gone for a tumble. Silence followed. Then a scream. As all eyes watched Turk, Rand moved unhindered to the bottom of the stairs. He clicked the lighter and lit the Alpha up. Then came the real screams.

A clammy hand, no longer translucent, fell on Rand's shoulder. "And he thought that substance you rubbed on him burned."

Rand shrugged off the creature's touch. As panic overtook the crowd, they rushed for the exits. The people in the back slammed into those in front before they could open the doors, and Rand's own panic intensified. D-Rod could not be allowed to escape. "Henry! The doors!"

With blurry speed, the Henry-thing flashed through students to the front door, then out of the room, then back at Rand's side. "They are locked," it said, grinning with the zeal of a child on Christmas morning. "As promised."

As if to prove the Henry-thing's point, the crowd smartened enough to allow those in front to try the door. No matter which way they turned the knob or swung the dead bolt, it would not open, sealed shut by some force Rand couldn't understand and didn't want to. Had the masses of students been thinking more clearly, they might have taken Rand out easily enough. Someone still upstairs might have jumped him from behind. But none of them cared about their fellow man. They only cared for themselves.

He lifted the makeshift flamethrower and aimed it at the students fighting with the door. "Henry was better than all of you," he said to no one in particular. But he didn't fire.

The students took the chance to flee. Some shrank into corners or behind furniture while others ran from the room. The rug around Turk's now-still body was smoldering. Rand skirted the growing blaze as he moved into the living room.

Three Alphas came in to meet him, lining up horizontally, each with a yard or so between him and his brother as if squaring off for another dance sequence. They were spreading out, flanking, and preparing to rush him. The basketball werewolf stood to Rand's left. A tall werewolf in a grayish V-neck sweater, with yellow eyes, fangs, and what looked like a hipster beard and sideburns stained in blood, took the center spot. And to his right stood Patrick, who'd resembled Seth Green to begin with, decked out as Oz from *Buffy the Vampire Slayer*. Rand had liked that show. The character, not so much.

He liked Patrick even less. The Alpha took a step toward Rand. "Put that thing down, Rand. It's not too late to make this—"

Rand torched him. Patrick howled as the flames encased the fake hair on his face and melted the glue that held it there. It smelled worse than real hair burning. The brother had been fourth on his list. Whether he died or not was not crucial. Rand would have been content with severe disfigurement.

He only had a moment to appreciate Patrick's pain before the tall werewolf rushed him. He grabbed the sprayer's nozzle and shifted it upward, his gloves apparently insulating his hands from the heat as Rand shot fire onto the ceiling. Ash and embers rained down around them. Those still hiding in the room dispersed, all except the third Alpha, who seemed confused as to what he should do. Had he joined the fray, Rand would have been bested easily. As it was, he had only managed to wrestle the tall Alpha to a standstill, the awkward claw mitts likely hindering the frat boy's size advantage.

It wouldn't last. Rand's strength was waning. "Who are you supposed to be, anyway?" he grunted, trying to distract the Alpha as he willed the Henry-thing to help him.

"Spader. *Wolf.* Man . . . fuck you!" The Alpha searched for a comrade as fire spread around them. "D-Rod! Help!"

The basketball werewolf broke out of his apparent fog. He took one step toward the struggling pair, paused, then shook his head. He turned and dove through the picture window.

D-Rod! Number One on Rand's list was getting away. "Henry! Where the fuck are you?"

"Yes?" The Henry-thing stood behind the Alpha, looking taller, thicker, more solid, and less like Henry than it ever had. It inhaled deeply, its eyes closing and its salacious grin widening as it turned its head up to the blazing ceiling, basking in its euphoric light. "All this terror . . . all this misery . . . You have done well, Rand." It fixed its black orbs upon him. "Kill them! Kill them all!"

Its arm and hand elongated, stretching like taffy and re-forming until it resembled a claw like that of a gigantic hairless bear. It raked that claw down the Alpha's back. He cried out in agony then fell prone. Gashes scored his back so deeply that Rand could see his spine.

"He . . . He wasn't on the list."

"Neither were any of them," the Henry-thing said, waving his bloody claw.

Rand glanced about the room. Partygoers clambered over the windowsill, and the student at the bottom of the pile had gone limp and leaked from his midsection. Others rolled on the ground, trying to put out burning clothes but only spreading the flames to the alcohol-drenched carpet. Still others cowered, curled up in balls with their faces buried in their costumes, waiting for someone to save them as they sucked in the poison air.

And D-Rod had gotten away. Rand tried to see out the broken window but caught no sign of the yellow jersey. He coughed. The smoke stung his eyes. He could no longer see very far ahead of him, much less outside. Under cover of the smoke, he held his breath and felt his way back toward the cellar door, stepping over and on top of others. Hands reached for him. Voices begged for help. Rand heeded none.

"He's gone." Rand gulped down the moist cellar air, which was hazy but not yet ablaze. He began to cry, doubtful he would ever get another chance at the Alphas' alpha. "I'm so sorry, Henry."

He sprayed fire all over the basement before ditching his tank and retrieved his butcher knife from the dryer. Hoping to find D-Rod outside, he crawled out the same window through which he'd entered. As he rounded the front of the house, something hard connected with the side of his head. He dropped the knife as darkness claimed him.

"You can still stop this, Rand." Henry's voice, as gentle and kind as it had always been before his final moments, called to him from behind closed eyes.

As he opened them and the world slowly came into focus, Rand lay on his back on the fraternity house's front lawn. A conflagration silently burned the house to cinders—no crackles, no screams, no nothing. Just the warmth of a large bonfire and the deeper warmth of a friend.

But if I'm deaf, how can I hear him?

Rand looked up at Henry, who appeared as he had in life, his eyes radiant and alive. The imposter's lines of contempt were absent from his expression. But he knew, inexplicably yet undeniably, that this being was neither Henry nor the creature who'd helped him avenge his roommate. The only difference between the being standing over Rand and the real Henry was that the warm glow it radiated was actually tangible.

It offered Rand a hand up. "You are not deaf. Merely dreaming."

Rand took its hand. "You're not Henry."

"No." It grinned, borrowing Henry's crooked smile but with

none of the malice the Henry-thing had borne. "But it pleases me to think men like Henry are still part of this world. Men like you may yet become, Rand. You may think you are lost, and surely you have strayed from the noble warrior's path. You have done things your heart knows Henry would not have condoned. But where there yet is life, there may be redemption."

"I've killed people." Rand studied the grass. "Not all of them deserved it. I don't deserve redemption."

"My brother's grip is strong, young friend. Your will is stronger. You must break his hold on you before it is too late. With all your hate, all your rage, with all the pain and misery and death you cause, he grows stronger."

"Brother?"

"He who has led you astray. We are but a dichotomy, light and dark, kindred spirits who have lived alongside the inhabitants of this land for ages before your kind. What I seek to raise up, he seeks to destroy. A cunning deceiver, he feeds off destruction, chaos, and misery. Make no mistake: to walk with him is to advance derision and conflict that will consume all. It will consume you."

"What do I do?"

"Let go of your hate and your desire for revenge. Survive the night. Feed him no more. I am here now in spirit but will come in body with the dawn."

"And just let D-Rod get away with what he did?"

"If justice is not served in this world, it may yet be claimed in the next. Your justice hurts you more than it does him, and like you, he may yet find his true path."

"And be forgiven?" Rand growled. "I will never forgive him. He should be tortured for all eternity for what he's done."

"Maybe so. But is morning so long a wait when eternity is the end? I only ask that you delay your judgment and let time decide if you shall forego it entirely. My brother has grown too strong at a time when the veil is thinnest. If freed, the pain you have suffered will spread like a sickness. Your wrath is nothing against his." The spirit laid a hand on Rand's shoulder, sending warmth tingling through his tired muscles. "I will do all I can for you, but you must not give in to him or despair before first light." The figure began to flicker like a dying light bulb. "My strength wanes in his shadow. I will banish him again on the morrow, but you must feed him no more."

Rand came to in the back seat of a police cruiser. A conversation between the large man driving and the passenger beside him ensued.

"I'm just saying he deserves worse," the passenger said, his voice familiar. "He killed your son."

"Don't you think I know that?" the driver shouted, whipping his head to his right to glare at the passenger. Sitting behind the passenger, Rand got a good look at the driver's face as he turned: Deputy Tewksbury. He did some quick math in his head. Everything added up to his being arrested, at best. It sounded as though the person seated in front of Rand objected to that.

He tried to reach for the door, only to find his hands cuffed behind his back. A form blinked into existence beside him. Its sudden appearance and the mutation of its features forced a quiet squeak out of Rand's mouth. He shifted farther to his right, away from the creature.

The Henry-thing had become far more thing than Henry. It had nearly doubled in size, so large that its neck and shoulders pressed against the roof, its head drooping in front of its chest like a vulture's. Its black orb eyes had grown into portals, vertically slit vortexes stretching upward like bullets standing on end, flickering with pale lights lost in a vast darkness. Its nose and mouth protruded to form a stubby snout. Interlocking teeth jutted like stalactites and stalagmites from a massive jaw, each tooth sharp and treacherous. Even with such a menacing maw, it still appeared to be smiling, less shark-like and more piranha-like than before, no doubt lusting for a feeding frenzy.

Rand shrank from that grin, heeding the words of the dream entity. Whether he'd really been visited by a benevolent spirit or had merely experienced the ramblings of an unconscious mind, he understood that the thing sitting beside him was evil, plain and simple. The fact that he had used it as a tool for revenge perhaps made him evil as well. *Or is it using me?*

The philosophical point seemed moot. Rand could do nothing in his current predicament and was heading off either to jail or to some place much, much worse. The Henry-thing extended an elongated arm, taut and corpse-like with too many joints, and rested a veiny mat of a hand on Rand's leg. It was webbed and membranous like a frog's but much thicker. Each impossibly long finger ended with a curved, scythe-like claw.

"What are you?" Rand asked.

"Do you care?" The thing raised its eyebrows, one of the few remaining parts of it that still seemed human. "To you, I am a friend, just as I have been."

Rand was dubious but low on options. Keeping his voice to a whisper, he said, "Then help me . . . friend. D-Rod got away. I can't go to jail until—"

"Oh, you won't be going to jail, dickhead." The passenger turned in his seat and stared through the partition. D-Rod had removed much of his costume and makeup. He sneered with confidence, appearing not to notice the monstrous creature sitting right next to Rand. "And you're damn right I got away. Did you really think a little faggot like you could take me down?"

Rand looked to his left. The Henry-thing was gone, if it had ever been there at all. "Then . . . where are you taking me?"

"Don't you worry about it, bitch. You'll find out soon enough."

Deputy Tewksbury, who kept his gaze forward through the entire exchange, hit his sirens. The swirling red and blue illuminated the woods that stretched out on both sides. A moment later, students dropping bottles and joints ran past the car as it trolled forward. Rand slapped the window, trying to get their attention, but no one even slowed. He sighed, uncertain what he'd hoped to accomplish anyway.

He shuffled to his left and peered between the seats. In the headlight beams, he saw a moonlit sky. Before it, a familiar railing.

D-Rod leered back at him. "Yeah, that's right. You know this place, don't you?" A smug grin made his face even more repugnant. "It's where that faggot boyfriend of yours jumped." He snickered. "You should have saved everyone a whole lot of trouble and joined him then, but this is kinda romantic, don't you think?"

Rand didn't answer. His hate festered like an infection that no amount of antibiotics could cure. D-Rod needed to get what was coming to him, the consequences be damned.

"You know? You wanting to join him and all. It's like Romeo and . . . well, Romeo, I guess."

Deputy Tewksbury slammed a palm into his steering wheel.

"You're going to pay for what you did to my son." He brought the car to a halt and jerked the gear shift into park. For the first time since Rand had awoken, he and the deputy locked eyes. Tewksbury's were red and puffy.

Rand locked away any pity he might have for the man. "For what *I* did to him? Your fat pig of a rapist son deserved everything he got. Maybe you should blame yourself for what happened, for not raising him right or for not doing your goddamn job in the first place and arresting him for what he did to me and Henry. Or maybe you should blame the sicko sitting next to you for instigating the whole thing to begin with, huh? You know, violence begets violence and all that shit."

Deputy Tewksbury grimaced. He looked at D-Rod with the same contempt in his eyes he'd shown Rand.

"Shut the fuck up!" D-Rod blurted. "Say what you want about me and Turk. We didn't kill anyone. You killed a lot of people tonight. And not just Turk and the Alphas, either. People who had nothing to do with any of this." He jammed a finger against the partition. "Now it's your turn to die."

Rand chuckled. Tewksbury and D-Rod turned to watch him, their puzzlement written all over the faces. The chuckle blossomed into raucous laughter. "That's too funny, D-Rod," he managed between laughs. "You taking the high road, like you're somehow in the right." Rand's laughter died down. He stared at D-Rod with renewed hate. "And the worst part: you probably believe it."

The deputy exited the car. As Tewksbury circled to Rand's door, D-Rod said in a hushed tone, "You're lucky he's even here. I'd have my way with you again, all night, for what you did. And only after I had my fill and you were left squashed into nothing more than the little shit you are, then I'd kill you. Slowly. And no one would ever know what happened to you or even care."

The door beside him opened. Rough hands clamped around his arm and hauled him out of the car. Unable to get his feet under him in time, Rand fell onto the cool, hard ground, jarring his shoulder.

As he tried to rise, a sneakered foot slammed into his ribs, knocking the wind from his lungs. A sharp pain stabbed at his side, worse than any cramp he'd ever felt. He thought a rib might have broken and pierced something. Again, he tried to rise to his knees and catch his breath, tasks made difficult by the pain and the handcuffs. A second kick caught him in the stomach, a third in the face. His eyes teared, and blood and snot ran from his nose as he fell to his back.

"That's enough," Tewksbury said.

"Why?" D-Rod kicked Rand again. "What's the difference? Ain't like the coroner will be able to tell what wounds came before the fall and what came from it. And even if he could, you, Patrick's dad, and the rest of our parents would never let it show up in any report. We could do whatever we want to him right now, in front of everyone, and no one would ever give two shits."

He flipped Rand onto his stomach, punched him in the back of his head, then pressed a knee into his back. "If you want, I'll hold him down, and you can have a go at him. You know, for Turk."

"You really are sick, Derek." Deputy Tewksbury pushed D-Rod off Rand. "After this, I never want to see your face again. Got it?"

D-Rod stood and held up his hands. "You're the boss."

"Stand him up."

As D-Rod and Tewksbury lifted him to his feet, Rand searched the area for his so-called friend. "Where are you, Henry?"

"Aw," D-Rod chided. "He's looking for his dead lover boy. I must have knocked him pretty good with that last punch." He grabbed Rand by the chin and forced him to meet his eyes. "Don't worry, bitch. You'll be with your Henry soon enough."

"I am with you as always, Rand," the Henry-thing said, appearing behind Deputy Tewksbury and towering over the large man. It looked as though, had it wanted to, it could open its impossibly large snout and consume the officer's head in one bite. And yet it stood there, doing nothing.

Rand glowered at it. "I thought you were my friend."

"Me?" D-Rod laughed. "Can I be honest with you, Rand? You and your faggot boyfriend were never going to get in. Turk and I had plans for you right from the start. Had to send a message to any other queers looking to join the Alphas. It's no place for your kind." He backhanded Rand. "But you just couldn't learn your place with all the other bitches, could you, Rand? Well, you're gonna learn it now, that's for sure."

"Let's just get this over with." Tewksbury shoved Rand toward the cliff.

Rand spit blood. "It wasn't supposed to be like this." He leaned against the hands at his back, but they were too strong. His feet slid along a wet patch of grass. "This wasn't the deal. My life . . . fine. But he's supposed to die, too."

"Yoo-hoo." D-Rod waved a hand in front of Rand's eyes. "I think he's losing it. Who the fuck's he talking to?"

"Who knows?" Tewksbury grunted. "Hold him a second. We can't toss him with the cuffs on."

"You worry too much about the details, but . . . " D-Rod punched Rand in the stomach. "Like I said, you're the boss."

As Rand keeled over from the blow, the Henry-thing crouched by his side. Even squatting and ducking its head, it loomed over Rand. "The deal was that I help you kill the Alphas at the party. As you can see, we are no longer at the party. I already threw in your parents to sweeten my end of the bargain."

"My . . . parents?"

"Aw." D-Rod rubbed his eyes. "Now he wants his mommy and daddy."

"Your father, I mean." It stood and laughed, an eerie chittering that grew into a full cackle. "What is the point of deception? You know in your heart that we killed your mother, too. Her misery and blood were sweet as strawberries on the tongue."

My mother . . . Rand tried to shake off the image of his mother lying gutted on the kitchen floor, either having been blocked from his mind by the Henry-thing or repressed by his own subconscious before then. A hairless bear-thing had feasted upon her innards.

Even as his arms came free, he met the force guiding him to the cliff's edge with minimal resistance. Tears raced down his cheeks. Henry, his mother, and all those innocent people at the party who might not have gotten out—he had been responsible for their deaths.

Well, him and D-Rod. "He dies, too!" Rand wrenched himself free and shoved D-Rod to the ground.

The Henry-thing shrugged and sighed. "Very well." His form lost its wispiness, becoming more solid. More seen.

Deputy Tewksbury drew his gun. "What the hell is that?" He aimed at the Henry-thing, the pistol trembling in his hands. He opened fire.

The creature zigzagged, its movements almost too quick for Rand to catch. In a blur, it was behind Deputy Tewksbury, rising to its full height. The officer stood with his mouth agape, his chin quivering, and his wide eyes set forward, as if he knew what was behind him but lacked the courage to turn and face it.

And just as Rand had imagined earlier, the Henry-thing unhinged its jaw and clamped it over Tewksbury's head. The decapitated body fell away as the creature kicked back its mouthful like a baby bird choking down a regurgitated worm and swallowed. The head squeezed down the creature's narrow throat like a cartoon character swallowing a whole turkey.

It wiped its mouth. "I can read your thoughts, remember?"

Rand stood motionless, stunned, terrified, and uncertain. He glanced at D-Rod, who lay cowering on the ground, lacking the wits to get up and run even as the Henry-thing stalked toward him. As the creature moved, sleek like a predator on all fours, its prey cornered, Rand's trembling didn't quite subside. And yet a sick sort of pleasure washed over him, making his skin crawl.

"Make it hurt," he heard himself say, though he couldn't remember forming the thought.

"G-Get back. Leave me alone!" D-Rod shuffled back on his palms and heels, getting closer and closer to the railing.

The Henry-thing crept forward at an equal pace, its nostrils expanding as if inhaling the Alpha's terror. Blood and viscera dripped from its lips.

"That's Henry." Rand smiled through his hate. "You remember Henry, don't you? Looks like he's the Alpha now."

"W-Wait! I'm sorry." D-Rod's head tapped against the railing. "Call it off! Please, I'll do anything. Just call it off!"

As the Henry-thing lowered its head, it huge black tongue lolling almost to the ground, Rand took particular glee in D-Rod's closed eyes and turned-away face. "Now, why would I want to do that?"

The creature buried its snout in D-Rod's groin. What emitted from D-Rod's throat didn't sound human, the cries of a wolf caught in a trap. But D-Rod could not even chew off his own paw to escape. He tried to turn to his stomach, to claw his way toward the cliff, perhaps believing the fall would be a cleaner, better death than what he faced. But the Henry-thing pawed and swiped at him, buried its claws into his thighs and buttocks, and effortlessly dragged him back into its awaiting jaws. D-Rod screamed, begged God, Rand, and anyone else who might listen for help, until his voice went hoarse. Soon after, he blanched, and blood sputtered from his mouth like a tiny geyser. Only a moment later, he was dead. It served as no deterrent to the Henry-thing's feasting. When it had satiated itself, and D-Rod lay eviscerated, it stood on its hind legs and grinned a mouthful of guts. "Did you enjoy that as much as I did?"

Rand crossed his arms. "It was too quick. Better than he deserved." He studied the carnage and the monstrous thing that stood before him. He knew he should be afraid or perhaps horrified at what he himself had done, but he only felt empty.

Until a dam inside him broke. With it came the resurgence of grief. It had been locked away only long enough to get the job done. But now that the last Alpha on his list was dead, it all came rushing back in to fill the void with something blacker. It swept the breath from his lungs. He staggered to the railing and sat down, his legs suddenly gone feeble, turning away from all that he had sown. "What now?"

The Henry-thing sat beside him, just as Henry had the last time Rand had seen him. It was nothing like Henry and never had been. Rand wasn't much like his previous self either.

"Now?" The creature closed its eyes and turned its snout up to the moon. Its skin, graying like rotten meat, rippled in the glow. "Now our time together is done." It stood and started away, its movements sluggish, as though it were waiting for a response, just as it had when Rand had first encountered it, waiting for Rand to come to his own decision.

"I mean . . . What do *I* do now?" Rand had been so hell-bent on revenge, so convinced that he would die in the effort, he'd never given a single thought to what might come next should he survive. He'd done so much and, if the creature and D-Rod were to be believed, hurt so many who hadn't deserved to be hurt. Deputy Tewksbury and Patrick were acceptable losses, both complicit in covering up what had happened. The only crime the Alpha in the sweater had committed was being an Alpha who'd gotten in Rand's way. And his mother? She had been a victim, too.

But she did nothing to prevent Dad's violence against me or herself. Rand tried to find some justice in the thought but couldn't. His mom had loved him, and he'd loved her, but he had . . . *What? Let her die? Or did I kill her myself?*

As faceless as those at the party were, their numbers unknown, Rand wasn't sure he could live with their deaths on his conscience. Maybe he should run, keep them faceless, and leave only his mother and Henry to haunt him. And what about Henry? It would be too easy for Rand to say he'd done it all for him, but that would be his guilt trying to pass the buck. No, he'd done it all, everything, for himself. Henry had been the excuse.

He took a deep breath, ready to take ownership of his actions. "How . . . how many did I kill?"

The Henry-thing turned, its smile all teeth. "Are we including these two? Technically, I killed them. Or . . . " Its gaze fell upon Rand's hands.

Rand looked down. Under the pale light, his fingers seemed elongated. They were crusted with blood. He gasped and closed his eyes. When he opened them again, his hands appeared normal. *A trick of the moonlight?* Some blood did stain his skin, but he could have gotten that from wiping his mouth after D-Rod kicked him.

Or a trick of the deceiver?

He swallowed. "How many?"

"My dear friend, as much as I would like to claim otherwise, I am not an all-knowing being like the idol you worship. But between the noxious air and the fire itself, the Alphas we disbursed, that deputy, and—" It chuckled. "Your parents. I would guess dozens. Not as many as I would have liked but enough to satiate my hunger. To restore me . . . nearly." It tapped Rand's shoulder with a rancid claw. "You have proven an adequate apostle. You have killed many. Your friend would be so proud. Your mother, too, if they were alive to see it."

"Why did you kill my mother?"

"Me? I may have been the tool, but . . . thy will be done." It laughed. "Am I using it correctly? Your spirits are so strange to me, but to be worshipped as you do them . . . "

"No, I wouldn't have wanted that. She . . . I . . . I loved her."

The Henry-thing chortled. "And yet I am called a liar." It leaned close to Rand's ear, bumping his shoulder playfully. Hot, foul breath moistened and slithered over his skin like sauna steam. "Remember. All of it."

And Rand did. He begged the Henry-thing to give him the strength to kill his father as the man berated him for being victimized. The creature had filled him with strength and rage enough to spur an army to slaughter. It had given of itself, and Rand had known true debasement, how good it could feel to release malevolence upon the world. He'd torn his father apart like an animal and had loved every second of it. And when he'd finished with his father, his bloodlust peaking, he'd craved more. The only person left was his sniveling mother, who had let his father beat, humiliate, and degrade them both.

"But I wouldn't . . . I didn't want to . . . "

"Oh, but you did! For all those times the bitch let him hit you. All the times she lay down and took it herself. So weak. So pathetic. She was just a bitch, Rand. *You* were just a bitch. But now? Now, you are the Alpha."

"No." He rose, his hands curling. "I'm not like them. I just wanted to make things right."

"Right?"

"Even then."

"Do you remember the female who asked if you were all right after the Alphas had played with you?" When Rand didn't respond, the Henry-thing smiled. "She died in the fire." It crouched to be at Rand's eye level, fixed him with its black gaze. "But they all deserved it, did they not? They stood by while you and Henry were raped, even watched it on their tiny screens and laughed at you, at all your wonderful pain and misery." A bear-trap grin spread over its sallow cheeks. "But they are not laughing anymore, are they, Rand?"

"It was just supposed to be the Alphas—"

"It was never just the Alphas!" The Henry-thing snarled. "Now, end this whining. We are only beginning. Through you, I have much work to be done."

"But you said . . . " Rand backed away from the creature, creeping slowly toward the cliff's edge. "You said we were done."

"I lied. I do that, Rand. It is over when I say it is over. You, pathetic pale face, have no say in the matter. Did you really think you ever did?" It leaped over the railing and stalked toward Rand on all fours, just as it had D-Rod before it fed. "You are mine, boy, and through you, this new world. I will drown myself in the filth of humanity and soak in the vast depths of its misery, and you—" it raised a claw to point at Rand, "—you, boy, will be my vessel." It licked its lips. "My bitch."

Rand shivered. He didn't know what the thing wanted from him but guessed it was more of the same. A lot more. He had planned to live only long enough to see vengeance done. He had nothing left, inside or out, except for the chance to be with his one real friend again.

"God forgive me." On shaky legs, he continued to shuffle backward. "I'm nobody's bitch." His foot touched down on open air. He screamed as he fell over the drop.

But he never hit bottom. Instead, he plummeted to within forty feet of the ravine, where soft hands seemed to catch him. *The hands of God?* He hovered in the air, his body as light and incorporeal as the air itself. Assuming he had died, he was simply thankful there had been no pain. An invisible force drew him horizontally toward the cliff's face and a tall, narrow opening therein. As his momentum increased, he threw up his arms and closed his eyes, bracing for impact.

He opened his eyes to find himself surrounded by the deepest dark, the only light coming from the stars outside the narrow gap. Wind whistled through the fissure, its chilling touch prickling his skin, which felt real and solid again.

A hand appeared in the gap, then a torso, filling the opening and closing off the light. Rand tried to shrink away from the approaching figure, only to find his lower half encased in stone. His abnormally wide and membranous hands searched for some kind of release but found none.

The figure drew near. His breaths short, Rand peered up at the stranger silhouetted by the light from the gap, hoping blindly that whoever it was would help him.

The figure leaned in close. Rand stared back at himself, a wide, wicked grin plastered across his cheeks.

"What?" Rand swatted wildly at the face that was his. "How?"

"Your predecessors lived at one with the spirits and we alongside them. Not like your absentee god. You pale faces do not seem to have any real comprehension of the spirit world, and because of that, our influence has waned. But even this remains true among the more enlightened of you simpletons: at this time of the cycle, what your kind calls 'Halloween', our worlds converge. You tell each other that darkness is benign, make up stories to laugh at what you fear. And even while you tell yourself that I cannot be real, that I am a product of your dysfunctional mind, I cross unchallenged into your world, not only in spirit but also in body." He turned to walk away. "And you, boy, may cross into mine."

Stretching with all his might, Rand reached for the creature that had become him, but even his new, elongated arms couldn't breach the gap. "Please! Don't leave me here! I've done everything you wanted. Please!"

The thing that looked like Rand but was not Rand laughed. "Ah, you understand that now. I really must leave. The sun will be upon us soon, and my brother will come. Yet, I could never resist an opportunity to gloat. Although I barter in lies, I will grant you the truth this one time, boy. I am thankful for your misery and all that you have spread. I am particularly thankful to you for taking my place."

"No . . . You can't . . . I . . . "

As his doppelganger squeezed through the gap and disappeared, Rand's panic grew. He tried to squeeze himself out of the encasement. He searched frantically for a latch or other mechanism again and again, probing every inch. When that proved futile, he swatted at it in hopes it would break before he would.

Rand broke first. His alien hands mangled and bleeding, he cried, thrashing and battering himself into exhaustion. He was near passing out when the first rays of sunlight trickled through the gap. With them, an amorphous body of white light entered. It materialized into a Native American warrior. Tall and proud, he displayed none of the savagery history's conquerors had attributed to his kin.

"Tawiskaron," it called in an Iroquois tongue Rand should not have understood yet did. "Have you not learned anything in your exile?"

Rand raised a feeble hand. "I'm not—"

"I will hear none of your lies!" A solid object as hard as rock smashed into his mouth. Chips of his teeth scratched his throat as he swallowed them down with blood. He clawed at the object affixed over his mouth, but like the stone around his legs, he could neither remove it nor determine how it was attached. He screamed through it but could form no words.

"It pains me to see you like this, brother. How many cycles will it take before your evil dies? To protect the humans from your influence, I'm afraid I have no choice but to seal you off completely." The warrior spirit sighed. "When the day comes that you are ready, I will return. Until then, I will continue my vigil, hoping you let peace into your heart. As I told the mortal you sought to corrupt, where there yet is life, there may be redemption. And your life, brother, offers you an eternity to find it."

The spirit vanished. A minor earthquake shook the cave, peppering Rand with pebbles and dust, forcing his eyes shut. When he opened them again, the darkness had become eternal, just as he had become. The gap had been shut, the air already as stale as a tomb.

THE END?

Not if you want to dive into more of Crystal Lake Publishing's Tales from the Darkest Depths!

Check out our amazing website and online store
or download our latest catalog here.

We always have great new projects and content on the website to dive into, as well as a newsletter, behind the scenes options, social media platforms, our own dark fiction shared-world series and our very own webstore. If you use the IGotMyCLPBook! coupon code in the store (at the checkout), you'll get a one-time-only 50% discount on your first eBook purchase!

Our webstore even has categories specifically for KU books, non-fiction, anthologies, and of course more novels and novellas.

Subscribe to Crystal Lake Publishing's Dark Tide series for updates, specials, behind-the-scenes content, and a special selection of bonus stories - http://eepurl.com/hKVGkr

ABOUT THE AUTHORS

Kevin Lucia is the ebook and trade paperback editor at Cemetery Dance Publications. His short fiction has been published in many venues, most notably with Neil Gaiman, Clive Barker, David Morell, Peter Straub, Bentley Little, and Robert McCammon.

His first short story collection, *Things Slip Through*, was published by Crystal Lake Publishing in November, 2013. He's followed that with the collections *Through A Mirror, Darkly, Devourer of Souls, Things You Need, October Nights*, and the novellas *Mystery Road, A Night at Old Webb*, and *The Night Road*. His first novel, *The Horror at Pleasant Brook* is forthcoming from Crystal Lake Publications, October 2023.

USA TODAY and #1 AMAZON bestselling author **Jeremy Bates** has published more than twenty novels and novellas. They have sold more than one million copies, been translated into several languages, and been optioned for film and TV by major studios. Midwest Book Review compares his work to "Stephen King, Joe Lansdale, and other masters of the art." He has won both an Australian Shadows Award and a Canadian Arthur Ellis Award. He was also a finalist in the Goodreads Choice Awards, the only major book awards decided by readers. The novels in the "World's Scariest Places" series are set in real locations and include Suicide Forest in Japan, The Catacombs in Paris, Helltown in Ohio, Island of the Dolls in Mexico, Mountain of the Dead in Russia, and Hotel Chelsea in New York City. The novels in the "World's Scariest Legends" series are based on real legends and include Mosquito Man, The Sleep Experiment, The Man From Taured, Merfolk, and The Dancing Plague. You can check out any of these places or legends on the web. Also, visit JEREMYBATESBOOKS.COM to receive Black Canyon, WINNER of The Lou Allin Memorial Award.

Jason Parent is an author of horror, thrillers, mysteries, science fiction and dark humor, though his many novels, novellas, and short stories tend to blur the boundaries between genres. From his EPIC and eFestival Independent Book Award finalist first novel, *What Hides Within*, to his widely applauded police procedural/supernatural thriller, *Seeing Evil*, to his fast and furious sci-fi horror, *The Apocalypse Strain*, Jason's work has won him praise from both critics and fans of diverse genres alike. He currently lives in Rhode Island, surrounded by chewed furniture thanks to his corgi and mini Aussie pups.

Crystal Lake Publishing's most popular anthologies:

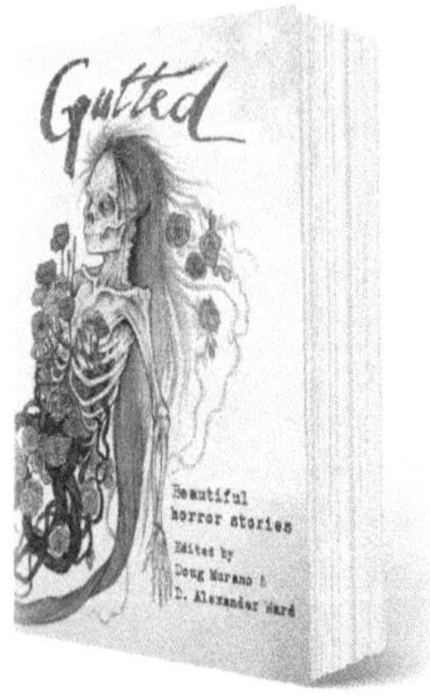

Readers . . .

Thank you for reading *October's End*. We hope you enjoyed this 3rd book in our Dark Tide series.

If you have a moment, please review *October's End* at the store where you bought it.

Help other readers by telling them why you enjoyed this book. No need to write an in-depth discussion. Even a single sentence will be greatly appreciated. Reviews go a long way to helping a book sell, and is great for an author's career. It'll also help us to continue publishing quality books. You can also share a photo of yourself holding this book with the hashtag #IGotMyCLPBook!

Thank you again for taking the time to journey with Crystal Lake Publishing.

Visit our Linktree page for a list of our social media platforms. https://linktr.ee/CrystalLakePublishing

Our Mission Statement:

Since its founding in August 2012, Crystal Lake Publishing has quickly become one of the world's leading publishers of Dark Fiction and Horror books in print, eBook, and audio formats.

While we strive to present only the highest quality fiction and entertainment, we also endeavour to support authors along their writing journey. We offer our time and experience in non-fiction projects, as well as author mentoring and services, at competitive prices.

With several Bram Stoker Award wins and many other wins and nominations (including the HWA's Specialty Press Award), Crystal Lake Publishing puts integrity, honor, and respect at the forefront of our publishing operations.

We strive for each book and outreach program we spearhead to not only entertain and touch or comment on issues that affect our readers, but also to strengthen and support the Dark Fiction field and its authors.

Not only do we find and publish authors we believe are destined for greatness, but we strive to work with men and woman who endeavour to be decent human beings who care more for others than themselves, while still being hard working, driven, and passionate artists and storytellers.

Crystal Lake Publishing is and will always be a beacon of what passion and dedication, combined with overwhelming teamwork and respect, can accomplish. We endeavour to know each and every one of our readers, while building personal relationships with our authors, reviewers, bloggers, podcasters, bookstores, and libraries.

We will be as trustworthy, forthright, and transparent as any business can be, while also keeping most of the headaches away from our authors, since it's our job to solve the problems so they can stay in a creative mind. Which of course also means paying our authors.

We do not just publish books, we present to you worlds within your world, doors within your mind, from talented authors who sacrifice so much for a moment of your time.

There are some amazing small presses out there, and through collaboration and open forums we will continue to support other presses in the goal of helping authors and showing the world what quality small presses are capable of accomplishing. No one wins when a small press goes down, so we will always be there to support hardworking, legitimate presses and their authors. We don't see Crystal Lake as the best press out there, but we will always strive to be the best, strive to be the most interactive and grateful, and even blessed press around. No matter what happens over time, we will also take our mission very seriously while appreciating where we are and enjoying the journey.

What do we offer our authors that they can't do for themselves through self-publishing?

We are big supporters of self-publishing (especially hybrid publishing), if done with care, patience, and planning. However, not every author has the time or inclination to do market research, advertise, and set up book launch strategies. Although a lot of authors are successful in doing it all, strong small presses will always be there for the authors who just want to do what they do best: write.

What we offer is experience, industry knowledge, contacts and trust built up over years. And due to our strong brand and trusting fanbase, every Crystal Lake Publishing book comes with weight of respect. In time our fans begin to trust our judgment and will try a new author purely based on our support of said author.

With each launch we strive to fine-tune our approach, learn from our mistakes, and increase our reach. We continue to assure our authors that we're here for them and that we'll carry the weight of the launch and dealing with third parties while they focus on their strengths—be it writing, interviews, blogs, signings, etc.

We also offer several mentoring packages to authors that include knowledge and skills they can use in both traditional and self-publishing endeavours.

We look forward to launching many new careers.

This is what we believe in. What we stand for. This will be our legacy.

Welcome to Crystal Lake Publishing— Tales from the Darkest Depths.

www.ingramcontent.com/pod-product-compliance
Lightning Source LLC
Chambersburg PA
CBHW070455200726
48293CB00007B/2221